BATTLE AXE

Praise for LAMBDA Literary Award Finalist Carsen Taite

"Real Life defense attorney Carsen Taite polishes her fifth work of lesbian fiction, *The Best Defense*, with the realism she daily encounters in the office and in the courts. And that polish is something that makes *The Best Defense* shine as an excellent read."—*Out & About Newspaper*

"Taite is a real-life attorney so the prose jumps off the page with authority and authenticity. [*It Should be a Crime*] is just Taite's second novel...but it's as if she has bookshelves full of bestsellers under her belt. In fact, she manages to make the courtroom more exciting than Judge Judy bursting into flames while delivering a verdict. Like this book, that's something we'd pay to see."—*Gay List Daily*

"Taite, a criminal defense attorney herself, has given her readers a behind the scenes look at what goes on during the days before a trial. Her descriptions of lawyer/client talks, investigations, police procedures, etc. are fascinating. Taite keeps the action moving, her characters clear, and never allows her story to get bogged down in paperwork. *It Should be a Crime* has a fast-moving plot and some extraordinarily hot sex."—*Just About Write*

In *Do Not Disturb*..."Taite's tale of sexual tension is entertaining in itself, but a number of secondary characters...add substantial color to romantic inevitability."—Richard Labonté, *Bookmarks*

In *Nothing but the Truth*..."Author Taite is really a Dallas defense attorney herself, and it's obvious her viewpoint adds considerable realism to her story, making it especially riveting as a mystery. ...I give it four stars out of five."—Bob Lind, *Echo Magazine*

"Taite has written an excellent courtroom drama with two interesting women leading the cast of characters. Taite herself is a practicing defense attorney, and her courtroom scenes are clearly based on real knowledge. [*Nothing But the Truth*] should be another winner for Taite."—*Lambda Literary*

Visit us at www.boldstrokesbooks.com

By the Author

truelesbianlove.com

It Should Be a Crime

Do Not Disturb

Nothing but the Truth

The Best Defense

Beyond Innocence

The Luca Bennett Mystery Series:

Slingshot

Battle Axe

BATTLE AXE

by
Carsen Taite

2013

BATTLE AXE

ISBN 10: 1-60282-871-7
ISBN 13: 978-1-60282-871-1

This Trade Paperback Original Is Published By
Bold Strokes Books, Inc.
P.O. Box 249
Valley Falls, NY 12185

First Edition: May 2013

Credits
Editor: Cindy Cresap
Production Design: Susan Ramundo
Cover Design By Sheri (graphicartist2020@hotmail.com)

Acknowledgments

Thanks for all the readers who've written to tell me how much they enjoy Luca Bennett, her mysteries, and her messed-up life. Special thanks to Jean Redmann and Greg Herren who invited me to submit a story for their anthology, *Women of the Mean Streets*. "Boomerang," the story I submitted for that book, is where Luca was born. I also owe a shout out and huge thanks to my pal Ashley Bartlett, who beta-read this book for me up until the very second before I turned it in.

To Len Barot, Cindy, Sheri, and all the other folks at Bold Strokes Books—you make the publishing process seamless, and I can't imagine taking this journey without you.

And extra special thanks to Lainey, love of my life, who encouraged me to keep writing about Luca from the time she read the first few pages of "Boomerang" and who has read every word with a watchful eye to make sure I don't mess with her favorite character.

Dedication

For Lainey. Here's to living our dreams!

CHAPTER ONE

I don't think I'd ever seen a bigger burger. The guy in the booth across from me grasped it with both hands, but they were no match for the one and a half pounds of meat and fifteen bacon slices sandwiched between two buns. A Triple Bypass. I wasn't sure if I'd ever been that hungry.

My guy ordered a Double Bypass. Only one patty less, but it didn't look nearly as daunting, and I know I'd been that hungry. Hell, I was that hungry now.

He tacked on a side of Flatliner fries, a butterfat milkshake, and a pack of Lucky Strikes. I shook my head. He wouldn't eat like that in the joint. Not only was I earning a living by picking him up, I was saving him from himself. I was practically a Good Samaritan.

I waited in my seat until he hefted the large bag and waddled from the restaurant. Excellent. I'd thought I'd have to watch, drooling, while he finished off his meal and then lit up a few cancer sticks. When I saw him turn toward the parking lot, I made my move. My strides were like four of his, and it didn't take me long to catch up to him.

"Excuse me, sir?"

He turned toward me, clutching the bag against his hefty middle. "Can I help you?" He edged away as he spoke the words. If I had to guess, he was more scared about losing his lunch than he was about being caught by the law.

"I work for Hardin Jones. I need to talk to you about the court date you missed last week."

I barely got the last words out of my mouth before he took off running. All three hundred plus pounds of him shook like jelly as he tore across the parking lot, dodging pedestrians and cars alike. I'd taken his size for granted and figured he was an easy mark, but he was a tornado, and I quickly realized I'd have to push hard to catch him.

As I sprinted toward him, he risked a backward glance, which is probably why he didn't see the car careening toward him. I did, but I charged ahead anyway, pulling up short just as he glanced off the front bumper. He staggered a little but then charged forward again, gripping the bag from the Heart Attack Cafe like it was his last meal. The way he was running, it might very well be. I wished I had on tennis shoes instead of heavy boots, but my next meal was at risk too, so I accelerated my speed and pulled alongside him.

"You're just making things worse," I yelled.

"Don't…care," he huffed, but I could tell he was losing steam. Still, I wasn't in the mood to spend all day chasing a fat man through the streets of downtown Dallas. We were near the famous grassy knoll, a perfect place for a comfortable landing. I pulled up short and crouched. He looked over his shoulder, probably wondering why he could no longer hear my pounding pace. When he saw me standing in place, he grinned, but as I leapt through the air, I watched his grin change to dismay.

My Olympic jump took him so by surprise that he remained rooted in place until I landed on his back and took him to the ground. We rolled, and I took advantage of being on top to whip out a pair of handcuffs and secure them to one of his wrists. The other wrist was connected to the hand that still clutched his bag of lunch, and he wasn't letting go. After a struggle, I managed to snap the steel bracelet in place and worked on prying his fingers loose from the bag, finally tearing the brown paper just below his grasp. When I pulled the bag away, I thought he might cry.

As I marched him away, I heard a thousand tiny clicks, and I turned back to check it out. A band of tourists was snapping pictures of our little incident. I smiled and bowed for the camera.

❖

I turned Mr. Heart Attack in to the sheriff's department and drove directly to Hardin Jones Bail Bond Agency. While I waited for Hardin to visit his safe, I started in on my lunch. Everything was cold and a little smashed, but still good. Free is always good.

"You're going to die young if you keep eating shit like that." Hardin didn't beat around the bush.

"I'll probably die young anyway. May as well enjoy myself until then."

"I suppose." He handed over a stack of bills. "You should be able to enjoy yourself for a while on this, but if you feel like working, I have a bunch of small cases for you."

I didn't count the money. The bounty on Mr. Heart Attack was twenty-five hundred dollars, ten percent of his bond. Hardin would never short me even though he hated parting with money. Paying me was cheaper than paying the court the full twenty-five large he would owe if Mr. Heart Attack went AWOL.

Work had a tendency to dry up, so I told him I'd be happy to take anything he wanted to throw my way. He had one ready and handed me the file and told me to come back Monday for more.

I glanced at the clock in my Bronco. All these years and it still worked. I was late.

When I reached the parking lot of the softball field, I shucked out of my boots and pulled on a pair of tennis shoes. I left my leather jacket in the Bronco and strode across the field in jeans and a tank top. Chance would have a jersey for me to wear. And a glove. And a bat. I wasn't big on sporting equipment.

"Hey, Luca, over here!"

I turned toward the voice. Nancy Walters, one of the cops who played on Chance's team. I headed over to her and she met me halfway.

"We're over there this week. Thanks for filling in. I've got your jersey, although it's a shame to cover up that chest." She faux leered and I play snarled back at her. We did this role-play every time we saw each other. She was harmless. At least I'd never been drunk enough to try to get into her pants. Chance would've killed me, and she was the only cop whose pants I cared to transgress. I tugged on my jersey and glanced around the field.

Jessica Chance stood at the pitcher's mound, deep in conversation with the team's star pitcher. Tall, blond, trim, and fit, Chance made a softball jersey seem sexy. Yet, even in sporty mode, everything about her—from her intense stare to the way she feigned a relaxed stance—screamed cop. The only time I ever saw her really relaxed was when she was in the throes of an orgasm. Even then, I always suspected she held a little back, like she couldn't quite let down her guard even for sex. I remembered, even though it had been a while. I planned to remedy that after the game.

"Come on, Luca. You've only got a couple of minutes to warm up." Nancy led me to the space in front of the dugout and pointed to the bats. I shrugged and lifted a few, swinging them through the air. I could hit okay, but I didn't need to be great. Once on base, my real skill was running round the bases faster than any fastball could throw me out, and the sole reason Chance made me sub in. I hoped my Double Bypass wouldn't hold me back today.

While I swung the bats, Nancy rattled off the usual gossip. "Gail couldn't be here today. I hear one of the security guards that works for her had a fling with one of her clients. She went into full takedown mode today. You know how she is."

I did. Gail Laramore may have retired, but she would always be a cop. She owned a security company that provided protective detail to local celebs and politicos. I was playing her spot today. Nancy's gossip sometimes helped me out on a case, so I encouraged it. "Any idea which client?"

She leaned in and whispered, loud enough for the entire dugout to hear. "Sylvia Romero."

"Really?" I was surprised. The queen of Dallas real estate development had a pristine reputation. I don't know why this kind of stuff continually surprises me. Just last summer, I'd uncovered a ring of weird sex flings that included the grand dame of Dallas society and our former pristine U.S. senator. "I guess being horny makes folks lose their good judgment." I'm so wise.

"I guess so. Speaking of which, you still seeing that defense attorney? The hot Latin one?"

"Smooth segue, Nance." She needn't have specified hot and Latin. I'd only bedded one criminal defense attorney, and her name was Ronnie Moreno. She'd been my summer fling. "Watched her get on a plane last month. She's got a job in D.C."

"You didn't go along? I'm sure you could find lots of work there."

"Thought never crossed my mind." I wasn't the type to move across the country over a woman. I wasn't the type to do anything for the sake of a woman other than lose sleep and drink more than I should. "We had fun, but we've both moved on."

"You ever going to settle down, Luca?"

I opened my mouth to answer, but another voice chimed in. "Yeah, Bennett. When are you going to actually stick with a relationship?"

I turned to see Chance standing behind us. Figured she was ribbing me like always, but a stern look in her eyes said she was scolding instead. Whatever. She was one to talk. Her relationships consisted of a series of one-night stands interspersed with familiar visits to my bed. Or hers. Our casual sex sessions were the longest running relationship either of us had ever had. I reminded her that I wasn't the only one with commitment issues. "Pot. Kettle. Which one you wanna be?"

I could tell she was trying not to smile, but it didn't last. Her smile got even bigger as she looked away from me up into the bleachers. Decent sized crowd today, probably because summer's heat had finally faded into a semblance of fall. I didn't pay too much attention to who had come to watch. I figured most of them were partnered up with players on both teams. But Chance's gaze lingered on the women gathered to watch us kick up dirt around the bases.

"Looking for someone?"

The flinch was slight, but I saw it. She jerked her eyes away from the spectators. "Nope. You ready to play? I need you in the outfield today."

I didn't attend these games to show off athletic prowess. I was supposed to stand in for some not-so-important position and then run like hell when it was my turn at bat. Gail played outfield and she was stellar. No way could I fill her shoes. "You sure that's where you want me?"

"Just do your best to catch the ball and then run it to the infield. Don't try to throw anyone out." With those sternly delivered instructions, she started to walk away.

"Hey, Jess."

She turned and raised her eyebrows, probably because I'd used her first name. Not something I normally do in public. "Yeah?"

"If I catch the ball, what will you give me?"

She grinned. "You're impossible."

"Seriously, you don't think I put on this butt ugly shirt for fun, do you?"

"You don't have to play if you don't want."

I couldn't read her expression, but she sounded a little pissed. I stepped closer, but not too close. After all, we were surrounded by loads of our friends and Jess's co-workers. "You busy after?" I assumed I already knew the answer. We'd play here, get sweaty, go to her place or mine, shower, play, and get sweaty again. It's what we did.

"I might be."

Well, those were three little words I hadn't expected. We had a regular deal. I subbed in and she paid me back. No equivocation. "I might be." Fuck that. I wasn't a beggar. I'd offered my services, but seemed like Chance wanted to keep me in the outfield.

"Cool. Check you later." I strode away, trying to disguise my anger as nonchalance.

The game lasted forever, but I shined. Totally against my nature, but I knew I was showing off for Chance and her maybes. At least that's how it started. In the third inning, after a particularly showy slide into home plate, a new motivation appeared on the scene. A tall, gorgeous redhead. A little overdressed for a softball game, she wore a tan pantsuit and high-heeled boots.

I don't normally go for redheads. In my experience, they have a tendency to flame up for no reason whatsoever. At least none that I can fathom, and I don't have much use for volcanic eruptions unless they are orgasmic. But Jess's snub made me feel like making an exception. Red seemed to be looking right at me, so I tossed her a casual wave. She smiled. I tugged my cap and turned to jog into the dugout when I ran smack into Jess. Both of us backed up fast. "Sorry," I mumbled.

She didn't hear me, distracted by something up in the stands. I followed her line of sight and my eyes landed on the redhead again.

Didn't surprise me. We had the same taste. Part of the reason we got along so well. "She's a hot one."

I wasn't prepared for the angry look Jess shot my way. She seriously needed to get laid. I shrugged and joined the rest of the team.

Four innings later, while the rest of the team took a victory lap, I sifted through the cooler, wishing beer was allowed on these fields.

"I wouldn't mind something cold to drink if you have any extra."

I looked up into sea green eyes and wondered if a cold drink was what Red really thirsted for. "Not much here, but you're welcome to anything you see."

Her knowing look told me she knew what I was offering. She extended a hand. "I'm Heather. What's your name?"

Jess burst into view. If I didn't know better I'd think the game was still going and she was sliding into home base. "Her name's trouble." She slid a possessive arm around Heather's waist and flashed me a look that dared me to make a smart remark.

I didn't have any smart remarks. The contrast between Red's tailored ensemble and Chance's sweaty, dirty uniform jammed up my thinking bones. These two knew each other. Well enough for Chance to engage in a public display of affection. Well enough that she didn't care about making put together girl all sweaty. This would take a while to process. All I knew right now was I wasn't getting laid tonight. At least not with Jess.

As if she could hear my thoughts, Jess added an exclamation point. "We're headed out. Thanks for standing in. See you later."

Wow, she'd managed to pull out of enchantment mode to say three whole sentences. But she couldn't be bothered introducing me to her…her whatever. I watched them stroll over to a brand new silver BMW sedan and climb in.

A BMW? Seriously? I tried not to care that Jess had ditched me for the hottest chick at the game. Besides, no matter how put together Chance's date looked and how sweet of a ride she drove, Heather sounded like a stripper name to me.

CHAPTER TWO

My crumbling apartment complex was dark. A perfect cover for rent dodgers like myself. It wasn't that I didn't feel some responsibility to pay my bills; it's just that I had priorities, and shelling out cash for this dump was low on my list. Besides, I was still in hock for medical bills related to my last big case. A case for which I hadn't been and would never be paid.

I parked my Bronco far from my front door, hoping to sneak in under my landlord's watchful gaze. As I approached the door, I saw a shadow lurking. I took the direct approach.

"I'll get you your money, Withers. Quit stalking me."

"You? Paying me? That would be a switch."

The voice was low and throaty. Sultry. Delicious. Wasn't Withers, but familiar all the same. Diamond Collier. I'd always wondered if Diamond was her real name. We'd known each other, intimately, but not the personal details kind of intimately. She stepped out of the shadows. I hadn't seen her in months, but she hadn't changed one bit. Her formerly blond hair was now brunette, but she was still as sexy as I remembered. And, I could tell by the bulge under her jacket, she was still packing.

"Hello, Agent Collier."

"Hello, Luca Bennett. And it's Marshal Collier now." She pointed at the door. "Aren't you going to invite me in?"

My mind ran through the contents of my apartment, sparse, but in complete disarray. I didn't have much to offer in terms of hospitality.

My fridge was empty and my sheets were a couple of weeks dirty. Plus, I was pretty sure I had a couple of unregistered weapons on the kitchen counter. But I wanted to show her some hospitality. Boy, did I.

I had a sudden blast of brilliance. A few drinks might make my place look better than it was. "I have an idea. Come with me." I walked back toward the parking lot, listening for her footsteps behind me. She didn't ask where we were going. Either she trusted me or she wanted something bad enough to follow me anywhere. Maybe a little of both.

I passed the Bronco and kept walking. About a hundred yards later, we wound up in front of Maggie's, my local bar of choice. Mostly because it was within walking distance of my place.

Diamond nodded her head when I held the door open. Kind of appropriate to bring her to this bar considering months ago I'd met her here. At least I'd met a picture of her. In a file from Hardin's bond agency. He'd hired me to find what we all thought was a murderer, but it turned out Diamond was just a federal agent posing as a stripper turned socialite. I got to pretend to haul her in and collected a reward instead of a bounty, but I didn't much care what the money had been called since it was in cash. As a bonus, I'd gotten to play with my catch.

I wasn't naive enough to think she was back because I was such a good lay. It'd been months. Still, I could hope. Maybe a few drinks would do the trick. I led her to a booth and we sat down. "I'm ordering beer unless you want something stronger. If you say you're on duty, I'm moving to the bar."

"I'll have a Jameson's. Neat."

Perfect. After Chance left with the stripper dressed like an insurance saleswoman, I'd been mentally prepared for a difficult evening. Looks like my concerns were unwarranted. A few drinks and I'd feel safe bringing Diamond back to my messy lair.

"Luca Bennett, you don't think your tab's high enough?"

Diamond and I both turned toward the feisty little woman tapping her pen on our table. Maggie wore her Saturday night best, a tiger print miniskirt with a not so coordinating flaming orange sweater that showed more cleavage than I cared to see on a woman who'd gone on several dates with my dad. She didn't normally make a point of mentioning my growing tab unless she was annoyed with me. Maybe bringing Diamond here had been a bad idea. Should've just picked up a bottle of whisky at the corner store. I held up a hand to ward Maggie off, but Diamond beat me to the punch.

"Actually, I'm paying. So, you're Maggie? Is this your bar? It's great. Very comfortable feel."

Maggie's brash demeanor couldn't compete with Diamond's overdone praise, and she practically preened. "You think so? I was thinking of doing some work on the place, but I don't want to ruin the ambiance."

Good thing I didn't have a drink yet, or I would've choked on it. I watched while Diamond charmed Maggie and then Maggie offered her a drink on the house. Luckily, Diamond ordered a beer for me. I was convinced I would've stayed thirsty without her intervention. When Maggie finally wandered off, Diamond turned her attention back to me.

"You come here often?"

"Too much, I guess. Maggie treats me like shit, but I get to run a tab. Seems like a fair trade-off."

"Treats you like shit? Right."

"Okay, maybe shit is a relative term. She treats me like I'm her wayward teenage daughter."

"Something tells me you worked hard to get the part."

"So, you transferred to the Marshal Service." I wasn't in the mood to talk about my complicated pseudo familial relationships with Maggie or anyone else. I was curious about Diamond's shift in status. When I'd met her, she was working organized crime, undercover. Deep. As a federal marshal, she wore her badge on the outside and did what I do—chase down fugitives. Not exactly competition since her client was the United States government and she got a salary, and my client was usually a seedy bail bondsman, like Hardin, and I only got paid if I was actually successful.

"Kind of hard to stay undercover when the entire Russian mob thinks you turncoated them."

"You could've moved away, dyed your hair, gotten plastic surgery."

"I like it here. And I did dye my hair, but my face? You wouldn't want me to change that, would you?"

"Yeah, I like it here too." I wasn't falling for the flirt. I knew she hadn't shown up on my doorstep to fall into bed. Not that I'd mind that action, but I wanted to know the real story first, get the business out of the way.

She feigned a quick pout and then plunged in. "I could use your help."

"I bet you could, but let's finish our drinks first. Otherwise, I'll feel like a cheap date. Don't worry. You don't have to buy me dinner."

"Be serious for two minutes, will you? Most of your work comes from Hardin Jones, right?"

There are no client confidentiality rules between bondsmen and the muscle, like me, they hire to find wayward criminals, but I hesitated before answering. Maybe she was just making an assumption, since when she'd posed as one of those wayward criminals, Hardin was her bondsman. But something about the way she asked told me she already knew that most of my business came from him. It bothered me that she knew more about me than I knew about her. I settled on a semi-cagey response. "We have a good working relationship."

Her nod was perfunctory. "He has the bonds on a couple of guys we're interested in."

"So go get them. Isn't that what you do?"

"Well, yes, if they have federal warrants. These guys are small-time. No pending federal charges. Yet."

I wasn't following. Wasn't sure I wanted to. Complicated wasn't my thing. I'd chosen this profession for the sheer simplicity of it. Find the jumper, turn them in. "I'm sure you'll figure something out."

She reached into her jacket and pulled out two photos. Not mug shots, action shots. Guy number one was driving a van. His face was hard to make out in the grainy surveillance shot, but enough details came through to make an ID possible. Guy number two was walking. Judging by the look on his face, he either feared where he'd come from or dreaded his destination.

"These the guys?" Rhetorical question designed to get her talking.

"Yes. Sandy Amato and Vince Picone. Lower links on Geno Vedda's chain of command."

Geno Vedda was legend among organized crime families in Dallas. Part of his legend was his ability to lead a double life. Successful entrepreneur and hardened criminal. "And you're interested in them because?"

"We want Vedda."

"What's new about that? Not like he hasn't been breaking laws his entire life."

"He's gone missing, and my team has been assigned to find him."

I waved at the pictures on the table between us. "And you think these two flunkies are going to lead you to him?"

"Can't hurt. Why don't you track them down? Maybe they'll lead us to Vedda."

"'Us'? I work alone."

"I'm not asking you to find Vedda, just his guys. Find them, collect the cash, and let me know. I'll take it from there."

"Why don't I just find Vedda for you? Probably be a lot easier." Visions of a healthy payout danced in my mind.

"No," she barked. "I mean, leave Vedda to us. Besides," she added as if she could read my thoughts, "there's no bounty."

"So you only want me to do part of your work for you."

"You don't have to do any of it. I just figured we could all win here. You collect a bounty from Hardin on Amato and Picone, and we may get a lead on Vedda. If you're not interested, just say so."

I was interested. Not necessarily because I might make a few extra bucks, but because U.S. Marshal Diamond Collier had deigned to come see me in person to ask this favor. Either finding these guys was way more important than she led me to believe, or seeing me in the flesh was a bonus she had to have. I'm not conceited, but I preferred to believe the latter because it fit in with my plans.

I leaned across the table and caught her lips with mine. I held the kiss for only a few seconds and couldn't help but smile at her surprise when I sat back in the booth. I gave her a minute to get on my wavelength before I gave her my answer. "Yeah, I'm interested."

❖

Sunday morning, I woke up alone. Just the way I like. The fact that my solitude followed a night of rowdy sex was a bonus.

I glanced at my cell phone. I'd turned the ringer off the night before and I'd missed a late night call. Didn't recognize the number and there was no message. Glad it hadn't interrupted sex with Diamond. I dragged my ass to the kitchen and wished for the thousandth time that I'd remember to buy a new coffee maker. The one my father had handed down to me when I graduated from the academy had met an untimely death last year when I accidently smashed it with a baseball bat when one of my one-night houseguests had startled me during the night. I was a much lighter sleeper now, but still too cheap to buy something as dull as a home appliance.

I don't like owning stuff. Comes with too much responsibility. I made just enough money to get by and indulge in a few important habits. Like guns and gambling. And beer. Said out loud, my list of important things sounds kind of nefarious, but I don't care what anyone thinks. I'm happy. At least as happy as I know how to be.

Diamond hadn't left a note. The only evidence she'd been in the place was a copy of her card with her cell phone number scrawled on the back. She'd asked me to call her if I found out anything about the two Guidos she wanted me to track. I hadn't decided if I was going to pitch in on her case, but I figured I could at least talk to Hardin and see if he wanted me to pick these guys up for him. At least then I'd make a few bucks. Otherwise, I wasn't sure if sexual favors from Diamond made it worth the effort. Fresh from last night, I was convinced, but in a few days, the bliss would probably fade.

In the meantime, I had the file Hardin had handed me yesterday. I took a quick shower, grabbed the file, and headed out in search of coffee. It was past noon, so I wouldn't have to go far. Maggie had recently decided to open for lunch. She especially liked the new hours on the weekends since it was her way to capture the hungover brunch crowd. Since she was responsible for most of her patrons' hangovers, me included, it was a steady business. Besides, this way I wouldn't have to spend my newly earned cash on something as frivolous as food.

I strolled into the bar. The empty bar. Big Harry waved in my direction and shouted, "Miss Maggie's in the office. She'll be right out."

He needn't have shouted since he and I were the only folks in the place. I waved back but didn't return the loud greeting. My head couldn't take the ruckus. I settled onto a barstool and spread open the file.

Henry Marcher. White male, age twenty-two. Bond posted by his mother, Daisy Marcher. The only address information in the file was hers. Guess Henry was still dependent on dear old Mom and she hadn't seen fit to kick him out even though he had an extensive record of minor offenses. This last was a robbery. Mr. Marcher was escalating. Probably had a drug problem, which resulted in all the stealing for money to buy drugs. Getting an apartment for himself was likely last on his list, and I had a hunch I'd find him at his mother's house, safe and sound, probably eating a home cooked meal. Maybe I'd make a trip over there after lunch.

When Maggie finally emerged from the back, she was trailed by something else my head couldn't take. Make that someone. My father, Joe Bennett.

Holy hell, what was he doing here? Noon on a Sunday was Dad's prime sleep it off time. He usually waited until after the sun went down on the weekend to show his face in public. But his face was not only out in public, it was shiny and awake. His eyes were clear and the last three or four strands of hair he had left were combed into some semblance of style.

"Luca! Great to see you," he bellowed.

I mumbled a response that hopefully sounded like "great to see you too." What I really wanted to say was why are you in my bar on a Sunday morning, but Maggie flounced over to my barstool, and I had my answer. She was decked in her finest purple dress complete with a sash so full of geometric design and color it made me dizzy. They were both so awake and cheerful it was exhausting to look at them.

I'd managed to push the reality of my pushy neighborhood bartender dating my deadbeat dad to the far recesses of my mind, mainly because I never saw them together. They'd met months ago when I was in the hospital recovering from my last nonpaying case. Concern over my well-being turned into interest in each other's well-being. For the last few months, they'd spent all their special alone time out of my sight. Okay by me. I'd just as soon they kept their private lives really, really private. Looks like I'd need to shell out some of my hard earned cash to feed myself today.

"I just stopped by to say hi," I lied, not that they'd fall for my play at niceties. "I've got somewhere I need to be."

"Nonsense." Maggie pushed me back onto the barstool, no small feat for a woman half my size. "I made a special lunch for Joe. Plenty for both of you. Blue Moon?"

She poured a frosty mug before I answered. Made me reconsider. Maggie wasn't big on handing out her good beer to folks who ran up tabs. Her dating Dad might have some perks. Guess I could have one beer before I hit the road. "Yeah, okay. Beer would be good."

She poured with one hand and motioned my dad onto the barstool next to me. She set our beers down and waved a hand between us. "Talk. I'll get lunch. We'll eat. Catch up."

In a flash, she was gone, and an awkward silence filled the space she left. I did my part to fill it. "Cold beer."

"Sure is."

"How's the house?"

"Good. Fixed that patch of fence last week." He took a deep drink. "Talked to your brother yesterday."

I couldn't remember the last time I'd spoken to Mark. He'd taken off from the hellhole that was our childhood home the minute he graduated from high school and never looked back. We spoke a couple of times a year, not necessarily related to any particular occasion. I didn't resent him for not sticking around, but I didn't have to cater to his need to cozy up to what was left of his family whenever he felt guilty about it. "He still alive?"

He smiled over his beer. "He's working for one of those fancy computer companies. I can't even pronounce what he does. He's getting married."

I nearly choked at the non sequitur. Married? The boy who spent his youth with his head buried in a book, graduated top of his class because he had no personal life. He'd sworn after witnessing the demise of Mom and Dad's happily ever after that he'd never commit to a relationship. If Dad had said he was dating, I would have been surprised, but married? "Did he get a girl pregnant?" The question spilled out before I realized I asked it out loud. Dad's angry stare sent me back to my beer and a muttered, "Never mind."

"You should be happy for your brother. Talk to him more than once in a blue moon. Then you'd know he's been dating a lovely girl for months. Her name is Lydia. Or Linda. Something like that."

Made me feel a little better that he could hardly remember the love of my brother's life's name. Still, how could Mark have mated and I not know about it? I still harbored the notion that the lovely girl might be knocked up. Time would tell. I suppose I should be expecting an engraved invitation in the mail any day now. Then it would be real. We could talk about it then. In the meantime, I'd blown off any thoughts about getting work done over lunch. I had another idea. I had cash burning a hole in my pocket and a potential accomplice right in front of me. "Hey, Dad, you interested in taking a trip up I-35 after lunch?"

"It's Sunday!" Maggie reappeared by Dad's side with her announcement of the obvious.

I looked around the bar. "You have a church service scheduled over drinks?"

"Don't be silly. But we're going to have brunch and then go to the farmer's market."

Seriously? I shot a look at Dad, but instead of a conspiratorial scowl, his expression told me he was excited at the prospect of "brunch" and a lazy trip to gaze upon fruits and vegetables. In the span of a day, my world had turned upside down. Jess was dating a stripper, my nerd brother was betrothed to a lovely girl, and my father turned down a trip to the casino for produce. I suddenly lost my appetite. This particular Sunday was probably best spent in bed.

I drained the last of my beer and slid off the barstool. "I just remembered something I have to do. I'll catch you later." I ignored their protests and entreaties to join them and walked home. Home, where I could depend on everything to be just the way I liked it. The same.

CHAPTER THREE

The Marcher house was a quiet place. I'd gotten here early on Monday, hoping to catch Momma Marcher headed off to work. Once she was gone, my plan involved some light breaking and entering. I figured poor little Henry probably slept in. Shouldn't be hard to roust him out of bed and haul him downtown.

No such luck. It was nine thirty a.m. and the house was still. Even from across the street I could see that the only car Momma owned was still in the garage. Guess the whole house had decided to sleep in. Lucky them. Lucky me, I hadn't had that second cup of coffee I wanted, or this stakeout would be short-lived.

This house was in a nicer neighborhood than mine, which supported my theory that Henry would probably rather hole up at home than stay on the run. Momma's cooking had to be better than what he might find lining a Dumpster. I decided to give this stakeout another hour before I figured out a plan B.

The hour seemed more like a whole day. I'd even fallen asleep at one point and woke up with a trace of drool on my chin. Guess I should've had that second cup of coffee after all. At least the car was still in the garage. If anyone had snuck past my sleeping self, they'd done it on foot.

I needed to walk around, stretch my legs, or I wasn't going to make it much longer. I climbed out of the car and walked a few yards away from the house as if it were perfectly natural for me to take a stroll through a strange neighborhood. I could never live in such a cookie cutter place. Every house looked the same. Four windows facing front, brick veneer, two trees. Reminded me of the house I'd grown up in, although that neighborhood was way older.

When I turned around to head back to my car, I detected movement in front of the house next to the Marcher's residence. Excellent. Time to make a move. I ducked behind some bushes at the house next door and waited. I saw a shadow slip around the side of Marcher's house, but I couldn't make out who it was. Whoever it was crouched low and moved along the fence. Had to be Henry, trying to sneak out. I unzipped my jacket for easy access to the long Colt in my shoulder holster and snuck across the lawn toward his place. The wide-open front yard meant I was probably visible to anyone who felt like peering out their windows at the tall, crazy woman slinking through what was probably a normally quiet neighborhood. Wouldn't be quiet today. Today, this place would be the scene of a takedown.

Once I reached the brick wing wall in front of Marcher's place, I tugged the Colt from my jacket and leaned around the low brick wall, letting the gun barrel lead. "Freeze."

"No, you freeze. And drop the weapon."

My guy had a really girly voice.

I followed my gun and peered around the wall. Not a sign of Henry Marcher, but an androgynous brunette who looked mighty fine in her Dallas Police Department uniform had a gun pointed at me. My gun was bigger, but the uniform won the fight. I may not like to wear one, but there's a reason we all like to see them on women. 'Cause they're super hot. No way was I going to duke it out with her.

I held one hand in the air and crouched low to set the Colt on the ground. "I'm a P.I. You can check my license. It's in my wallet, left inside pocket." I hoped she'd take me up on it, probably be the closest I could get to some action today.

She declined. "Reach in slow and toss it over here." I did and she studied it long enough to memorize every detail. "We got a report of some suspicious activity in this neighborhood. You mind explaining why you're slinking through people's front yards?"

"I'm working a case." I didn't bother telling her I was a bounty hunter on the prowl. Despite the rumors, cops don't necessarily hate

P.I.s, but they loathe bounty hunters. I have to be licensed as a P.I. to work as a bounty hunter, a fact that came in handy every once in a while. Like now, when I'd just gotten caught carrying a gun, something a bounty hunter isn't supposed to do when they are in the process of picking up a jumper. I shrugged. "Didn't know it was illegal to sit in my car or walk around a neighborhood."

"And the gun?"

Well, that was a sticky one. A concealed carry permit means just that—concealed. I'm not supposed to be running around waving my weapon in the air. I hustled for an explanation. "Sorry, I saw someone acting funny. Kinda spooked me."

I could tell she was considering the fact that she was the one who'd been acting funny, sneaking around the fence line. She jerked her chin at the gun on the ground next to me. "Looks like you're off the case for today. Why don't you clear out and leave these folks in peace?" It wasn't a question. She stood firm, legs spread, arms crossed. I dug in. I wasn't ready to leave. Hell, I'd spent the entire morning waiting to catch Henry. I was invested and, as much as I didn't want her to know what I was up to, I couldn't help a quick glance at the Marchers' house. That very moment, the garage door rumbled to life and slowly rose to reveal a boxy Olds Cutlass, circa 1985. Older than my Bronco. Made me feel a little better about my current state of financial well-being.

"Did you hear me? I said clear out."

I glanced back at Officer Hotstuff. I needed to lose her so I could take care of Mr. Marcher. The Cutlass was on its way out of the drive. Henry was at the wheel. That clinched it. "Great. I'll be on my way." I shot a look at the gun and she nodded. I grabbed it and rushed toward my truck, using every bit of restraint I could muster to keep from peeling out after Henry. I saw my new officer friend standing slack-jawed on the sidewalk, and I gave her a friendly wave.

Once I turned the corner, I hauled ass after Henry, slowing down as soon as I spotted him stopped at a light at the next intersection. I tapped my fingers on the steering wheel, impatient for the light to change while I made a plan. I needn't have worked so hard to fashion a strategy. Judging by the time it took him to accelerate from the light, Bronco would beat Cutlass in a drag race. In a drive through residential streets, I owned him. It pained me to drive so slowly, but I resigned myself to following him to his destination rather than cutting him off and taking him in the street.

We drove block after block at a painful pace. Finally, he pulled into the parking lot of an elementary school. Not a lot of action in the parking lot at eleven a.m. I parked a few yards away, contemplating my next move, while he sat behind the wheel of his ride, waiting. For what? A drug deal with a sixth grader? An opportunity to steal some school supplies?

I didn't have to wait long. He craned his neck at someone coming out the double doors of the school building and then got out of his car. He moved as slowly as his car and I rushed over to intercept. "Mr. Marcher?" He turned, his expression puzzled.

"Do you have Leonard?" he asked.

My turn to be confused. Who was Leonard? "I have a message from Hardin Jones. He said that you missed court and he sent me to help you get it straightened out." I'd chosen my most subtle approach. If it didn't work, I was prepared to tackle him.

"Oh, yeah. Well, I need to get Leonard now. I can come see Mr. Hardin later." He took a step away from me, toward the double doors.

I took two long steps and was at his side, cuffs in one hand, the other on my now concealed Colt. He looked back and I could tell when he fixed on the shiny silver of the handcuffs. I spread my hands, preparing to catch him when he bolted. He stood on his toes, ready to run, but before he could launch, the school doors burst open and we both turned to look.

"Ree-Ree!"

I watched as a skinny little guy ran and jumped into Henry's arms. Instead of looking shocked, like I would if a miniature person slammed into me, Henry smiled and patted the intruder on the head. "Hey, Lenny, I thought you weren't feeling so good."

"He has a fever."

The woman who spoke looked fierce, like school teachers were supposed to. I wondered what she would think about the fact a felon, make that a fugitive, had one of her charges in his arms. I thought about tipping her off, but decided she would be the type to call the cops. I wasn't sharing my catch. I decided on discretion. "Ma'am, I'm going to need you to take Leonard, or Lenny, back inside. I have some business with Mr. Marcher."

"You know Ree-Ree?"

When I'd left the house this morning, my plans did not involve having a conversation with a tiny person about someone named "Ree-Ree." Thankfully, Henry intervened.

"He's my little brother. The school called and he's sick. Momma's sick too, so she sent me to pick him up." He shot a glance at the fierce looking schoolteacher, and whispered, "I really need to take him home or my momma will whip me."

I wanted to meet the woman who could whip Henry Marcher, all six foot three inches, two hundred and fifty pounds of him. Again, I considered my options. Take him in now and leave little Lenny to rough out the rest of the school day with a tummy ache, while taking a chance the school marm wouldn't call the cops. I didn't need another run-in with the cops today, especially since I was carrying a gun on school property—enough to get me arrested for sure. The remaining option was equally distasteful, but legal and less likely to land me in trouble.

I leaned down and directed my comment to Lenny, not yet a felon. "How'd you like to ride in a Bronco?"

❖

It was nice to be standing in Hardin's office collecting money, two out of the last three days. I could get used to this. I was feeling so flush, I considered a middle of the week trip to the casino.

"That was fast. Ready for the other files?" Hardin asked.

"Sure." He handed me several files. "Hey, you have two of Geno Vedda's guys on bond?" I fished in my pocket for the scrap of paper where I'd written down their names. "Amato and Picone."

"What if I do?"

My antennae went up. Hardin wasn't usually cagey with me. "Just curious. Heard they were on the lam, figured I could roust them for you."

"Look at you, a regular entrepreneur. Stick to the cases I give you. You'll never find Geno's guys if he doesn't want them found."

"Any reason you wrote the bonds if you know they're such a risk?"

"Now you're scaring me." His expression told me exactly the opposite. He was amused, like I was a toddler trying to learn the biz. "You trying to go into business for yourself? Want me to tell you exactly how it's done? Everyone's a risk, but Geno sends enough work my way, I can afford to let some go. You want to look for them, go for it, but you're wasting your time." He reached in his desk, pulled a couple of files, and handed them over.

They were thinner than usual. As if he could read my mind, Hardin said, "Not much to go on, and what is there is probably a pack of lies."

"You'll pay the usual?"

"Ten percent of nothing is nothing. Good luck."

I took the files and left. A prickly feeling kept me from telling him that Geno himself had gone missing. Hardin didn't care about these guys, and Diamond cared enough to track me to my apartment and give up sexual favors. Maybe I'd find them, maybe I wouldn't, but I was curious enough to try.

It was only three o'clock, but it'd been a long day for me. Surveillance, almost being arrested, a car chase, apprehension, and turning in a jumper. The money in my pocket ached to be spent, but I was too spent to care. I pointed the Bronco in the direction of home and a nap.

I skulked through the small complex and managed to reach my door without running into Withers. I would've felt bad putting him off on the rent with a pocket full of cash. I tossed my jacket and holster on the kitchen counter and started toward the bedroom.

"You should get a better lock on the door."

Jess was lucky I recognized her voice and that I didn't have my gun in my hand. I strode over to the couch where she'd spread out. I refused to give her the pleasure of having both surprised and scared the fuck out of me. "You should take naps at your own place."

"I wasn't napping. I was waiting for you."

"I like 'em waiting, but next time wait in the bedroom."

"You wish."

I noted an edge to our banter. I'd known Jess since we both entered the police academy, more years ago than I cared to admit. She stayed on, and I bailed soon after we got our badges. Too many rules. She loved rules and she loved to remind me about them. Despite our differences, we'd both had similar needs, which resulted in a fuck buddy friendship that had outlasted any other relationship I'd ever had. After seeing her possessive way with the chick from the softball game, I sensed a shift between us. I could tell she wasn't here for a social call, but I couldn't resist testing the waters. I leaned over the back of the couch and brushed my lips against her neck. Her body froze, but her breath was quick and rough. Maybe I'd been wrong. Maybe she was here for the usual. I pushed my point by sliding my hand down her shoulder, across her chest. A stranger wouldn't have noticed how slightly she arched into my touch, but I was no stranger. Still, she was guarded and I wanted to know where I stood, so I said, "I'm tired. If you want to get laid, we'll need to get to it."

She sprung from the couch. "You should be so lucky. I'm here because someone should worry about how you're going to make a living when your license gets suspended. Again."

Guess that answered that. She hadn't dropped in for a quickie and, even if pleasure had crossed her mind a second ago, the moment had passed. Fine.

"What are you talking about?" I knew what she was talking about, but I wasn't going to make it easy on her to bust into my place and boss me around. I imagined Officer Hotstuff from this morning couldn't wait to tell Chance that I'd been waving a gun around a jumper's house this morning. No one seemed to care that he was the felon, not me.

I decided to play offense. "And you're one to talk about a license. How long you think you're going to keep your certification when I report you for breaking and entering?"

"You're kidding, right?"

I was half kidding. Well, I wasn't kidding at all, at least not about the angry part, but no way would I ever report her for anything. For a ton of reasons, one of which was she had enough dirt on me to take me out of commission for a very long time. She wouldn't, but she could. "Dial it back a notch. I assume you got a report from Officer Hotstuff."

She shot me a withering look. "That's Officer Pryor. Apparently, you think it's okay to carry a gun to round up bail jumpers."

"Maybe I was just taking a stroll through the neighborhood. I have a permit you know. Besides, turns out it was my lucky day. Officer Pryor is a hot number, and you know how much I like uniforms."

She didn't rise at the dig. She just sighed and stared at the floor. I hadn't expected jealously. What she and I had was casual, and it certainly wasn't exclusive, but I felt a little empty, like I'd expected more of a response. I dug a little deeper. "You know what I mean. I bet you put your uniform on for Red. Bet that really turns her on."

"Her name's not Red."

"Oh, I'm sorry, Heather, no last name, hottie from the softball game. You know if you shared a few more details, I might not be so crass."

"Lay off, Bennett." The three words were accompanied by a low growl. Finally, my shot had found its mark.

"Why? You want to keep this one all to yourself? Next thing you know you'll tell me you have feelings for her." I threw enough emphasis on the F word to make myself feel sick, and the strange look on Chance's face was a sucker punch to the gut. "Oh, shit. You do have feelings for her."

She stood. "I don't want to talk about it."

I strode over and poked her in the chest. "Say what you really mean. You don't want to talk about it with me."

"Yeah, okay. Maybe I don't."

I started to ask why, but bit back the words. It wasn't like we discussed everything. We'd known each other for a long time, but even so, we'd both been a bit cagey about sharing anything personal. The first time she'd met my father was just a few months ago, and then only because I'd managed to get myself in some deep shit. Since then, I'd shared a few more personal details about my lone wolf, super nerd brother and my get rich quick by marrying money mother, but beyond how she liked her coffee and what she craved in bed, the list of personal facts I knew about Jessica Chance could be counted on one hand. But I knew one thing. When a woman doesn't want to talk to her fuck buddy about another woman, she thinks it's serious. I hadn't wanted to talk to Jess about Ronnie Moreno, but I'd been delusional at the time. Jess wasn't the delusional type. I didn't think.

"You like her."

"I said I don't want to talk about it."

"That means you like her."

"If you were this persistent in your day job, you'd be rich."

"Quit trying to turn things around. And I don't have a J.O.B. I own my own business." A stretch of a description, but true nevertheless.

"Maybe you should have a job." She stared me down, dead serious. Something big was up with her. She always hassled me about my choice of work, but there had always been a layer of play in her words. Not now. So she was all serious and I felt weird. Or jealous. Or something I didn't want to examine right now. I abruptly changed the subject.

"My brother's getting married." Not exactly a complete change of subject.

She didn't miss a beat. "You don't say. When did he meet her? What does she do? Big wedding? Will your mom be there?"

Funny, I hadn't asked any of these questions when my dad had broken the news. Not because I didn't care, but because I hadn't thought to. That Jess was all hopped up about the details made me uncomfortable. "It's all being worked out."

"Will you be in the wedding?"

"What?" I didn't try to hide the shock in my response.

"You know a bridesmaid, or usher, or someone to cut the cake. Whatever."

She trailed off like she'd exhausted her wedding-related vocabulary. I could relate. What I knew about weddings consisted of what I'd seen on the covers of magazines as I stood waiting to check out with a six-pack at the grocery store. "I don't know. I mean, I don't think so." Her interest bothered me. I'd never figured Jess for one of those lesbians who dreams about weddings, walking down the aisle, two brides on a big, tall, white cake. The details alone made me shudder; imagining Jess in them would make my head explode. I cast about for a safer topic of conversation. "What do you know about Geno Vedda?"

"Why? Is he going to be at the wedding?"

"Seriously, Jess. I'm looking for a couple of his guys. What can you tell me about him?"

"I can tell you that if he doesn't want his guys found, you won't find them. Geno is more connected than Yuri Petrov."

Diamond was hooked up with Petrov when I'd first met her. At least she was pretending to be while she worked undercover to nail Petrov's brother for a murder. If Geno was more connected than Yuri, then Jess was right. I'd never find his guys. No wonder Hardin didn't hold out much hope.

"Hardin thinks it's a lost cause, but I think I might take a look anyway. Any chance you could get me a few details on them? M.O.? Something?"

"What's up?"

"What are you talking about?"

"Something's up with you. You're acting strange. If Hardin isn't interested in you finding these guys, then why do you care?"

She was one to talk about acting strange, all closed mouth about Red. Red, who she liked and didn't want to talk to me about. Well, two could play that game. "Diamond Collier came to see me."

"Agent Collier? Are you sure her first name is really Diamond?"

"I don't know. Who cares? Anyway, she came by Saturday night." *You know, the night you hustled Red off the softball field.*

"What did she want?"

"Lots of things." I couldn't resist a sly grin. "Some she got already, some I still owe her."

"I have to go."

"What? Now I have something to say and you don't have time to stick around? Delivered your lecture and now you're off duty?"

"Something like that."

"At least Collier thinks I have a real job."

"Is she the one who asked you to look for Geno's guys? Hell, she's using you. She's a freaking Fed. If they wanted to find those guys, they could. She wouldn't have to sleep with a two-bit bounty hunter to get what she wants."

"Fuck you, Chance. Fuck you."

"That's your solution for everything. Maybe you should find a better way to solve your problems than sleeping your way to a solution."

She stormed out, and I sunk onto the couch and pretended to be glad she was gone.

CHAPTER FOUR

I have a list of three things that I use to work off stress: sex, beer, and gambling. I'm not averse to doing more than one at the same time. Some people use exercise to work off stress. I run most mornings, but that's not about stress. The only reason I exercise is so I can drink all the beer I want and still have a body that someone will want to have sex with. Oh, and so I don't wind up looking like my father.

It was too late to run in my neighborhood with anything less than an Uzi. My go-to sex pal was probably cuddling up with her new friend. I had no beer in the house, and I didn't want to risk running into Maggie, who I now considered Dad's girlfriend more than my neighborhood bartender slash confidant. I picked up my phone and debated calling Diamond, but Jess's words rang in my head. "Sleeping my way to a solution." She was wrong, but somehow it seemed like calling Diamond on the heels of Jess's remark made me the wrong one.

That left one stress reliever I could always rely on. I grabbed my keys and half the contents of the coffee can in my kitchen cabinet and left my apartment.

The drive to the nondescript house was short. I stopped a block away and bought a twelve-pack of whatever was on sale. The tiny man with the crooked toupee who answered the door took the beer from me and gave me a big hug. "Luca, it's been a while. Haven't seen your dad either. Figured you both decided to get on the wagon."

"Not likely." I made the broad statement, but wondered about Dad. Since he'd started dating Maggie, he'd stopped doing a lot of stuff that had previously defined him. The last few times I'd asked him to the casino, he'd turned me down, and he only drank a few beers at a sitting instead of a case. Completely out of character and pretty ironic since he was dating a bar owner. "I've been broke." I reached into my pocket and pulled out the usual buy-in. "I'm flush now. You got a few losers that feel like parting with their money?"

He folded the bills and placed them in the pocket of his purple satin smoking jacket, then he motioned for me to follow him into the kitchen. "Fraternity brothers. Their girlfriends are watching, so they'll show off. Want me to deal you in?"

I had mixed feelings. College kids generally sucked at poker. Especially when they brought their dates along. They watched too much TV and fancied themselves high rollers. I could beat them, but the stakes would be high because they would toss in everything Daddy sent to fund the incidentals of their education, confident a single phone call would replace anything they lost. I was flush for me, but flush is relative. And I couldn't call Daddy. He didn't have any money and what he did went for dates with Maggie.

"You got something else going tonight?"

"I have another game starting in a bit. More your speed. Have a beer and relax. The Mavs game's on in the living room."

I was edgy, but decided to wait. I pulled a Miller from the carton and followed Bingo to the living room. Every room in his house had a theme, and this one was fat Elvis. Or mature Elvis as Bingo called him. He collected all manner of kitsch related to the King's reign in Vegas and was obsessed with conspiracy trivia about his idol's sudden death. I'd need a full case of beer to get through the night if we wound up playing in here.

I had an idea about how to deflect a night of Elvis trivia. Before Bingo could show me his latest collector's item, I asked him about Geno Vedda.

"What do you want to know? More importantly, why do you want to know? No offense, kid, but Geno's out of your league."

I didn't take offense. He only meant what Hardin and Jess had already implied. Bounty hunters like me look for loose ends. Guys like Geno didn't leave loose ends. I knew I wasn't going to find anything about Amato and Picone on the Internet. I'd given it a cursory look already, but pros don't leave traces. The only thing I found online was a record of their arrest and, since pros don't usually get arrested, I questioned whether the arrest had been a distraction from something bigger. No real way to tell. The best way to get intel on guys like this was the old-fashioned method. Ask around. The hard part was knowing who not to ask.

My dad had introduced me to Bingo when I was a kid. Bingo let me play with an extra set of poker chips while Dad blew our mortgage, then our grocery money, then traded beers for cards. Bingo knew most of our family secrets, and I trusted Bingo as much as I trusted anyone. "I'm looking for a couple of his guys. A favor for a friend."

"Since when do you do favors that could get you killed?"

I hoped that was a rhetorical question because I'd almost bought it on my last big job in a move that was part favor, part survival. I answered him with a question designed to appeal to his ego. "Special request. I guess you wouldn't know anything. Geno's a pretty big deal."

Worked like a charm. I watched Bingo puff up big, which made him look like a frog. Seriously, the smoking jacket would never give him the appearance of credibility he craved. "I know more than you think. Just concerned about my friend's daughter. If something happened to you, I'd never forgive myself." He leaned in and whispered in my ear. "Word is Geno's got a new business venture."

I patted my side where the Colt hung, ready for action. "I can take care of myself. Guess you'll be happy if Geno finds new work." In addition to his façade of restaurants and vending machines, Vedda was big into bookmaking, effectively shutting small players like Bingo out of that part of the gambling business. Bingo's advantage was his connection with cops. On any given night, off duty officers could be found in his living room, betting away their meager earnings. In exchange for the opportunity, they looked the other way when it came to Bingo's other customers.

"Geno and I run in different circles. My business doesn't leave a dent in his operation, and he leaves me alone. Besides, I send him a referral every now and then." Code for bets too big for Bingo to handle.

"So what do you know about this new venture of his?" I was pretty sure that Geno's new business was the reason U.S. Marshals were on his tail.

"Now's not a good time to discuss this." He motioned to the other room, teaming with young testosterone. "Come back tomorrow. During the day. We can talk then."

I got it. Some of Geno's guys ran games like Bingo's, and it wouldn't do to be talking about the competition when customers could listen in. Okay by me. I was already several beers in and I wasn't going hunting for mobsters tonight. I reached into my back pocket and pulled out the small notebook I kept with my wallet—a throwback to my cop days. I scrawled Amato and Picone's names, tore the sheet, folded it in half, and handed it over. "I'll come by tomorrow, but I still want a game tonight. We still on?"

He tucked the paper in his jacket. "Always, Luca. Always."

I'm sure he meant it at the time.

❖

I woke the following afternoon with shooting pains in my head and limited recall about how I'd made it back to my bed. I turned over to check the clock and was stabbed in the side by my holstered Colt. Couldn't remember the last time I'd been too drunk to take off my gun. Instinctively, I reached into my pockets and quickly realized I hadn't come home with any money. Thank God, I'd only withdrawn half the money in my coffee can bank or I'd be broke and hung over.

It was four p.m. I wanted to write off the day, but any thoughts about rolling over and going back to sleep went the way of my clear head. I stumbled out of bed and stripped down to my underwear. Shower or run? Both, I decided, mostly because a run would net me a cup of coffee from the corner grocery.

I pulled on a pair of sweats and a T-shirt that had only been in the dirty clothes pile a few days and traded my heavy black boots for ratty sneakers. A few stretches later and I was out the door. I left my gun behind. I didn't have the energy to pull the trigger. Took about a mile before I sweated out enough alcohol to start to feel human again. It was a cold, crisp afternoon, and I could see my breath as puffs of air, letting me know I was still alive. I ran another mile before I rewarded my efforts with a cup of black coffee, large and scalding hot. I drank the brew, letting it burn my tongue as I walked back to my apartment. A shower and I'd be ready for the day. Good thing since I needed to pick up the next jumper on my list if I was going to eat the rest of the week.

Fresh from the shower, wrapped in a towel, I studied the file for Laura Tanner, aka Lana Tease, stripper on the run. Laura had a bit of a drug problem and had been arrested for possession of a controlled substance, meth, enough to get tagged with a third degree felony. Range of punishment two to ten years as a guest of the state penitentiary. And she had a lengthy history so she was likely to do some time, which is probably why she took off the minute her lawyer had given her the bad news.

I didn't blame the girl for doing drugs. Hell, I'd have to be full under to strip for a bunch of pot-bellied, middle-aged men who spent their days nursing drinks and shoving dollar bills in G-strings. I shuddered at the very thought. I wasn't out to judge her, just bring her in. Someone else could do the judging.

Her last job had been at the Foxy Lady. I knew the place well. It's where I'd met Ronnie Moreno, fiery Latin lawyer lady who'd swept me up in her personal and professional drama and left me without a paycheck when she went to DC to work for a high dollar firm. Bitch. The Foxy Lady had closed down when its owner turned up dead and his business partners all went to the pokey. If Lana had worked there long, she'd need drugs—the place was a cover for a kinky sex club where the rich and powerful used the strippers as their personal playthings.

Unlike a usual case, I didn't start with a last known home address. I doubted Lana would bother returning to whatever flophouse she'd spent her strung out existence crashing in. Strippers had to strip, and they generally had no particular allegiance to a particular club. I decided to start in the same area of town as the Foxy Lady and work my way through the clubs. I'd bet the money I had left I'd find her in time to collect my fee before dinner. I hoped so anyway, since drinking my way through the bars could get expensive fast.

Thirty minutes later, I drove past the Foxy Lady and surveyed the choices. Slice of Heaven would be my last stop, if I had to check it out. It was owned by Yuri Petrov and he wasn't likely to welcome me in his establishment. Not after I'd played a part in his brother Andrei's arrest last year. Ah, good memories. I'd met Diamond working that case, and learned what an elusive and mysterious woman she could be.

I swung into a parking lot that connected several clubs and trudged into the dumpiest looking one first, Black Lace. I decided the name stood for the dark ambience. The whole place was dark except for a spotlight centered on the pole in the middle of the stage. Apparently, I was just in time, the music cued up, and seconds later, a tall blonde appeared and the DJ announced Magic had just taken the stage.

I didn't need to look at the picture in my pocket to know this dancer wasn't Lana. Rather than waste time watching Magic gyrate, and risk having to spend money on a drink for the dubious pleasure, I decided to poke around. The dressing room, such as it was, was pretty easy to find. It was still early so the crowd was scant. Clothing was scant too. When I walked in, no one seemed phased at the interruption, but they clearly wanted to let me know the roster was full.

"Try Slice of Heaven, down the street."

No thanks. "I'm not looking for work. I'm looking for someone." I pretended to consult the pad in my pocket. "Laura Tanner. Her stage name is Lana Tease." I dropped my voice to a whisper. "She's going to get an inheritance. Big one."

"Girl!" The dancer nearest me stood and walked over. "You're barking up the wrong tree. No one named Laura or Lana here." She slid an arm around my waist. "How about you give me that inheritance?"

I delicately removed her arm, which was way too close to my holster. A holster holding a gun that the law forbade me to carry into a bar. I doubted this woman would care, but you never know. "You ever seen Lana at any of the clubs?"

Strippers aren't the most loyal beings. They aren't actually employees. They are independent contractors, and though they might settle in at a place they liked, they had a tendency to move from club to club when business got slow. The owners didn't care—variety was good for business, and as long as they had a stable of pretty girls willing to shed their clothes, it was all good. Chances were good at least one of these three rock stars had run across her at some point. I didn't want to whip out the picture I had since it was a mug shot, but I would if I had to.

"Nope. Don't know Miss Soon to be Rich."

"I do." A mousy voice piped up, and a petite brunette walked toward me. "She's at the Dusty Rose. At least she was there last night. It's next to Slice of Heaven."

Of course it was. "Thanks, uh…"

"Marigold."

I didn't think naming yourself after a pungent flower that repels insects was necessarily a good marketing move, but I wasn't in the business so I couldn't really talk. "You think she may be headed back there tonight?"

"She raked in the cash last night. Pretty sure she'll be back. She didn't show up until about eight last night."

My work here was done. "Thanks, Mari—" I just couldn't bring myself to say it. "Um, thanks very much."

Within a few minutes, I was back in the Bronco. I hadn't had to spend a dime yet and I had a good lead. And a few hours to kill I decided now might be a good time to catch Bingo before his games started up and find out if he'd had any luck getting intel on Geno's guys.

He was in, but I was out of luck. He answered my knock, but instead of inviting me in to see his Elvis collection, he stepped out onto the front porch and shut the door behind him.

"Go away, Luca." The command was quiet and firm.

All I remembered about last night was that I woke up today with no money. I drew a conclusion that led me to mistake the source of his concern. "I'm not here to play. Don't worry—looks like I got cleaned out last night. Just checking in to see what you found out."

"I don't know what you're talking about." He shook his head and repeated his opening line. "Go away, Luca."

I hadn't been that drunk, but something had happened between last night's glad-handing promises to find out what he could and the cold shoulder he was offering now. I could tell by the stern expression on his face, it wasn't going to be easy to find out what. I peered over his shoulder as if I could see into the house. "What's up? You have people over?"

He shrugged, but his face remained impassive. "You need to go."

I stepped closer, but he held up both hands as if to ward off an attack. From me. Crazy.

I stepped back. "Okay, okay. I need to go. I'll go." As I left, I couldn't resist a parting shot. "Guess you aren't as connected as you think you are."

"You have no idea what you're doing, Luca. If I'd bothered to look at those names you gave me last night, I would have sent you packing then. Listen closely. You should find other work."

I didn't bother answering. We both knew that was never going to happen. I had skills. And now I was curious. The combination meant I was going to see this case through.

CHAPTER FIVE

What seemed like hours later, I'd blown twenty-five bucks on two watered-down drinks at the Dusty Rose, and I was ready to go. The dressing room in this place was guarded by a big barrel-chested guy who looked like he could stop bullets with his bare fists. I glanced at my watch. It was still early, and I resolved to nurse the shitty bourbon for another hour before giving up.

The next dancer to take the stage looked promising, but her name was Yvonna Hump. She had the same body type as Laura, aka Lana, but instead of blond hair, she sported flaming red waves. No way it was her natural color, but I'd have to wait until the lights went up to see if she was my gal.

"You like what you see?"

The voice came from behind, and I was certain I was about to be sold on the virtues of a good lap dance. I held up a hand to wave off interest, but the woman grasped it rather than walking away. "I think I'll have a seat and see what you find so captivating."

Now I recognized the voice. Diamond. "What the hell are you doing here?"

"Better question is what the hell are you doing? I thought you were going to find Amato and Picone? But instead, here you are getting your thrills watching cheap dancers." She pointed at the stage. "She's pretty hot, even with the fake hair color, but if you wanted a show, you have my number. Don't you know I'm an accomplished performer?"

She was, although I'd never seen her dance. On a stage, anyway. She'd started her last undercover gig as a stripper in one of Yuri's clubs, but had quickly morphed into socialite when he'd chosen her to become his arm candy at high society events. I'd never had a chance to see her dance, but I had seen her perform in other ways that convinced me of her flexibility. Tonight wasn't going to be one of them. I was focused on my long-term success and a little leery about the fact she seemed to be spying on me. "Why don't you buy me a drink?"

She signaled the waitress and ordered drinks for both of us. And she paid. The night was improving drastically.

"Anything to report?" she asked.

"Nope."

"Really? Bingo didn't have any information for you?"

I struggled to hide how pissed off I was at the confirmation she'd been following me. I decided to punish her by withholding info. "Nope."

"Surprising. I thought he was connected."

She could goad me all she wanted, but I wasn't giving up intel until she did. "Tell me more about why you are so interested in Geno."

"Seriously? He's a mobster? Isn't that enough?"

She tossed off the comment, her eyes trained on Ms. Hump. I waved a hand in front of her face. "Uh, no. He's always been a mobster. Why now? Is it because he's into something new?"

Her face lit up. Damn, I hadn't meant to say that last part out loud, but it was too late. She latched on and wouldn't let go.

"So you did find out something. Care to share? There might be more in it for you than the bounty on Geno's guys."

"Oh yeah, like what?"

She licked her lips. Really? She was great, but I didn't need to catch bad guys to get laid, and I told her so.

"All right then. What do you want?"

I looked up on stage and she followed my glance. The music was winding down and so was Yvonna, but like a true star she gave it her all and wound herself around the pole one last time. As she curved her body up and over, her hair color morphed from red to blonde. It wasn't a magic trick. Her wig started to slip, and she almost fell when she released the pole to try to push the wig back into place. The DJ caught the action and cut the lights and music before we could witness her complete demise.

I turned to Diamond. "That's my jumper. You want my help, then help me get her." I didn't wait for a response, didn't expect one. I jumped off my stool and strode to the dressing room. Barrel-chested bullet stopper was in position. "I need to see Yvonna. It's very important."

He didn't bother with words, but he held out a hand and shook his head.

Diamond's voice cut through the crap. "We're here on an important federal matter. She has information crucial to our nation's security."

I looked over my shoulder and tried not to laugh at Diamond's look of exaggerated importance. Oh, and the badge she shoved at the big guy. That almost sent me over the edge. I looked back at big guy and muscled a stern look back on my face. "She's right. It's imperative that we speak with her immediately."

He looked from me to Diamond, probably assessing whether we were kooks or cops. Finally, he stepped aside and motioned us through. Once we were a few steps away from him, I whispered in Diamond's ear, "'Crucial to our nation's security'?"

She shrugged. "It worked, didn't it?"

I ignored her comment and pushed the double doors that led to the dressing room. This one looked just like all the others. Worn tables with bright mirrors and clothes strewn on every surface. I counted four girls before I lasered in on the one I was after. I silently willed Diamond to follow my lead.

"Yvonna?"

She didn't respond, so I took a step closer and tried a different tack. "Laura?"

That got her attention, but not in a good way. Even in a thong and five-inch heels, she was faster than me. She dashed to the opposite side of the room, but Diamond was waiting there and blocked her exit through the fire door. Talk about fast. She must have moved when I wasn't looking. I mouthed a begrudging thank you. She nodded and then leaned down and whispered something in Laura's ear, which seemed to deflate her enthusiasm for flight. They even seemed to get cozy for a minute, and I saw a flash of burnt orange as Laura reached her hand inside Diamond's jacket. I strode over to assess the situation—she was my jumper, after all—but by the time I reached them, they'd finished their cuddling. Despite shouts from the other girls warning her not to go with us, Laura accompanied Diamond out of the club without resisting. I followed like a useless appendage.

When we finally reached the parking lot, Diamond thrust her toward me. "Do your stuff."

I cuffed Laura and put her in the backseat of the Bronco. Before I joined her, I pulled Diamond aside. "I could have taken her. What was going on between you two back there?"

"Maybe I was just calming her down, by telling her what a good time the two of us had when you apprehended me."

She was lying, but I couldn't figure out why. "She was all over you."

"Jealous?"

"You wish. I could've taken her myself."

"I have no doubt, but I had fun helping you out. Now it's your turn."

She was leaving lots of stuff out. I could feel it. I brushed aside the odd interaction she'd just had with my jumper and focused on the reason Diamond had contacted me in the first place. "Tell me why it's so important you find these guys, Amato and Picone. Or why it's so important *I* find these guys."

That last was the part I really wanted to know. She had access to all the weight and power of the mighty U.S. government. Surely, they could locate two mid-level mobsters without help from me. Unless maybe the pursuit for Geno wasn't an authorized case, which made me both question why I'd want to get involved and get excited about the prospect at that same time. "You going to tell me it's a matter of national security or is that just a line you use to pick up strippers?"

She shook her head and laughed. "Don't you know by now? Everything's a matter of national security. But seriously, you're right; we can find those guys on our own. I just figured someone may as well profit from it, and I figured finding them would be an easy job for you. Find them or not. It's your choice."

Right, my choice. We didn't know each other well enough for her to have such a good handle on my desire for easy money. On the other hand, maybe finding Amato and Picone would be easy. Besides asking Bingo for info, I hadn't really tried. Maybe I'd turn Lana/Yvonna/Laura in, collect my money, and get Geno's guys. Show the Feds how easy it was to find lost souls. Collect the bounty and then collect a little something else from one of the Fed's finest. The prospect of cash and carnal pursuits spurred me to make a brash promise. "Oh, I'll find them. You just better be ready to pay up."

I waited with Laura in the car and watched Diamond walk away. I'd hoped she parked nearby so I could get a fix on how she was getting around. No telling how that information could be useful, but I wanted it. There were too many cars, though, and she disappeared in the shadows. Once I settled on the fact I'd lost her, I started the Bronco and pulled forward only to be blocked by a Bentley that swerved into my path. I shot the driver the finger, for my personal satisfaction since I doubted he would give a shit about being cursed by someone in an old SUV. To my surprise, the car stopped and a passenger emerged. A huge passenger, and rather than emerge, he kind of unfolded from the interior of the car. I recognized this guy. I didn't know his name, but he was Yuri Petrov's chief muscleman.

Shit. I shifted into reverse and glanced in the rearview mirror, only to realize I wasn't going anywhere. The car blocking me from behind wasn't a Bentley, but a midnight black Hummer. Not the small-scale version yuppies buy, but the full-size luxury SUV only the truly rich could afford. I knew it had to be one of Yuri's.

I had no way out, and muscleman was headed my way. I slid my hand into my jacket and made sure the Colt was ready for action. My ride was packed with guns, but only two were currently in my reach and I didn't want to act too suspicious. On that front, I turned to Laura and warned her to be quiet. "Don't say a word. Let me do all the talking. If you want to live."

Maybe she was the reason behind this roadblock. Maybe she was one of Yuri's favorite girls and he didn't want her hauled in. Maybe he'd pay me the bounty himself. Yeah, right.

Muscleman tapped on my window and I cracked it just enough to hear him say, "Luca Bennett."

It's not good when they remember your name, but no sense playing dumb now. "Yeah?"

"Mr. Petrov would like a word with you."

I bet he wanted more than a word. "Tell him to call my secretary and schedule an appointment."

He nodded at Laura. "This woman? Is she your secretary?"

I couldn't tell if he was kidding or just plain dumb. Yep, I always cart my secretary around in the backseat of my car, in handcuffs. Then I remembered who I was dealing with and realized this guy might be serious. I needed to placate him long enough to get out of here and back to the relative safety of my crappy, but well arsenaled apartment. I pointed at the handcuffs circling Laura's wrists. "She's off duty at the moment."

"I see. She seems content to stay where she is." He pointed to a guy standing next to him. "My associate will watch her while you talk to Mr. Petrov. He's waiting." He jerked open my door and waited. I climbed down rather than be pulled from my own vehicle, and followed him back to the Bentley. He frisked me and took the Colt, then opened the rear passenger door and waved me inside.

Yuri sat in the back, an Afghan dog at his feet. Probably the most unscary animal on earth, but I had a healthy fear of being trapped in someone else's vehicle with nothing more than a .22 in my boot.

"Luca Bennett, bounty hunter. How nice to see you again."

"Hey, Yuri, nice ride." I didn't know what else to say, and it was a nice ride even if I could imagine a million other places I'd rather be.

"You like my ladies? You like them very much."

I didn't have a clue where he was headed with this. Had he seen me with Diamond and recognized her? That wouldn't be good. Maybe he just thought I'd come from one of his clubs. I decided to play along. "The woman in the truck? She's not a date, she's a payday." Maybe he had business with her and wanted to take her off my hands. Her bond was seventy-five hundred; my fee would be ten percent, which was a small price to pay for my freedom. "If you have a more pressing matter with her, we can deal."

"You like to deal, that is true."

It wasn't a question so I didn't respond. I didn't have a clue where this conversation was going, and with every passing second, I felt more claustrophobic, which diluted what little manners I usually possessed. "Yuri, I'd love to stay and chat, but I really need to get going."

"Morris Hubbard, Bingo, you know him, right?"

Holy shit. I'd heard Bingo's real name only once before, and it was when Chance found out I spent most of my take at his place. She made some snarky comment about how at least I'd picked the most untouchable gambling house in town to lose every penny I made. I didn't think she meant it as a compliment, and I didn't think Yuri brought up Bingo to find out where he could catch a game. Bingo's last words to me, "You need to find another line of work," rang loud. Right now, in this moment, I had a tendency to agree with him. "What about him?"

"You are friends, yes?"

"Depends. What do you want?" Yuri didn't like the direct approach, but I was convinced if I stayed on track, I could shortcut to whatever he wanted or needed from me.

"I would like you to talk to him. Convince him his business partners aren't working in his interest. He needs a new patron. That patron is me. You will tell him."

I wasn't going to be telling Bingo anything, but right now I'd promise Yuri whatever he wanted if he'd just let me out of the damn car. Bentley or not, right now it felt like a tomb. "I'm just a bounty hunter. I thought you knew that."

"As I recall, you are good at what you do. You like bounty? Then do as I say." He nodded at the guy who'd sat across from us, pretending not to listen to our conversation, and he pushed open the door. I didn't waste any time scrambling to exit, but Yuri's hand pulled me back.

He stuck his hand at me and I instinctively took it, curious about the cold metal he left in my fist when he withdrew, but more concerned with getting out of the car. His last words rung in my ear as I walked briskly back to my car.

"Bounty is good. Do as I say."

❖

"Who were they?"

I turned to Laura, semi surprised she was still cuffed and seated in my ride. The deal with Yuri had lasted only ten minutes, but it felt like hours since Diamond and I, mostly Diamond, had apprehended Laura at the club. Surreal. The only thing that assured me the whole event had indeed been real was the piece of metal still clenched in my hand. I slowly spread my fingers and gazed at the gold coin. The writing on it was in what looked like Russian—lots of vowels and hard consonants. It was big, bigger than a half dollar. And heavy.

Bounty. I'd just been paid in advance. But for what?

"That looks valuable."

Laura was chock full of keen observations. Pretty annoying while I was trying to process what had just happened. Strange night. First Bingo, make that Morris Hubbard, shunned me. Then Diamond tailed me and basically took over my job. Then Yuri and his band of muscle waylaid me in a strip club parking lot and left treasure in their wake. And something else had happened, something that nibbled at the edge of my memory. Like a rat feeding its hunger on whatever it can find. I stared out the window, trying to remember, when Laura interrupted again.

"What are you going to do with me?"

Laura. That was it. I'd have sworn I saw Laura give Diamond something back at the club, or Diamond took something from her. The whole exchange had been off. As if they'd known each other. I remembered how intently Diamond had watched the stage, even before I told her Laura was my jumper. I'd been sure Diamond was at the club for me, but what if Laura was the reason Diamond had been at the club in the first place?

I considered Laura's question and decided the answer depended on how willing she was to share whatever information she had. "That woman who was with me, do you know her?"

"What woman?"

"Seriously?" Diamond wasn't the kind of woman you missed, whether you preferred chicks or guys. Either you wanted to fuck her or you thought your man wanted to. I wasn't in the mood to play games. I pulled the Colt from my shoulder holster, cocked it, and pointed it at her thigh. "You need that leg to dance, don't you? Or do you have a side job you'd care to tell me about?"

"I don't know her."

Her voice shook, but I knew she wasn't being completely honest. I waved the gun. "You talked to her."

"She talked to me."

She could drag this on forever. I leaned over the seat and, with my free hand, I started searching the scant clothing she wore. She wriggled away in protest. "What are you doing?"

"Looking for answers. You handed her something. What was it?"

"Get your hands off me. I don't have it anymore."

I pressed the barrel of the Colt against her flesh. "Tell me."

She whimpered, but she was close to breaking. "Meds. They were mine. It was nothing."

She wasn't making any sense. "You gave her medicine? What was it?"

"T-bars. Just a few. They were mine. Prescription."

Xanax. I didn't believe her because it didn't make sense that Diamond would ask for drugs from a stripper or that a stripper would offer drugs to a federal agent. Then again, I had seen a flash of burnt orange pass between them. Could've been a prescription bottle. Still didn't make sense. "You just up and gave her a bottle of pills that belonged to you. What? Were you trying to bribe her not to haul you in?"

"She knew I had them. She told me to hand them over."

No way. "You'd never seen her before, but she just walked up to you said, 'May I have your Xanax prescription please?'"

Laura crossed her arms. "Ask her yourself, if you don't believe me. She grabbed me and said, 'Give me the prescription, fast and quiet.' Hell, I didn't know who she was or how she knew I even had it. I still don't know who she is, but she had a gun. I wasn't going to tell her no." She gave the gun pressed against her leg a pointed look. I uncocked the Colt and placed it in my lap, still in sight, but not as threatening.

A thought hit me. "The script wasn't yours, was it?"

"It had my name on it."

The queen of literal. "Where did you get it?"

The look of fear in her eyes told me what I needed to know. Well, it gave me a hint anyway. "Do you have more?"

She nodded slowly and I considered my options. Her bond wasn't a huge amount, but enough to keep me in beer and housing for another month. But I was curious, and with a list of jumpers to catch, I was feeling rich. Rich enough to feed my curiosity. "Tell you what, you give me a bottle of exactly what you gave her, tell me where you got it, and I'll let you go." I holstered the gun as a show of good faith.

She didn't have much choice, but she was bent on wrangling some of the details. "I'll do it, but you can't do anything with the info until tomorrow. I need to get out of town."

"Deal."

She gave me turn by turn directions to a shack, posing as a house in a neighborhood worse than mine. I was no stranger to this part of town, but I was sure glad I didn't live here. I wanted to wait in the car while she went in to get me some of what she promised, but I didn't trust her. Funny, since she was either too trusting or too dumb to realize she'd led me to where she lived. Guess she figured I'd either keep my word not to come looking for her or that I wouldn't want to return.

I followed her inside. The place was the very definition of squalor, but I tried to act like I visited dumps every day. She offered me water, which I'm sure would be poison once poured into any of the nasty glasses lining what I'm sure were roach-filled cabinets. It amazed me what some people do with their freedom. Jail would be a step up for her.

She ducked into the bathroom, and I chose not to follow. I have some standards, and frankly, I was scared of contracting one of those flesh-eating strains of bacteria. She popped out in less than a minute and shoved a prescription bottle in my hand. I read the label.

"This is just like the one you gave Di—I mean my partner?" No sense disclosing Diamond's name, real or not.

"Exactly."

I rolled it over in my palm and read the label. Laura's name, address, and an official looking patient number. And a logo for a pharmacy I'd never heard of. "I don't get it. What's so special about it?"

"I dunno."

She did and I told her so. "Deal was the bottle and info. Spill."

"I don't know much," she insisted. "I get it from this gal at Slice of Heaven. I don't know where she got it."

"You get what? The pills? And then what, you put them in an old bottle with your name?" Possession of an unauthorized script was a misdemeanor. Not Laura's most serious crime, but I could see why she'd want to minimize her exposure.

"No, I get the pills and the bottle. They come together. You know, the pills are in the bottle." She delivered the ramble as if I were the slowest person on the planet. Right now, I kinda felt that way.

"But your name is on the bottle."

"Right. They put it on there."

"Who's 'they'?"

"I dunno."

She probably didn't. "Okay, give me the name of the girl you got them from."

"She's one of Yuri's girls. She's not going to talk to you."

"Great, we won't talk. Give me her name."

"I don't know her real name." I stared her down and waited. Finally, she shook her head. "She goes by Candy."

Of course she did. I closed my fist over the pill bottle and contemplated my next move. It wouldn't involve Laura, aka Yvonna Hump. Looked like I was going to make a trip to Slice of Heaven whether I wanted to or not. But first, I needed some advice, and I knew just who to call.

I cut Laura loose and drove directly to Chance's place. It was late, but we regularly called on each other late at night. True, I usually showed up looking for something other than advice or information in the dead of night. I wasn't ruling out a little release if she was up for it. Spending the evening in strip clubs would affect anyone's libido. And brushing into Diamond hadn't helped.

As I pulled up to Chance's house, I plotted my approach. Sex first, then information. She was more likely to share when she was relaxed. But the minute I drew close, I realized my plan was just that—mine. Jess had other plans.

I recognized the snazzy car from the day Red had picked her up at the softball game. What I hadn't noticed at the game was the Illinois plate. Interesting, but Illinois or Texas, it really didn't matter. Jess was probably relaxing just fine without my help. I considered knocking on the door anyway. It was late; maybe Red would be leaving soon. Surely, she wouldn't mind an interruption from one of Jess's old friends. But I knew she would. Same way I would if Red came calling while I was visiting. Rather than put a name to what I felt, I did a petty thing and wrote down the tag number of Red's car, then peeled out in a move sure to disturb whatever activity was going on inside.

CHAPTER SIX

I started the next day early. Really early since I hadn't really slept. Instead, I'd spent a healthy amount of time on the Internet, looking up the coin Yuri had forced on me. It was a Russian Imperial 5 Ruble, 1885, worth several grand, depending on who you asked. Maybe I should be happy about scoring such a big reward, but I couldn't help but think about the consequences of accepting it.

I stuck the coin in my pocket, and turned to less professional pursuits, like the numbers and letters on the crumpled piece of paper I'd saved from last night. Chance wasn't my only friend on the force, and I'd called in a favor to get Red's plate run. Red, aka Heather Deveaux, not only drove a fancy car, she had a posh Chicago address. According to LinkedIn and Avvo, she was a doctor, an ophthalmologist, and part of a group of eye specialists located in the Windy City. Either she hadn't gotten around to updating her profile or she was between jobs. Or she was only here for a visit.

A doctor. Make that surgeon. Whatever. I wondered where Jess had met the good doctor. On a case was the most likely answer since she was a workaholic. Or maybe some do-gooder on the softball team finally decided to make good on their promises to find the coach a gal. They didn't understand that Jess didn't need any help getting dates; she just wasn't big on relationships. Other women our age seem to think all dates came with the possibility of more. I knew better. Jess was probably banging Dr. Deveaux for fun. And who could blame her? Dr. Red was a hottie. I'd have banged her if I'd seen her first.

But I hadn't, and the fact that Jess had, crawled under my skin and made me restless. I wasn't sure if my restlessness was more about Deveaux or Jess. I shut down my laptop and changed into tattered sweats and a Notre Dame sweatshirt left behind by a one-night stand. As I recalled, that particular Irish hadn't fought me. Not much anyway. I shook off the memory. Not getting laid last night had as much to do with my edgy mood as the string of questions I had about Diamond, Jess, and the surprise visit from Yuri. A run would calm me down.

My neighborhood woke slowly. It was after eight, and signs of life were limited to the garbage truck collecting the remains of last night's fun from local bars and convenience stores. Fine by me. I liked quiet mornings since I usually spent them tucked in bed. Not having regular hours worked well with my tendency to work at night and rest in the mornings.

I ran twice as far as usual, but the racing thoughts coursing through my brain were not to be outdistanced. I focused on the professional, not the personal. Yuri's instructions to me, to speak to Bingo, spooked me more than I liked to admit. For several reasons. First, even though I knew Bingo's gambling biz was illegal, I hadn't pegged him for being involved in organized crime. But Yuri wasn't the kind of guy to sling around rumors. So who was Bingo in business with and why did Yuri want a piece of it? Had to be big to draw his interest.

Jess might know. Or know someone who did. The cops were always trying to catch the Petrov family in the act, but usually it was the Feds who were on Yuri's tail. I honed in on Jess instead of the other person who might know about the Bingo angle—my dad. He'd known Bingo since before I was born. Surely, he had to have picked up some intel during hundreds of poker games over the years.

Where to start? Jess or Dad? It was still early by my standards. Dad wouldn't be up, or God forbid, he might be at Maggie's place, and/or she at his. Chance would either be at home or on the job. Or maybe she'd stayed in, brewed coffee, and scrambled eggs for Dr. Red. Ick. If that mess was happening, it needed to be interrupted.

After a quick shower, I made a call and then swung by her place. The Beemer was still parked in the drive. Lovely. I could stay or I could go. I didn't want to bear witness to the domestic bliss probably happening inside, but why should I change my habits because Jess had changed hers?

I resisted the urge to block the Beemer in and parked on the street. I was halfway to the door when it opened and Dr. Red strode down the walk. She wore a sharply tailored black suit with a light blue shirt. I don't know much about fancy clothes, but the shirt looked soft, like silk. She was taller than I remembered, partly because of the high-heeled black pumps. Where was she going, all dressed up?

I smiled and took a stab. "Job interview?"

"Excuse me?"

"Just a guess, Dr. Deveaux. Or maybe you've already landed a cush job at a private practice. That's what you're used to, right?"

"Do I know you?" She wrinkled her forehead for a moment, and then the shade of recognition fell. "Oh wait, you were at the softball game. You're a friend of Jessica." She said Chance's name, slow, enunciating each syllable.

Jess-i-ca? Did she really call Chance Jess-i-ca? What other special couple things did the two of them share?

"I am a friend. An *old* friend. And what are you?" I had intended to use a more subtle approach, but she had an edge about her that put me off. Confident, superior. Qualities I usually found attractive, but coming from her, the attributes left a sour taste. Like they weren't genuine, like they were covering something else. I stared her down until she answered.

"I'm a friend too. A *new* friend." She smiled. A smarmy smile, and added, "New friends are a treasure, don't you agree?"

Okay, that did it. I hated her. "Weren't you on your way out?"

She glanced back at Chance's front door, like the last thing she wanted to do was leave if I was staying. "Yes, I suppose I was."

"Well, don't let me keep you." I swept my arm in a grand gesture toward her car. Her very expensive car, which looked totally out of place in front of Jess's modest house.

She took a step, then stopped. "I do need to go, but I'll be back. Soon."

I watched her drive off. If her parting words were meant to be some sort of threat, I wasn't buying. No way was a woman like that going to steal Jess's heart. I tried not to wonder why I cared so much.

Jess's paper was still in the yard. I picked it up and carried it to the door, which swung open before I could raise my finger to press the bell.

"What're you doing up?" She stood in the doorway, her blond hair wet, her long-sleeve shirt unbuttoned to reveal a flat plane of well-toned muscle. Sexy. Delicious. I tried to ignore how freshly fucked she looked.

"Nice greeting. Thought you'd be in a better mood, *Jessica*."

She squinted at me, likely trying to divine what I meant without having to ask. I left her guessing. "Are you going to invite me in?"

"I need to get to work."

"You're late already. John will cover for a while longer." Chance had recently been reunited with her old partner. For the past few months, she'd been stuck with a loser named Elton, who thought the way up the ladder was on the back of his more experienced partner. Unlike Elton, John didn't consider me a near felon, and he knew Jess and I went way back. When I called him this morning, he'd let me know that Jess had called and said she was going to be late. I'd correctly assumed she was still at home and headed right over. Apparently, my timing had been perfect. Now that Dr. Red was gone, Jess could make coffee for me.

"Come on in. We can talk while I get ready." She didn't wait for an answer, and left me in the doorway while she strode off in the direction of her bedroom. I'd only been here a few times in the light of day. Normally, I showed up late at night and whatever happened between us occurred in the dark.

I liked her place. It looked lived in. Pictures on the walls, mementos on the shelves. The pots and pans hanging in the kitchen were used for cooking, not dust-gathering, potential weapons like they would be at my place. And she owned the place, which meant no nosy landlord snooping around. I followed her to the bedroom and made myself comfortable on the unmade bed while she finished getting dressed with a leisure I didn't usually see. I felt smug that I, not the doctor, had the pleasure of this particular intimacy.

She let me ogle for a few minutes before she asked, "Are you going to stare at me or tell me what you came for?"

"Maybe you'd like to come now." I patted a spot on the bed beside me. "Care to join me?" I was only partly kidding, but I added a laugh to give her an out and save face in case she blew me off.

She didn't laugh me off. No, she did something far worse.

"I'm seeing someone."

"What does that mean?"

"Don't make me say it."

Our casual relationship was over. I could read it in her eyes. I was torn about whether I wanted her to speak the words. We'd relieved each other's stress for ages. Was she really cutting me loose? For a hot broad in a fancy car?

Looks like I'd answered my own question, but I pushed the point. "Are things between you and Dr. Deveaux that serious?"

She whipped around. "How do you know her name?"

"Magic."

She shoved me in the shoulder. "Leave it be, Bennett. My girlfriend isn't one of your jumpers."

"Girlfriend?" I hadn't meant to say that out loud, but the word tumbled out before I could stop it.

She blushed. Apparently, my shout made Jess as uncomfortable as it made me. It's one thing to announce something and another again to have it reflected back at you. I stared at Jess's reddening face. I'd seen her face assume lots of different expressions—anger, pain, humor, passion—but never anything that resembled embarrassment. I grabbed her arm. "Sorry, didn't mean to yell. What's up with you?"

She shrugged out of my grasp and put several feet of distance between us. She was acting like I was a disease she might catch. I stared her down until I drilled through the surface. She wasn't embarrassed about calling Heather Deveaux her girlfriend. She was embarrassed about me. About the fact I'd still show up on her doorstep, looking for casual sex, when she'd probably already whispered words of promise to the doctor.

"So I guess you are pretty serious about her." I was the master of the obvious today.

"I like her. A lot."

"Tell me about her. Does she have a job yet? Is the job market better here than in Chicago?" I hated acting all casual about the subject, but I figured it was the only way I'd get any info at all. If pushed, I'd have to admit my curiosity was more about envy than interest.

"Let's not do this, Bennett. Did you have some other reason for dropping by? Mornings aren't usually your thing."

She knew me. And I'd come to rely on that. I wanted to tell her I'd come by the night before, but she'd been too busy for what we normally shared. I wanted to know details about Deveaux, but she didn't want to share what had become her preferred form of intimacy. I resolved to find out some other way and focused instead on the original reason for my visit.

"What's Yuri Petrov up to these days?"

Her face got stormy and I smiled. This was the Jess I knew. "Stay away from him."

"Don't have to tell me twice. Problem is he won't stay away from me." I described our chance meeting the night before and showed her the gold coin. "It's an Imperial Five Ruble. I Googled it."

"It's old. Bet it's worth a fortune."

"You know a good pawn shop?"

"Don't be stupid. Did Yuri give this to you?" She didn't wait for my answer. "You should give it back. You keep this, he owns you."

My turn to step back. "No one owns me." I stared hard to make sure she got the full implication of my words.

"Chill. I'm not telling you anything you don't already know. Yuri's people have been very active lately. I don't know what they're up to, but I think they're squaring up for a big move."

"Any reason it might have something to do with Bingo's place?"

She shook her head. "I don't get how Bingo could be involved. Yuri's not into gambling."

"But Vedda is. And when I showed up asking Bingo about Vedda's guys, he practically threw me off the property. There's something I'm missing, but I don't know what it is." I started to mention the prescription I'd gotten from Laura the night before, but she cut in to warn me off again.

"Is there a reason you care? Is Hardin not giving you enough work? Stick to what you do best and leave the detecting to those who get paid for it."

I thought about the other jumpers still on my list. Her comment about detecting pissed me off, but she was right. I wasn't a cop, nor did I want to be. Wasn't my job to stop crime. I should go for the sure thing and leave the loose ends for someone who cared. There was only one reason for me to chase down whatever Vedda, Petrov, and Bingo were into, and Jess named it before I could.

"Unless you're so hot for the Fed that you'd scare up trouble you don't need. That's never worked well for you before."

Diamond. We'd somehow circled back around to her. "Why don't you like her?"

"I don't know her. And neither do you. But I do know this—once you go as deep undercover as she did, it's hard to ever be honest." I started to protest, but she held up a hand to stop me. "Hear me out. Maybe honesty isn't the best word, but the line between truth and fiction becomes shady. It has to or you can't survive. I'm not faulting her, but I believe she'll use you to get what she needs. Don't count on her needs to be the same as yours. Be careful."

She cared enough to warn me from danger, but that kind of caring wasn't what I'd come looking for. I wasn't going to beg and she wasn't offering. The realization made me act like a spoiled two-year-old who couldn't stand to see someone else playing with her toy. "Why don't you stick to running the doctor's life, not mine? I can take care of myself."

"Then why don't you do that? As I recall, you showed up here without an invite. You can leave anytime you like."

She didn't deserve my anger, but I didn't have anything else to offer. I stood and started toward the door, pausing when she called my name.

"Luca."

I turned around. "Yeah?"

"Be careful. I mean it."

She frowned, with worry not anger. I recognized the look. I'd seen it before and had even welcomed her concern, but right now, I'd trade a pound of her concern for an ounce of something deeper. When had the balance between us shifted from need to want? I shoved the question deep. I didn't have answers. At least none I wanted to explore. I left without another word and she didn't try to stop me.

❖

I drove home and took a nap. I planned on a long one to compensate for getting up too early for absolutely no reason whatsoever, but precisely at the moment my eyeballs started REMing, a loud and unrelenting knocking jerked me out of sleep. At the same instant, my cell phone started ringing. Boy, was I popular. I glanced at the phone—unknown number. Again. That made at least five I'd gotten in the last week. I pushed ignore, grabbed the Colt from my nightstand, and strode to the door, ready to shoot up whoever felt the need to knock so damn loud at eleven in the morning. I swung the door wide and waved my gun. "What the hell do you want?"

"Put that thing away. You could kill somebody. And put some clothes on before you answer the door. Didn't your mama teach you any better?"

My landlord, Ernest Withers, averted his eyes, but his red face signaled he was truly mortified to have seen me half-dressed. I'd answered the door dressed only in an old, ratty T-shirt, sporting a big gun. I probably looked ridiculous, but I didn't care. He was the one who'd interrupted my nap, after all. "My mama taught me not to beat on people's doors in the middle of the day."

He shuffled in place, but he didn't back down. "I came for the rent you owe. Don't you own any clothes that don't have holes in them?"

The non sequitur didn't faze me. I was used to his eccentric ways. His ways, and the fact that he overlooked most of mine, were a large part of the reason I stayed in this dump. I usually paid my rent around the middle of the month, and considered the delay a free line of credit. This month, I'd gone into the third week before he'd caught me. It wasn't that I didn't have the cash. It was just that there were so many more fun things to do with money than pay for a roof over my head. I thought back to the other night when I'd blown a large part of my stash at Bingo's. That'd been fun, but paying Withers now would put another serious dent in my cash flow. I hunted around until I found my jeans on the floor where I'd shed them and pulled a small wad of bills from the pocket. I peeled off a few bills, about half the rent, and handed it to him. "Here's most of it," I exaggerated. "I've got steady work. I can get the rest to you next week."

He snatched the bills from my hand before I could change my mind and sighed heavily while he counted it out. "Luca, I have a business to run. You may be able to work whenever you like, and do God knows what in the middle of the day..." He cast a disparaging look from my smashed hair to my crumpled attire. "But I have bills to pay."

"Aw, come on, Withers. I'll get you your money. I always do." I waved the Colt again. "Now run along or I'll report you to the housing authority for being a slumlord." I had no idea if there was a housing authority who made sure cheapskates like me have decent housing for almost no money, but I played the bluff well. He scurried off and I hit the bed again, but this time sleep was elusive. Instead of counting sheep, I counted unanswered questions about Diamond, Bingo, Vedda, Petrov. And Jess. All subjects I knew less about than I should, but more than I wanted.

After an hour of futile ciphering, I gave up on sleep and consulted Hardin's list. The next jumper listed was Otis Shaw. Bond had been posted at fifty grand, a healthy payout. Time to collect some funds and forget about gamblers, gangsters, and girls. For now, anyway.

I'd saved this particular jumper for a reason. Apprehending him was going to be more work than the others. Otis Shaw wasn't a small-time thug. He'd been charged with murder, and he'd cut out the day his trial was supposed to begin. He wasn't a psycho kind of murderer. The person he shot down was a childhood friend turned rival in a dispute over drugs and a woman. To guys like these, the drugs were probably more important than the woman, but she'd probably been what had tipped the scale from anger to gunshots. Finding her would likely lead me to him.

The Internet gave her last known in just a few clicks. I dressed in the Colt, Sig, and my trusty switchblade, and headed out the door. By now it was one o'clock and I was starving. I should definitely eat before taking on Shaw. I glanced down the street. Maggie's place was open and it was easy. Maybe she'd have some good gossip. Maybe my dad wouldn't be there hanging on her arm. Wasn't sure why their relationship bothered me, but maybe I was just tired of seeing all the bachelors in my life suddenly coupled up. Jess, Dad, my brother.

Jess's words from the other day rang in my head. *Are you going to be in the wedding?* Hell no, I wasn't going to be in the wedding. Mark hadn't even told me there was a wedding. I didn't blame him. We didn't share much since he'd hightailed it out of town to get away from the life-sucking drain of our parents' house. He'd had it the hardest when they spiraled into divorce. Me, I'd never believed in happily ever afters, but he'd always harbored fancy notions about true love, destiny, and all that crap. When he finally figured out Mom and Dad would just as soon beat each other to death as look at each other, he was devastated. He told me once, when he was in college, he no longer believed in marriage.

Fast-forward and Mark was engaged. If it could happen to him, it could happen to anyone. Was no one safe?

Maggie's place was mostly empty. I grabbed a barstool and laid a twenty down. I had a tab, but lately I felt funny using it, like it was nepotism. Stupid, I know, but with everyone blurring lines around me, I clung to my independence. I can't always afford principles, but I liked it when I could.

Maggie bounced over and shoved the twenty into my breast pocket. Well, I'd tried to be principled. "You hungry?" she asked.

"Very."

She nodded, poured me a glass of tea, and left with an "I'll be right back" tossed over her shoulder. The tea was okay, but I'd have preferred a beer. A couple actually. Probably best I didn't indulge. If I started drinking, I wouldn't be hungry anymore. I hoped for a burger. And fries. Protein and grease to fortify me for the job ahead.

She returned in a few minutes. "Your lunch will be ready in a minute. Have you talked to your brother?"

"You sound like my mother. You bucking for the role?"

She didn't flinch. "Not a chance, girl. But it would make your dad happy if you were involved in the wedding."

"I haven't been asked. Hell, I've barely been told about it."

"I don't think it's been long in the making."

"Really?" Mark was the last person I'd expect to get married on the fly. "Is she pregnant? Maybe they'll elope."

"Not a chance. Girl's parents want a big shindig. They have money. Society folks. It's going to be quite a to-do."

With that threat, she took off again, hopefully to check on my lunch. While she was gone, I tried to picture my dad stuffed into a rental tux, standing alongside fancy rich folks, making a toast to his son, the groom. I wondered which of my mother's husbands she'd choose to bring to the affair. She'd remarried so often, I stopped keeping track. Her string of husbands all had money, the primary prerequisite for marrying my mother. Dad and I would be out of place at a society wedding. High school educated, blue-collar misfits. Nerdy Mark should be out of place too. How he had gotten hooked up with money, high-class money at that? Last time I'd talked to him, the most exciting thing in his life was being on the brink of cracking some kind of code. I didn't understand a word of what he'd said, but I knew it had been the most important thing in his life. Granted, our conversation was several months ago, but what happened to change all that?

"Here you go." Maggie slid a plate in front of me, a huge smile on her face. I decided her smile had to do with the joke she was playing on me. Instead of a big burger and crispy fries, I was staring at a turkey sandwich on wheat bread. With leafy greens that looked suspiciously like spinach. And a fruit cup where the fries should be. Fresh fruit.

I pushed the plate back toward her. "You running low on food back there?"

"What's that supposed to mean?"

"I mean this looks a little healthy. I eat this, I might have a reaction."

"Like feeling good?"

"I feel just fine."

"You eat crap. This is good food."

"You force feed your other customers with this stuff?"

"You're not a customer. This is on the house."

I pulled the twenty back out of my pocket and tossed it on the bar. "How many French fries will that buy?"

She sighed. "You're just like your father." It wasn't a compliment.

"You try to get him to eat like this?"

"He says he likes it, but I think he sneaks off and eats junk when I'm not around."

I grinned because I knew he did. My mother had given up trying to get him to eat right when I was still in diapers. "You can't change people."

"That right, Luca? Bet you thought your brother would never get married."

We'd talked about my family before she'd ever met my father. Bartender/drinker kind of talk. Didn't think she'd retain or remember anything I'd whispered into my beer. "You're right about that."

"What about you? You ever going to get married? Whatever happened to that nice cop that helped Billy out? You two seemed to get along real well."

And there went my appetite. Maggie didn't usually refer to cops as "nice." They were pesky rule-mongers who badgered suffering business folks. But she'd taken a shine to Jess after Jess had helped her no-good brother out of a jam.

I started to reply with a "we're just friends," but stopped myself when I wasn't sure if "friends" was an accurate characterization of what we were to each other. We'd gone to the police academy together, bonded over a shooting that got out of hand, and had been fuck buddies ever since. I used Chance when I needed info on a case. She used me to fill in on her softball team. I didn't know what to call our relationship, but friends seemed both too much and too little. Didn't really matter anymore because Jess had a girlfriend and, like all women who hook up for the long haul, their friends become second-class citizens.

I felt even lower than that.

CHAPTER SEVEN

A fter I left Maggie's, I stopped at Whataburger and ordered a double with cheese. And a large order of fries. Turkey sandwiches on wheat bread don't stick to your ribs. I scarfed it all on the way to find Shaw. My only real lead was his girlfriend, Dalia Franklin. She'd posted the bond and put up the house as collateral. It wasn't so much a house, but a bunch of sticks propped up to look like shelter. One big wind and it would come tumbling down.

I knocked three times and was about to leave, when the door finally swung open. One look at the under-aged girl holding a crying baby standing in the doorway, and I decided Shaw was in more trouble than he thought. "Dalia?"

She shook her head. "She ain't here, but she's supposed to be. She and that jerkwad baby daddy of hers. They left me here with their snotty kids, and I got places to be. She'll come back late tonight and forget she promised to pay me five bucks, as if that's enough."

She had a lot more to say on the subject. Her rant took on a surreal quality, and as she continued, all I could hear was blah, blah, blah. I pegged her for all of fourteen, maybe fifteen. Wherever she had to be was likely somewhere she wasn't supposed to be. I had no idea if five dollars was good wages for a night of babysitting. I only knew no amount of money would cause me to switch places with her. I'd never sat babies a day in my life, and I figured her complaints were justified. Didn't mean I wanted to be the one to hear them. I watched for her to take a breath and jumped in. "Do you know where either of them are?"

"Dunno where Dirty is, but Dalia's at work."

"Where does Dalia work?"

She opened her mouth to answer and then shut it and squinted her eyes at me. "Who are you?"

I started to tell a lie, but why burn a good one when the truth will work just as well. "I work for Dirty, er, Mr. Shaw's, bondsman. He missed court and I came by to remind him."

She looked me over, nodding her head. No doubt she noticed the bulges under my jacket and decided I meant business. Business she wanted no part of.

"You leave Dalia out of this. She's a pain, but she's my sister and she never did nothing wrong except gettin' hooked up with him." She paused and punctuated her threats with crossed arms and a fierce look. "You tell anyone I talked to you and I'll cut you."

I smothered a laugh by faking a coughing fit. Once I recovered, I made a solemn vow to keep her identity a secret, and I scribbled the address and hours she gave me into a tattered notebook I keep on hand. I didn't intend to show up at Dalia's work, but now that I knew her hours, I wouldn't have to hang around waiting.

It had been a full day already. I'd exercised, eaten, worked a little. The one thing I hadn't done was get laid. Jess was out on that front, but someone owed me. I just needed to find something to trade. Time to find Sandy Amato and Vince Picone.

I was half tempted to go by Bingo's and bully him into talking to me, but after last night's revelations, I figured his place was being watched. I wasn't in the mood to have my every move caught by either the Feds or Petrov's men, but there was someone I knew who could go to Bingo's without drawing any suspicion. And it was time I paid him a visit.

I fished the key from underneath the dirt-filled flowerpot and opened the door. My childhood home was exactly like it was when I was sixteen. Frozen in time, every stick of furniture was exactly the same, every creepy knickknack was in exactly the same place, and every family photo hung in exactly the same position on the wall. No one entering would know that this place housed only one person—an aging, lonely, alcoholic whose family had scattered and dreams had shattered. As much as Maggie had become a fixture in Dad's life, nothing about this place had changed. It may have gotten worse, since Dad spent most nights at her house, making this place seem even more desolate. I walked the halls, sure I would find him here. It was carly afternoon. His favorite time to drink, and no way would he start drinking this early in front of Maggie, the reformer.

He was out back, smoking a cigar and drinking from a can of Pabst. Three empty cans lined the concrete patio.

"Hey, Dad."

He turned in slow motion, and I could tell it took him a minute to decide if I was someone he knew. A few second later, his eyes lit up. "Luca! What a nice surprise. Join your old man and we'll toast this great weather."

I pulled a beer from the plastic rings and snapped the top. "Pretty cold day to be sitting outside."

He pointed at the cigar. "Your mother trained me well. No cigar smoke in the house. Guess I got in the habit of being outside with them." He pulled another from his jacket. "You want one?"

I waved him off. "Maggie know where you are?"

"She's fine."

"She thinks she's teaching you to eat right, be healthy."

"She doesn't put real mayonnaise on her sandwiches."

"I know." I put a hand on his. "She used to push greasy food on everyone in sight. You know what it must have taken for her to change her own ways. She cares about you."

"She's a good woman." His tone was wistful. He hadn't changed for my mother and he wasn't going to change for Maggie, no matter how much of a catch she was. Wasn't in our DNA to change. Except for my brother Mark. Apparently, something or someone had prompted a change in him.

"What does Mark say about the girl? You know, the one he says he's going to marry?"

"Their picture's on the fridge. Fancy, professional job. I think it's going to happen."

Curiosity won. I walked inside to the kitchen and studied the happy couple. She wasn't stunning, but her smile was bright, and the way she looked at my brother spoke volumes. She was in love. Not hard to imagine. He was a catch. Smart, good-looking. We didn't talk about money, but I felt sure he did okay. Hard to believe this was the same guy who hid under his bed when our parents fought, which was often.

He looked at his future bride like she was the most important person on the planet. I glanced at the caption. *Save the Date, November 19th, Dallas, Texas.*

When I joined Dad back on the patio, I asked, "They're getting married here?"

"Yep. She's a doctor. Something about a fellowship here in town. Don't really know what that means, but he's got a line on a new job, and since her parents live out here, they decided to tie the knot in Dallas. Your mom's on cloud nine. Think they're making a big deal of it. The girl's parents are loaded. That's what I hear anyway."

The girl. Guess Dad hadn't met the bride to be yet. At least he'd been told about the wedding. Jess's words echoed. *Are you going to be in the wedding?* Guess I wasn't going to be there at all since I hadn't been asked. Not that I wanted to be. Big fancy to-dos weren't my thing. If I couldn't wear jeans, I pretty much didn't go.

My mom was probably having a field day, helping plan a fancy party with other people's money. Well, she could have her party. If I got an invite, I'd scrape up money for a gift. Maybe even manage to buy something they wanted, but I could pass on the ceremony.

I started to feel like my family wasn't mine. Only the bloated old man sitting across from me punching out beer cans. A strange desire to solidify our relationship caused me to offer an invitation I hadn't planned on. Amato and Picone could wait. "You up for a little road trip?"

The buzz delayed his response. "Road trip?"

"You know. Just me and you. How about it?" I glanced at my phone. I had seven hours before Dalia was supposed be home from work.

"I think I'm supposed to see Maggie later."

"Maybe you can buy her a nice prize with your winnings. I have work later. I'll get you back long before the bar closes."

He was already out of his seat, surprisingly nimble for an old guy who'd sucked down as many beers as he had. I knew I wouldn't have to do any more convincing. I packed him in the Bronco, and we took off for the hour and a half trip to the casino. Maggie would be pissed, but I didn't care. Dad was family, and right now I needed that, more than I wanted to admit. The road to hell, and casinos, is paved with good intentions.

❖

I took advantage of the ride to pump Dad about Bingo, but instead of background, all I got from him was the suggestion we go by his place and catch a game. "I'm craving a drive," was my lame response. I wanted him to go to Bingo's, but I didn't want to have to explain that I wasn't welcome. I had the evening to figure out a way to get him to go there and find out why Bingo was pissed off at me. This trip was just to whet his appetite for more. He didn't argue. He liked Bingo's place just fine, but he preferred the Winstar Casino for their better looking dealers. He was right about that.

I did learn he hadn't been to Bingo's in a month or so, probably due to Maggie's watchful eye. When my father had been married to my mother, he'd had to sneak out to fulfill most of his vices. Maggie wasn't at all like my mother, thank God, but she did have a bit of maternal instinct about her, which led to the healthy meals and no beer before noon rule. Dad was one of those guys women just loved to take care of. He'd had the Widow Teeter, from down the street, on a string since my mom had walked out years ago. I hadn't pegged Maggie as one of the ones who'd line up to care for the old guy, but love does strange things to people. A good reason to stay far from it.

The casino was hopping for early evening on a Wednesday. No sharp-dressed high rollers. Mostly grizzly looking folks, likely gambling away their government assistance. I didn't judge. Not like I had a retirement plan other than dying early. If death cheated me, one day I'd be old, right there with them, pulling a lever from my

Medicare approved scooter. I'd sooner shoot myself. But I could see Dad in their place. Maybe hooking up with someone like Maggie would save him from such a fate.

I settled him at a poker table and left to get us drinks. I didn't make it far before I ran into a surprise. Literally.

"Geez, Diamond, you think the United States government wouldn't want their agents gambling with the common folk."

She grabbed my arm and steered me to a not so quiet corner. "What are you doing here?"

"Bonding. You?"

"Any progress on Vedda's guys?"

"Your contract employee has nothing new to report. Except that I'm taking a few hours off, which considering you're not paying me, is none of your business. Don't you have some strippers to hustle?"

She tried to fake a puzzled look, but I saw through it. Now she knew that I knew she'd had more on her mind when it came to Laura Tanner than helping me catch a jumper. "Care to tell me why you were interested in a two-bit stripper?"

I watched her face while she went through the mental gyrations, wondering if I already knew what she'd told Laura, what she'd gotten from her. Her features settled into resignation. "I can't help it if cases sometimes overlap."

"I don't believe in coincidences." I mentally scrolled through the improbable list. She'd tailed me to one of the cases Hardin had given me and gotten me to commit to looking for a couple of his other jumpers. She'd followed me to Bingo's, followed me to the strip club. And she conveniently disappeared when her faux old flame, Yuri Petrov showed. She was using me for something, and it was time for her to spill. "I have a few questions for you." I shot a look over at the table where Dad was steadily losing money. Any second now, he'd start wondering where I was with the drink I'd promised. "Wait here."

She followed my gaze and nodded. "I'll meet you in Paris."

She wasn't envisioning a romantic rendezvous under the Eiffel Tower, not the real one anyway. We were in the Winstar World Casino and faux French architecture was just one of the cheesy landmarks. I shoved one of the beers I held into her hand. "Hold this. Makes you look less like a cop. I'll be there in a minute."

I delivered Dad's drink and told him I was going to give the slots a try. He barely looked up from his cards, but wished me good luck. I don't play slots—too mindless—but leave it to him not to remember details about his oldest child. I shrugged his inattention off and left for gay Paree.

Diamond was waiting. I'd had my doubts she'd stick around. She was a wily woman. Before I could get out a word, she grabbed my arm and led me to the far end of the casino, to a bank of elevators. I didn't question our destination. Figured there wasn't any point. I was just encouraged she hadn't taken off the minute I turned my back.

We got off on the twelfth floor. A long walk down an empty hallway, a dip of a card into the lock, and next thing I knew, we were alone in a hotel room. Not what I'd had in mind, but a bonus for sure. I sat on the bed. "You wanted me so bad, you followed me to Oklahoma? Hell, Diamond, I would have given it up in Texas. You want to answer my questions before or after?"

She paced the room. Nervous, not excited, pacing. Not exactly a prelude to hot sex. On her third lap, I reached out and grabbed her arm. "Sit. You're making me dizzy." I didn't wait for an answer, but pulled her into my lap, circling her waist with a strong grasp, rubbing her skin when her shirt came untucked. She gasped at my touch. A swallowed moan, really. That was all it took. Within seconds, I was totally turned on, and the only question I cared about was how fast I could get Diamond undressed and begging beneath me. I rolled us over and started unbuttoning her shirt.

She stilled my hand with hers and panted, "Wait."

"Don't want to," I managed to say before I covered her mouth with mine. I craved closeness. I tugged off her shirt, then mine, and pulled her close, but I couldn't erase the feeling she was still distant.

"Take off your pants." I spoke the words into her mouth and held her tight while she complied, surrendering to my pressing need. I nipped and sucked her lips, then moved to her breasts. She unbuttoned my jeans and inched her hand inside. I groaned when her hand slid down to finger my wet center. My clit hardened. It felt good, but I needed more. I bucked against her, forcing her hand where I wanted it most, but none of my thrusts brought me close enough. Close enough to Diamond. Close enough to coming.

She entered me, one finger, two fingers, three. My jeans were halfway down my ass, but I didn't care. I could feel my walls closing. I was going to come, but something was missing. I felt the orgasm building, but I could've bluffed anyone watching into thinking I was playing cards instead of coming at the hands of a beautiful blonde vixen.

I kept the rhythm, fighting to drown out my ticking brain. Why did it matter? Why was I even noticing this? I'd had my share of one-night stands where orgasm was the only goal and any stray emotions were only strings to be cut as quickly as possible. I buried my face in her tits, hoping the taste of skin would force me somewhere physical. Some place where I didn't care who was fucking me. It didn't work.

Maybe all the talk lately about relationships and marriage had frozen my emotions so all I could manage were rote physical reactions. I needed to shut down the computer running through my brain or I was never going to enjoy a sexual encounter again.

She was pumping me hard now. Stretching me, pulling me, demanding my attention. Or at least the attention of my clit. It agreed with her. I came quietly and rolled over. She sat up, shot me a questioning look, and then started to get dressed. I waved her back. "Your turn."

"I'm good."

She wasn't and neither was I, but I didn't want to talk about it. We both dressed in silence. I waited until she was all buttoned-up before I asked my first question, figuring I should at least get half of what I came for—information. "How do you know Laura Tanner?"

"I don't. At least not well. I got her name from a contact. Heard she had a lead on Vedda's guys, so I showed up at the club. Imagine my luck when you were there to bring her in."

"And you took her prescription bottle because you were in need of some pain relief?"

"All I did was tell her she was going back in, not to fight back. She gave up the bottle to keep from having it on her when she got booked in. Smart girl."

She was lying. Big time. I didn't know why, and an hour ago I may not have cared, but now I cared deeply. Maybe it was because the lie came on the heels of something sweaty. What had gotten into me lately? Intimacy wasn't something I relied on in making judgments in my everyday living. This slow bleed of caring needed to stop now. It was only going to get in the way of my ability to do my work. And my work was all I had.

CHAPTER EIGHT

I rolled out of bed the next morning with the second fuzzy head in less than a week. The only difference today was that I had money in my pockets and the bed wasn't mine. Oh, and there was a guy snoring in the other bed.

Dad. With empty pockets.

Diamond had shoved the room key in my pocket the night before as a down payment for helping her out. As pissed as I was that she wasn't being truthful with me, I kept it. I planned to do some serious drinking and, since Dad was tying one on, staying the night in Oklahoma seemed like a great idea. I wasn't in the mood to track down Shaw anyway. Too distracted to take on a dangerous felon. Instead of a bounty, I earned my living at the tables and had apparently managed to make it back to the room with my winnings intact. I did feel a little funky about staying in a room that had been bought on government dollars, but I figured all the surveillance cameras were likely to catch was footage of two drunks, snoring off a night on the town.

I roused Dad and we were on the road, munching on to-go food in the car. Dad didn't have a big win to brag about so he was pretty quiet. He did moan a bit about how Maggie was going to wonder where he'd been. I pointed out they weren't married and he had a right to do what he wanted in his free time. He sighed and I wondered again about DNA. Thank the stars I hadn't gotten the pussy-whipped gene. No one cared if I came or went. Fine by me.

As we pulled up to Dad's house, I pulled out a wad of cash and stuffed it in his shirt pocket. "Those tables were rigged. Go to Bingo's. He'll set you up nice."

He smiled and patted his pocket. "Thanks, Luca. I'll do you proud." I'd woken the beast and there was only one way to tame it. He'd be at Bingo's within twenty-four hours. Surely, Bingo wouldn't be able to resist sharing gossip about why he'd kicked me out. All I'd have to do is pay another visit to dear old Dad and get some answers.

My plan for the day was ambitious. First, lose the tail. Next, track down Shaw's girlfriend, find Amato and Picone, and trace the prescription bottle Laura had given me. By midnight, I'd have some answers. Winning got my blood flowing.

I was certain Diamond or one of her lackeys was following me, and I decided to have fun with them. I drove by Chance's place three times, approaching from different angles each time. My stomach clenched when I saw Dr. Deveaux's car in the driveway. It was ten o'clock and I was sure Jess was at work, because, using my keen detective skills, I'd called there and hung up when she answered. What was the doctor doing in Jess's house all by herself? I considered going to the door and feigning surprise to find her there, but instead resigned myself to being satisfied by the fact the Feds were probably running her license plate. I laughed when I thought about them doing a background check, and the idea was so funny that on my next drive-by, I slowed to a crawl and snapped a few pics of the car with my camera phone. Then I took off to my next stop.

Hardin had been in the bail bond business for thirty years. He'd bought this building, a former combo convenience store gas station, when he first opened, and he hadn't made a change to it since. The awning was tattered and the windows still boasted that tobacco, gas, and "candie" were all for sale. Hardin and I were a lot alike. Don't fix it unless it's broken. Don't buy new when the old works just fine. But Hardin was rich, and I wasn't. I'm thinking that's because he confined his gambling to criminal defendants instead of cards.

We can't all be perfect.

I parked the Bronco in one of the bays he liked to leave open in the cooler fall weather. Once a year, he hosted a big party for his best clients. Lawyers in suits and a judge or six would stand around in the garage and gnaw on ribs and chug from beer bottles they pulled from icy metal tubs. Every other day of the year, he parked his dually in the first bay. His missing pickup signaled he wasn't in. Good. He wasn't who I wanted to see.

I pulled the bay door down and walked in the side door to the office. Sally Jesse, Hardin's right hand, was on the phone, but she waved me into a seat close by. She was way young, but she'd worked for Hardin since high school, accompanying her mom to work. Her mom had been forced to retire last year when emphysema took hold. Sally's mom had never liked me. She didn't think bounty hunting was women's work, didn't understand why I wasn't home, barefoot and pregnant. But Sally and I saw eye to eye. More than her mother would ever realize. I remember the first time I'd ever seen Sally out at the bar, gyrating with a crazy regular that the patrons of the place had nicknamed Liquor Lucy. Sally had seen me watching and we bonded instantly. And that's why I knew I could count on her for a favor.

She hung up and lit up. "What's shaking, Luca?"

I pointed at the cigarette dangling from her lips. "Those kill people."

"Lose all your vices and then you can lecture me. You come by for cash? I thought you were all paid up."

"I am. Just need a favor."

"Name it."

"Let me borrow your car for a few hours."

She hesitated, and I knew it wasn't because she thought I would mistreat her ride. She drove a beat-up Chevy. Wasn't much I could do to it that hadn't already been done.

"And when someone comes in wanting to know where you are?"

She was even smarter than I'd pegged her for. "You could tell them I'm in the restroom?"

She laughed. "That should work for a bit. Seriously, Luca, you in trouble?"

"Not a lick." At least not yet. I mentally flashed on the Russian, but I doubted he'd had me tailed this morning. I'd only noticed one suspicious car, and it was plain vanilla Fed. Besides, the Russians liked Hardin and used his services regularly. They weren't going to cause Sally any trouble. And what would the Feds say? She borrowed your car—that's illegal! No, I wasn't in the kind of trouble she was worried about. "I just need a new ride for a few hours."

She shot a skeptical look my way and then tossed me her keys. "Tank's full."

"Got it. Thanks." I started to walk to the back, then stopped. "Got a cap I can borrow?" She pointed to a drawer. "Hardin keeps them in there. Don't tell him I gave one up."

I shoved my hair up high, pulled the black baseball cap low on my brow, and took off out the back door. I slunk behind the wheel of Sally's trashy ride and escaped down the alley. A few blocks away, I was finally satisfied no one was following me. Step one down. A dozen more to go.

❖

Ladies who work at night usually sleep in. I was counting on that when I knocked hard on Dalia's door. I heard a healthy dose of cussing and banging around before the door finally opened an inch. "Whadda you want?"

"I have a package for Dalia Franklin."

The door swung wide. No one can resist a package; it was like Christmas. Except this time it wasn't. The only package I had was a Colt .45 that I kept out of sight for the moment. She'd obviously just rolled out of bed. Her hair stood on end and her gown was on backward. She had the sour expression any caffeine addict has before their first cup of black gold for the day. She thrust a hand in my direction. "Give it here."

I grabbed the door with my free hand and pushed my way in. Only took her a sec to spot the Colt and the sight was like a jolt of espresso right into her veins.

She did the one thing I can't stand. She started screaming. Loud, I'm being murdered screams. I slapped a hand over her mouth and prayed the neighbors wouldn't come running. "Shhh, shhh, I need you to be quiet and listen to me." After I repeated the chant several times, she finally settled down.

"I'm not going to hurt you. I'm looking for Otis. I work for his bondsman and he missed his court date. We can get it all straightened out if I can talk to him before the cops do. Do you know where he is?"

She just stared at me for a minute and I wondered if she'd scared herself senseless. Finally, she nodded her head.

"Okay, great. I'm going to move my hand. Don't scream. Okay?"

She nodded again and I moved slightly, but remained on alert in case she decided to resume her role as a human alarm system.

She crossed her arms and morphed instantly from scared to defiant. "How do I know you are for real?"

Because I'm standing right here? I knew what she meant. "His bondsman is Hardin Jones. You probably met Sally when you went in to post the bond? How would I know all that if I wasn't real?"

Her features wrinkled in thought as she considered my hard logic. She settled on another nod to indicate she believed me. She'd nodded so much since I'd gotten here I figured her neck muscles were worn to shreds.

"This house belongs to my momma. We put it up for the bond."

I silently thanked her for this tidbit. "Well, then, you definitely want to protect her house. If he comes to court, everything will be just fine." I lied with ease. I had no idea what would happen if I turned him in beyond the bounty I'd collect. The judge would probably decide the bond he'd already paid was insufficient and Hardin may or may not cash in on the collateral. Not my problem.

"He doesn't stay here."

"Do you know where he's staying?"

"With his other girl, Shante. She ain't had no baby yet. He don't like the baby crying all the time." Her desire to protect her double-dealing man was pathetic. All the more reason I would relish turning this guy in. "Do you know where she lives?"

"She stays with her auntie. In Cedar Hill." She referred to a suburb, south of Dallas. I pulled out my notebook and handed it to her. She scribbled a picture of a house, instead of an address. "I don't remember the house number, but it's on Jefferson Street. Looks like this. She pointed at the drawing. A big flaming sun hung from the porch. Shouldn't be hard to find.

I slipped the notebook back in my pocket. "When's the last time you talked to him?"

"Couple of days ago. He brought some diapers by. He's supposed to come by again tomorrow night."

I thanked her for the info, assured her she'd been very helpful, and left. I'd nab Shaw either today at his girlfriend's house, or tomorrow night back here at his baby mamma's place. But before I made a trip all the way out to Cedar Hill, I wanted to make the most efficient use of my time in this neighborhood, or at least not far from here.

Old Dallas legend says that the Sicilian mob inner circle used to meet in the backroom at the original location of Mangia restaurant. I didn't know for sure if the restaurant had a backroom, but I did know that most legends have a basis in truth. Couldn't hurt to check it out. Besides, Mangia had some of the best crab claws in town and I was starving. Tab or no tab, a dry turkey sandwich from Maggie's wasn't going to cut it.

Lunch was booming business at Mangia. Seemed like such good business would be enough to make all the mobsters go legit, but old habits and steady money are too tempting. I told the hostess I'd sit at the bar and she looked relieved she wouldn't have to waste a whole table on a single customer. When I saw the bartender's back, I lost my breath. Tall, lean, spiky blond hair. Tight ass. From behind, she was the spitting image of Jess. Only when she turned around was I completely sure Chance hadn't taken a second job.

"Just drinking or eating too?"

I caught my breath and found my voice. "Both. Draft and a menu." She poured with one hand and shoved a plastic covered menu my way with the other. She was hot and definitely not Italian. Blonde, blue eyes. She did something besides shake drinks to get biceps like those. I wouldn't mind working out with her.

"Start you out with something?"

She'd read my mind. I cracked a suggestive smile, but she only tapped a pen on a pad of paper. Oh, wait. She meant food. Well, I'd need food if I was going to go a few rounds with her. "Crab claws. Large order."

She jerked her head in approval and wandered back to the register to type in my order. Again, with her back to me, she looked just like Jess. Or maybe missing her was making me see things. It'd been less than a week since I'd discovered Jess's new penchant for doctors in fancy cars, but the distance was deep. I knew I wouldn't be welcome on her doorstep late in the night.

I wasn't being selfish, well, maybe a little, but the truth was Jess wasn't herself around Dr. Red. At least not the self I knew. And, in my opinion, the new relationship Jess wasn't an improved version. I wondered if any of her other friends had noticed. There was another softball game on Sunday. I knew because it was on a piece of paper hanging on my fridge. I hadn't been called up to play, but maybe I'd stop by and see if I could commiserate with Jess's teammates.

I nursed my musings by quickly downing my beer. Only took a few minutes before I had the perfect excuse to wander around in the back. I held up the mug, and when the barkeep asked if I wanted another, I said yes and could she hold my seat for a minute. I walked in the direction of the restroom, but once I was satisfied no one in the bustling crowd was paying attention to me, I veered off toward the kitchen. Guys in jeans and white chef jackets all nudged for the best positions in front of burners and ovens. I made it halfway through the line before anyone even noticed me.

"Hey, you can't be back here. Get out."

I looked at the guy holding a skillet in one hand, and I waved and held a hand to my ear, feigning inability to make out his words.

He shouted louder this time. "Get out!"

I shouted back. "I have a delivery outside. I'm new on this route. But it's COD. I need to talk to your manager." What the hell, I figured I could pass for a truck driver. Jeans, boots, leather jacket. Truth was I looked more like a hood, but it was the best I could do under the circumstances. Being this close to so much good food was making me dizzy. The drive thru breakfast I'd eaten in the car this morning was history.

He told me to wait outside and he disappeared behind a door labeled office. I doubted a secret room would be labeled, so while I pretended to walk back the way I'd come, I studied the room for another door. There it was, next to the walk-in. Could barely make out the outline of the door until I got real close. I eased over and, because I knew I didn't have much time, pushed hard, spilling into the space.

I scrambled to regain my footing, distracted by the strong odor of garlic. Three men sat around a table. A fancy table, complete with a white tablecloth and real silver and crystal. The surface was crowded with my favorite things. Crab claws dripping in butter and garlic, homemade pasta and meatballs, lasagna, and baskets of bread. Drool was imminent.

One of the younger guys half stood, pulling his napkin from his throat and tossing it to the table. He pointed to the door. "This is a private room."

I fought the fade of hunger and focused on the reason for my visit. "I'm looking for Geno Vedda." I decided to lead with the name of the big guy rather than hinting I was looking to apprehend some smaller fish.

Napkin Tosser walked toward me, and I could see him reaching around his waist. Hunger was about to be the least of my worries. I considered drawing a gun of my own, but you don't wave a weapon in front of mobsters unless you plan to use it. We weren't there yet.

I raised both hands in surrender. I wasn't really sure what to do next. Announcing I was looking for Geno's guys instead of Geno seemed like a bad idea. None of these guys were Geno, but the big guy with the white hair at the head of the table looked vaguely familiar. I shot him my best "Hey, I'm harmless look" and prayed that whatever happened here today, I would get to eat some of those crab claws.

My prayer was strong. Head of the table signaled for Napkin Tosser to sit. "I'll handle this." He addressed me. "Who sent you?"

Trick question and I wasn't falling for it. I knew I needed to be very careful about what I said next, but instinct took over and I blurted out, "Bingo."

The one word opened doors. "Sit, sit." He poked Napkin Tosser on the arm. "Get her a plate." He waved his fork at me. "You're hungry, right? I can see it in your eyes."

I was starving, but conflicted. Here I was sitting in a secret room with a trio of mobsters who, if they found out I'd just lied to them, would make sure this was my last meal.

Oh well, it would be an excellent last meal. I accepted the plate and loaded it up. White Hair raised a glass to toast the food, and a full five minutes passed with no sound other than the smacks and groans that accompanied a good meal. I should've spent the time thinking of what I'd say next, but my brain was paralyzed by garlic.

When my plate was empty, they offered more, but I didn't want to push my luck. I might need to be mobile soon and, as much as I would love to eat more of this amazing food, I decided throwing up while trying to fight off gangsters would be a bad move.

A waiter came in and cleared our plates and took orders for espresso. I could almost pretend we were at a social gathering. Almost.

White Hair tipped his espresso cup and downed the whole shot at once. Then he picked up his glass of grappa and swirled a bit on his tongue as if to rinse. Pretty much all grappa is good for. When he set his glass down, he cleared his throat and announced. "My son owns Bingo. Does my son own you?"

Finally, it clicked. This was Anthony Vedda, Geno's father. Word was the old man had retired and left the business to his oldest son, Geno. How much did Anthony know about his son's dealings? Did he know he'd gone missing? Or was Geno only missing to the Feds? Without knowing the answer to any of these questions, I was walking through a minefield, and there's only one way to make it safely to the other side. Run like hell.

I stood. As much as I wanted information, I needed some to get some. Time to regroup. "Thank you for lunch. I hope you'll excuse me. I have an appointment across town." I took two steps toward freedom before turning to face Anthony. Old, faded, yet still very powerful. "And to answer your question, no. Your son doesn't own me. No one owns me."

CHAPTER NINE

L unch and confrontation drained my earlier ambition. Once I was convinced I was no longer being followed, I traded Sally's car for mine and headed home. A nap seemed like the safest way to spend the afternoon. I stripped and fell into bed within seconds of returning to my apartment. Sleep came easy, but my dreams were full of activity.

My brother's wedding reception was a huge affair, mostly because of all the Cosa Nostra in attendance. Maggie directed caterers while my mom and dad sat on thrones in the front of the room, accepting plain white envelopes from the Italian strangers who filled the room. A Russian gymnast performed on a mat in the center of the room. Mark and his bride danced around the perimeter of the mat, holding each other with one hand and stuffing wedding cake into each other's mouths with the other. Jess stood in a corner, dressed in a low-cut black dress with a high slit up the side. When she caught me looking, she raised her glass. I started to walk over, but stopped when I saw a hand snake around her waist. Diamond Collier didn't stop there. She stepped in front of Jess and leaned in. I couldn't see what they were doing, but I was mad to find out. Unfortunately, I suffered from dream quicksand. No matter how fast I walked, I wasn't moving. Maggie passed by with a silver tray and offered me an icy shot of vodka, which I gladly downed. She said, "Love is in the air," before she flitted off to satisfy the thirst of the remaining guests.

I woke up sweating and I swore off grappa. So much for a refreshing nap. I'd have been better off hanging out with Anthony

Vedda, telling him the Feds were looking for his son. Of course, that probably wouldn't be a surprise to him. The Feds were always looking for his kind—came with the territory.

Still, I had the feeling that whatever Geno was involved in wasn't sanctioned by his daddy. And whatever it was involved Bingo. Bingo, to whom I'd instructed my dad to visit. Maybe we should all stay away until this blew over, let Bingo deal with whatever mess he'd gotten into on his own.

Wasn't going to happen. I tried not to care about Bingo's fate, but he was a fixture in my life. I spent the equivalent of a car payment at his place every month, and when I was a kid, he hung my pen and paper drawings on his fridge. I may not know much about him, but I knew enough to know he was probably in deeper than he realized.

Our last encounter had been bizarre. He'd been pissed, but anger is usually a placeholder for something else. His face had been flushed. He even shook a little when he'd ordered me out. In his case, I guessed the anger stood for fear. Maybe he realized how tangled up he was, but he definitely didn't have a way out. More than the potential loss of my second favorite indulgence motivated me to take an interest.

I couldn't trust Diamond to give me a straight answer about Bingo or anything else for that matter. Maybe I just wanted an excuse to call Chance. I was a little pissed at both of them after the dream I'd just had, but I needed info. Besides, it was only a dream.

I picked up my phone and it rang in my hand causing me to jump out of my skin. Hate when it does that. The display read private caller. Could be Diamond, but she'd know me well enough to leave a message. I punched ignore and set the phone down. I'd have better luck getting Chance to talk to me if I showed up in person.

Showered and semi-awake, I drove to the substation where Chance and her partner worked. Despite what you see on TV, once cops made detective, they rode a desk more than you'd think. Nowadays, investigations happened over the phone and Internet. Since it was late in the day, I was hoping to catch them in, finishing up paperwork for the day. When I hit the lobby, I told the desk sergeant I was looking for Detective John Ames. When John showed up, he looked surprised to see me, but talking to him first was part of my master plan.

"Hey, Luca. Chance just left. I expect her back though. You want me to tell her you stopped by?"

"No worries. Maybe you can help me. Can we take a walk?"

He looked around, then shrugged. "Sure. Give me a sec." He disappeared for a minute, then returned with his wallet in his hand. "Come on. I'll buy you a coffee."

We walked over to the diner across the street and settled into a booth. After we ordered, he leaned across the table. "If you're here to pump me for information on Jess, don't bother. She's as tight-lipped with me about her personal life as anyone."

It had occurred to me to try to mine personal details from him, but I hadn't planned to lead with it. I waved him off. "I get it. She probably doesn't want to talk about her flings."

"Fling?" He took a sip of coffee. "I guess you know about the doctor. Luca, I don't think she's a fling. I think she's moving in. I'm pretty sure Chance is with her now. About an hour ago, she got a call from her, sounded like an emergency. She left right away. Not like her, so I assume it's serious."

Serious? For who, her or the doctor? If Jess was in trouble, I wanted to know. I wanted to be there for her. But the doctor filled that role now. If whatever it was was serious for the doctor, I didn't want Jess to care, but there was nothing I could do about it. I didn't know what to do with these feelings. Didn't want to have to deal with them.

Focus, Luca. Get what you came for and get out. I plunged in. "I had lunch with Anthony Vedda today."

"No way."

Part of the reason I liked John so much was he didn't feel the need to maintain a cop poker face around people he trusted. And I liked being one of the people he trusted. "Damn straight. Grappa and everything."

"Want to tell me how you managed to score that invite?"

I told him about my trip to Mangia and how I'd essentially invited myself to lunch.

"Okay, now for the why? Any particular reason you want to rattle those guys' cages? You have a death wish?"

"I'm looking for a couple of Geno's guys. Looking for people—it's what I do, you know?"

"You need to stick to your day job." I raised my eyebrows and he continued, "Since when do you start hauling in mobsters? Did Hardin post their bond? I got a twenty says Hardin doesn't care if you find them."

I took a deep swallow of coffee and considered my options. I knew what I should do. Find Shaw, haul him in, collect a decent bounty. Tell Diamond Collier and her posse to do their own dirty work. Return Yuri's gold, Laura's RX. Get used to the fact Bingo's place was closed to me. Wasn't like me to let my life get so complicated.

But even if I didn't care for puzzles, this one had me tangled. Or maybe I was just avoiding the tangles in my personal life. Dad in a relationship, Mark getting married, Jess running off to be with her doctor—I couldn't wrap my tongue around the word girlfriend—at the drop of a hat. My stomach was twisted in knots and I knew it wasn't from a bad lunch.

"Hypothetically, you might be right. Hardin doesn't give a rat's ass if I find Amato and Picone, but what if the Feds do?"

"Then leave it to the Feds."

"I may have made a promise in a moment of, uh, weakness."

"She blonde or a redhead?"

"Shut up. She's a U.S. Marshal. And her hair color has nothing to do with her performance."

"She's using you. Doesn't seem like your style to do something for nothing."

"Sex isn't nothing." The words fell flat. "Besides, I got curious."

"Curiosity killed the—"

I held up a hand so he wouldn't finish the sentence. "I know, I know. If I tell you what I know, will you promise not to tell anyone else?"

"Anyone?"

I knew what he meant. "Yeah, even her. I just need to brainstorm for a minute and I can't hear myself think. I'll tell you what I know, you tell me what you think. We walk away and it's like we never talked. Cool?"

He shook his head, but I could tell by his expression, he was curious too. So I started talking, and once I did, he couldn't help himself. He hung on my every word.

I started with the day Diamond came knocking, and except for intervening real work episodes, I told him everything, closing with the surreal lunch hosted by the head of the Vedda family. When I finished, the first thing he asked was, "Do you have the Imperial with you?"

I sighed. "Really, that's all you've got? You want to see my coin collection?" I couldn't resist his enthusiasm, and I fished the coin from my pocket and shoved it toward him.

"Wow, this is amazing." He twisted it through his fingers and peered at the details on both sides. "Rare. Probably worth a grand."

"More, actually. I looked it up. Wanna buy it?"

"Really?"

"Since when did you become a coin collector?"

"Since always. My granddad was a collector, and I inherited his coin sets when he died. Nothing like this, but I've done a lot of research on international money."

"I don't know what to do with it. I wouldn't have taken it if I'd realized what it was at the time."

"You can't just give it back. It's a sign of disrespect. You have to find some appropriate way to return it."

"I don't have a clue what that means. All I know is for some reason, Petrov's focused on Bingo and he thinks I have some input there."

"Are you sure he's not really after Diamond and he's using the rest as a cover? He's got to have a vendetta for her."

True. He could have seen me with her. Wasn't like we'd been hiding that night. Still, why bring up Bingo? The Russian didn't strike me as the indirect type. "I think he would've just come right out and said so if he was looking for Diamond. I think she may be involved, but I think it's more complicated than that."

"You worried about Bingo? You want me to have someone run by and talk to him?"

I was worried, but I had a feeling that cops running by to check on him would drive him deeper into trouble. "No, but you can help me get a line on Amato and Picone. I have a feeling if I can find them, I might get some answers."

"Tell you what, you give up your lead on the prescription and I'll help. We've seen a lot of these fake meds showing up lately and I'd love to catch some of that action."

Diamond would be pissed. Didn't matter what she said about the exchange between her and Laura, I knew better. She'd gotten that prescription bottle, and it had something to do with the case she was working on. Not my problem. If she couldn't be bothered to tell me what was going on, well then, I'd just pass on whatever information I had to law enforcement who was interested. Good citizen that I am.

"Deal. How do you feel about going to a strip club tonight?"

Thursday nights are big in the world of strip clubs. Maybe folks like to start their weekends early or maybe it was that wives expected their husbands to be home for Friday night date night. Whatever the reason, I was glad Slice of Heaven was hopping since that made it less likely I'd be noticed.

In any event, Petrov didn't make a habit of hanging out in his own clubs. If he wanted a new woman or women, he would send one of his goons over to the club to pick one out. I knew this because Diamond had been one of the ones selected for him, once upon a time. And that was how she managed to infiltrate his inner circle and lead her team to arrest Yuri's brother for the murder of the head of a rival family. I didn't know how things would go down tonight, but I'd bet a fistful of those fancy gold coins the Russian handed out that I wouldn't run into Diamond here tonight or ever.

I'd shown up early, to get the lay of the land before John arrived. I'd been here once before, but a mostly naked woman in my lap had distracted me from the geography in the rest of the place. The waitress had already confirmed that Candy was working tonight. She'd be on stage around ten. I considered trying to pay her a preshow visit, but stalking the dancers in the back would draw too much attention. Better to let her do her thing, earn some money. She'd be in a better mood to talk once she had the hard part over with. I ordered another beer and settled in to wait.

No amount of beer could have taken the edge off what I saw next. I felt a tap on my shoulder and turned around. John stood behind me, grinning like a dog with a bone. The bone was a few steps behind him. Chance.

She was looking at the stage, not at me, so I took the opportunity to mouth "what the hell?" at John who lifted his shoulders and whispered, "She wanted to come along. What was I supposed to do?"

Uh, not tell her? I didn't bother stating the obvious. She was here and I suspected he'd told her everything. Note to self—don't trust John with confidential information. But secretly I was relieved. Jess knew what was going on, and I hadn't had to stumble over my feelings to tell her. I waved the waitress back over and motioned for them to sit.

John slid into one of the seats and then punched Jess in the arm and pointed at the other. She looked at him like she'd just realized they'd come here together and then sat down. She had yet to look at me.

"Hey, Chance. Heard you had a busy day today." My way of letting her know that John's inability to keep a secret went both ways.

She shot me a death stare. I hadn't expected such a visceral reaction, and I sure didn't think I deserved it. I did a mental rewind of the events of the past few days, but I couldn't think of any way in which I'd pissed her off. I decided to blow it off. Maybe her anger wasn't about me. "You get a night off from the doctor? She know you're at a strip club?"

Daggers. Okay, maybe the anger was about me after all. Only one way to find out for sure. "What's with the death ray? Mind explaining why you're so pissed off at me?"

We locked eyes. John cleared his throat, but neither of us turned toward him. She'd been acting strangely since last Saturday. Well, she'd been acting strangely toward me, anyway. I was done dancing around the subject. If she was mad at me, she could just say so.

"Dr. Deveaux is fine, no thanks to you."

Talk about out of left field. "I have no idea what you're talking about."

"I'm supposed to think it's no coincidence that days after you've started fucking a federal marshal, the FBI showed up on my doorstep, wanting to question my girlfriend?"

She'd just said a lot of really important stuff. Stuff I needed to wade through, process. But only one word stuck out. My internal sensors were completely broken, so I said, "She's your girlfriend?"

"Did you hear a word I said?"

"I heard everything you said." I wasn't sure that was true, but I plunged ahead. "How long have you been dating? How can you call someone your girlfriend when you barely know them? When your friends barely know her? What did the FBI want with her?" The last question was probably the most important in the scheme of things, but not to me. I didn't get how she and Deveaux had gotten to the "we have to give what we've got a name" stage of their relationship before I could even process they had a relationship. Crazy. That's what it was.

John cleared his throat again, and we all looked up to see the waitress waiting with our drinks. John paid and the table was quiet while she carefully arranged the coasters and drinks, showing off her stuff to John the entire time, undoubtedly hoping to earn a bigger tip. I think he finally gave her an extra five just to make her go away.

The air at the table had chilled. As much as I wanted answers to my questions, I was done talking. I'd done all the talking. If we were really friends, Jess could see fit to let me in. I hoped she would. That despite the acrimony between us in this very moment, she could find her way to sharing details about her life with me and that I would let her, even if I didn't approve.

"My friends do know her."

Sucker punch. Like any unexpected blow, it happened in slow motion and took what seemed like hours, but was really only seconds, to sink in. "Your friends?" I picked up my beer and drained it, and then slammed the empty mug on the table. "Your friends?" On some level, I knew I was saying the words out loud, but they were a constant chant in my head. Since when did her "friends" not include me? So Nancy knew? Gail knew? Probably everyone on the softball team, everyone she worked with, everyone who mattered to her. Except me. Why not me?

"I'm not your friend." I'd meant it to be a question, but that's not how it came out. Good thing, because I didn't want her to answer. I was scared of the answer. I stood, reached into my wallet and pulled out a ten, and threw it on the table. I turned to John. "The one you want is named Candy. She's supposed to go on at ten." I leaned over and pressed the bottle Laura had given me into his hand. "Take care of her."

He'd know who I meant. Without another glance at either of them, I stalked off. Angry, hurt, raw, I couldn't get away from these feelings fast enough.

I made it out the door before I had to stop, bend over, and catch my breath.

"Hey, lover, you okay?"

A hand settled on my back and I glanced up into kind eyes. And enormous tits. She spoke again before I could answer. "I'm early for my shift. You want to go somewhere and get a little private show?"

I straightened and mentally counted the contents of my wallet. I could afford a private show, and there was no shame in paying for it. Right? While I considered my options, the pressure on my back switched from her gentle touch to a rough hold.

"Fuck off, she's busy."

Jess?

"I was here first."

"Yeah? Well, she doesn't have to pay me."

Jess stared down my potential date until she raised her hands in surrender. "Fine, bitch. I got plenty to work with inside. Don't need to fight for it." She lifted her chin and pushed through the doors of the club, leaving me and Jess standing in the growing crowd of customers, her hand still on my back. She pulled me to the side of the building.

Once we were alone, she moved her hand to my face, cupping my chin, forcing me to look her in the eyes. "What is the matter with you?"

"What is the matter with you?" Childish repetition is all I could manage.

"Don't you want me to be happy?"

Wow. Loaded question. I started to say "of course," but held back. Sure, I want you to be happy, but do you have to be in a relationship to be happy? Do you have to be in a relationship with her? And what kind of trouble is she in, exactly? Finally, I drilled down to the real question. "Do you have to shut me out to be happy?"

She sighed and hung her head. "It's complicated."

"You're a chicken-shit."

"You don't understand. How could you?"

"What? I can't understand your little happily ever after fantasy? Oh, I understand it all right, but I also get it's a fantasy. If you don't get that, then you're in for a world of hurt."

"I'm happy, Luca."

"Really? Shutting me out of your life makes you happy?" I watched pain dull her expression, but I couldn't read the source. Maybe I couldn't read it because it was me. Did I cause her pain? Now that she'd found love, whatever we'd had probably seemed tarnished, trivial. But painful? I turned away as I spoke the next words. "Then go. Be happy. But don't think you can come back when the doctor doesn't get your late night need to drown your sorrow in a good strong fuck. When you don't feel like talking—you know how relationships are, they are all about the talking—and you just want to feel the press of naked flesh, hard, fast, rough. When the nightmares are so intense that you just want to blot them out, and tender kisses and talk about tomorrows isn't going to do the trick. When you feel the need so fiercely, don't you dare fucking call me." I punctuated my remarks by punching my finger into her chest. "Don't you—"

Her mouth was on mine before I could get out the last word. Against a lifetime of instinct, I pushed her away, but she held on tight. She surged forward and slammed me back into the wall, her tongue never leaving my mouth. My fight was fake, and within seconds, I surrendered to the familiar feel of Jess against me, in me. As close as she was, I wanted her closer.

I jerked out of her kiss and growled, "Touch me," in her ear. She knew exactly what I meant and slid her hand to my crotch, gripping hard, then stroking fast. I bucked with need and rode her hand while seeking her lips and tongue with my own. But she had a different idea. With her free hand, she tore at the zipper on my jacket and then ripped my shirt out of my pants, yanked it up to my neck. I groaned as she twisted one nipple while she sucked the other one to a hard point.

As weak as she made me, I wanted, needed to share. I pulled her closer and wrestled the buttons on her fly. I slid my hand down, between the rough denim and her soft panties. She was dripping through and I couldn't wait. I nudged aside the cloth and slipped two fingers in. Then out. Then in again. Her moans were magic. She was so ready for me—so open. And she had me so close—one more stroke. "Not yet," I panted in her ear.

"Yeah," she replied, and then she raised the bar by shoving her hand into my pants, not bothering to tease. She delivered long, hard, fast strokes against my dripping clit, while she kissed and nipped at my breasts. I could barely stand, and when the rush of climax crested, I arched from the wall, pulling her tight against my chest. She kissed my neck, sucking hard while I kept up my steady pace of penetration with my fingers, and rubbed her clit with the pad of my thumb. She would come with me. It was imperative.

The hitch in her breath told me she was on the brink, and I plunged in one last time to bring her home. She exploded and took me with her, linked by something far stronger than the physical hold we shared. I held her as she shuddered against me, kissed her hair, her face, her lips.

Finally, we both sagged against the wall. I pulled my shirt down and buttoned my fly. Jess was quiet. I didn't know what to say either, but the silence seemed dangerous, like the mend we'd just shared was floating away and now a bigger rift was building between us.

I slid my hand into her hers. She didn't react. She didn't squeeze my hand. She didn't pull away. Nothing.

Took me a minute, but I finally realized this, whatever it was, had meant nothing more to her than it ever had.

I slowly pulled myself off the ground. I'd walk funny for a few days, but the memory would be more painful than the soreness. She didn't even look up at me. Really, was I that much of an embarrassment?

I had to get out of there. Fast. I took two steps and stopped. I had to say something. To at least acknowledge what had just happened, even if she wouldn't.

I opened my mouth to say something nice, but true to my nature, I protected my own pain with my parting words. "At least you didn't have to pay me."

CHAPTER TEN

Friday morning came way too early.
I rolled out of bed and stiff-walked to the bathroom. I only knew two ways to soothe this kind of pain. Engage in the same exercise or die.

I wasn't going to be fucking Chance again anytime soon, and dying would mean she'd won. Guess I'd have to run off my pain. I pulled on a pair of sweats I was certain hadn't been on the floor more than a few days, grabbed my keys and a five dollar bill, and creaked out the door.

Instead of running in my neighborhood, I drove to White Rock Lake and took to the trail. It was as close to nature as I could manage, and for some reason I wanted to pretend I wasn't in the city.

A mile in, the physical pain subsided some, but I was still angry. How dare Chance start acting all holier than thou? *Look at me, I'm in a relationship, but I can fuck my best friend outside of a strip club and act like it means absolutely nothing.*

What pissed me off the most was why I even gave a shit. We weren't a thing, not the kind of thing she seemed to have with Deveaux, anyway. But we'd always had our own thing, undefined, but solid. She was there when I needed to talk, needed help, needed release. She'd always been there. And now she wasn't.

I could talk to Maggie, I had other friends on the force who could get me out of a jam, and the bars were full of willing women. So if it wasn't just about her availability, then why did I care so much that she was pulling back?

Because it was Jess. She'd cradled my broken body when I'd made a rookie mistake and gotten myself shot months out of the academy. She'd stood up to the veteran cop who blamed me for the incident. She remembered I liked my coffee black, and she could make me come in sixty seconds or sixty minutes, whichever I needed most. And she always knew what I needed most.

But my needs weren't her concern anymore. Yesterday, when I'd come to her for help, she was helping Deveaux. She was probably making coffee for Deveaux right now. She'd probably made slow, tender love to her last night after refusing to even hold my hand after we'd fucked.

I ran harder, trying with each footfall to drive these thoughts from my head. I didn't want to be this person. This jealous, possessive person. I wasn't this person, but I couldn't shake this fear that I was losing her. Was I losing her? And what did that mean?

Intent on my thoughts, I'd barely paid any attention to other runners on the path. When a hooded jogger nudged me, I practically growled.

She didn't flinch. "You look like you're in a bad mood."

I knew that voice. "Good morning, Marshall Collier. Find many fugitives here at the lake?"

"I'm taking the morning off. Looks like you are too."

"Nope. I'm working." She pissed me off being here, all sporty in her matching running suit, not even panting. I wanted her to leave me alone.

"Have another jumper on the loose you'd like me to help you catch?"

I hated her cheery voice. "Trust me, help from you isn't what I need."

"Uh, oh. I guess your cop friend got you all bent out of shape."

She had no idea. And neither did I. "What are you talking about?"

"Dr. Heather Deveaux?"

I should've had some coffee. My body was awake, but my brain was still on slow-mo. I kept running while the cogs fell into place. Jess had gone running to the doctor yesterday because Deveaux had gotten a visit from the Feds. Jess had been mad at me, like it was my fault the FBI was on Deveaux's tail. Why was that? Then I remembered my little game with the Feds the other day. I'd only been joking around when I'd taken pictures of her car. Had my tail turned their focus on her because of my stunt? Was there really a connection?

I was curious, but not enough to get involved. "I don't know what you're talking about."

She grabbed my arm, but I wrestled away. She wasn't giving up so easy. "Luca, you want to tell me how you know the doctor?"

I stopped and walked off the path. She followed. I crossed my arms. I might not be able to shake her, but I didn't have to have this conversation. "I don't."

"She's living with your buddy and you don't know anything about her?" She coughed into her hand and muttered, "Bullshit."

I glossed over everything she said, distracted by the fact she called Chance my "buddy." Really? Guess she and her team of super sleuths hadn't been tailing us last night when we were at the bar. If they had, she might have had to come up with a different word for our relationship, but I didn't have a clue what it would be. I resisted the urge to get into a conversation about my relationship with Chance, and focused on Diamond's question.

"I know she's a doctor. She moved here from Chicago. She drives a fancy car. She's hot, if you like redheaded supermodel types. That's about it."

"She's a person of interest."

"Maybe you think so. I prefer blondes."

"Don't play dumb. You know what I mean."

I did, but I'd purposely ignored her cop-speak. Diamond was telling me Heather Deveaux was the target of an investigation. My jealous self should've been elated. Maybe the Feds would haul her back to Chicago in a cross-country perp walk. Maybe she'd do time, lose her fancy car, her fancy clothes. Lose Jess.

My stomach clenched. Jess liked the girl. No matter what had happened between us last night, Jess was in a relationship with Deveaux. She would protect her with all the loyalty she saved for the people she cared the most about. I knew how fierce that loyalty was. If she found out I knew whatever Diamond was about to tell me, I would be on the other side, one of the ones Jess had to protect her girl against. I didn't want to be on that side.

But my own sense of loyalty kicked in. What if the good doctor wasn't everything Jess thought she was? What if she'd been lying to Jess, using her? Didn't I have a right to protect the person I cared about? How could I do that if I didn't know the whole story? I could at least listen to what Diamond had to say and then talk to Jess.

I knew it was a bad plan, but once I set it in motion, I couldn't stop. I motioned to a picnic bench about fifty feet from the trail, and we walked over and took a seat. "Okay, spill. And don't give me any crap about how it's an ongoing investigation and you can't give me specifics. You brought it up; you better have some details."

She nodded. "First off, it's not my case."

Already she was dancing around the subject. I pushed back from the table, but she raised a hand. "Wait, wait. I only said that so you don't blame me for whatever trouble your pals are in."

I cringed at the offhand reference to "pals." Jess was more than that. Way more. And because she was, the doctor would never be my pal. "Just tell the story."

"We've had a team following you for a few days. Shocked?" She smiled since she knew I'd made them. "One of the guys has been writing down the plate numbers every time you stop somewhere. We usually only run them if there's a reason to be suspicious, and we didn't have a reason until you started taking pictures of Deveaux's car."

Great. Guess I was partly to blame for the shiny spotlight the Feds had beamed onto Deveaux.

"They would've found her eventually."

I could tell she meant to be comforting, but the words fell flat. "Go on."

"She recently left a big, thriving practice in Chicago. All the doctors are super wealthy. Like way too wealthy for folks who treat hoards of Medicare patients. You get where I'm going?"

I did, but I also knew that law enforcement types, who don't make much, had a tendency to think rich folks all thrived from ill-gotten gains or at least stepping on the backs of little people. Still, Medicare practices don't usually translate into rich docs. "You think she's committed fraud, right?"

"Like I said, it's not my case. But yes, the agent in charge of the investigation thinks all the doctors are involved. They served some subpoenas, and all of the sudden, Deveaux takes off. Not a word to her partners. She just moves to Texas and starts living with a cop who knows enough to get her one of the best attorneys in town."

I had a million questions, but most of them weren't for Diamond. Good thing, since it wasn't her case and all. No, my questions were for Jess. Where had she met Deveaux? How much did she know about what was going on? If she knew it all, then what was she doing mixed up in something that could lose her badge—protecting a criminal?

Didn't matter how many questions I had, Jess wasn't likely to talk to me. Not after last night. She'd acted almost embarrassed, as if giving me a hand job outside of a strip club wasn't what she should've been doing last night. Maybe she thought she should've been home with Deveaux instead. And maybe she was right.

But Diamond owed me some answers, I started with the easy stuff. "Did your folks arrest the doctor?"

"No. Like I said, she's just a person of interest. But you might tell your pal that if her girlfriend wants to be one of the first in the door, I hear there's a deal to be made."

"You're assuming she's guilty of something."

"Innocent people don't run."

"Who said she ran? Maybe she just decided to spend her winter in a warmer climate."

"You under her spell too, huh?"

Too? "Not me. Just trying to see both sides."

"Well, make sure you keep an open mind. Detective Chance has decided we're the devil, picking on her girlfriend."

"I don't think they're that close." How close could they be if Jess was willing to leave her in her darkest hour and meet me at a strip club? I knew I was wrong, though. They were close, but how they got that way was the mystery I needed to solve. Diamond wasn't going to have those answers, so I changed the subject.

"By the way, I think you're about to get some help with your fake prescription case."

"Excuse me?"

"You remember our friend, Laura? I mean Yvonna Hump? She gave me her source, but don't worry, I gave the info to the cops. Like any good citizen would do."

"You're fucking kidding. Who did you tell?" She slammed a hand on the table. "Tell me now." I knew she'd be pissed that I'd given the lead to the locals, but I didn't have a clue she'd go ballistic. Her overblown reaction to details drove me to be vague. "I have some old friends on the force. I just passed along the info. They might not even do anything with it." I stood up. I'd gotten all I was going to get out of this conversation. Time to get out before I gave more than I got.

I couldn't resist a parting shot. "If you plan to follow me today, I plan to go home and take a big long nap. Then some food. Then maybe I'll get laid. Enjoy."

She couldn't help it. Her frown softened into a smile and I knew she'd enjoy watching at least one of those activities.

It may seem counterproductive to wake up, run, and then go right back to bed, but I'm convinced there is no better sleep than the kind cushioned by endorphins. Within minutes after getting back to my apartment, I fell into a deep sleep full of productive dreams. I got more done in those four hours than a week of awake time. And it was all easy. Totally unlike my dream from the afternoon before, I woke up refreshed and ready to take on the world. Or at least eat it. I was starving.

I considered ordering pizza. I don't usually order delivery since I hate waiting for food and it's just as easy to walk down the street to Maggie's, but I didn't feel like doing all the things I'd need to do in order to go outside. Like brush my teeth and put on shoes. I dialed the number stored in my phone and ordered a Big Brother, well done, and agreed to pay extra for delivery since I didn't live close enough. Would totally be worth it. I Fratelli's pizza was thin and crisp, unlike the cheap doughy crap with too much sauce like the pizza place around the corner served.

About thirty minutes later, my phone rang. I hoped it wasn't the pizza guy, calling to tell me he'd gotten lost. It wasn't, but it was an angry customer. I listened to my dad bluster for a few minutes before I cut in. "Dad, slow down and tell me what's wrong."

"What did you do to get me banned from Bingo's?"

Uh oh. "I don't know what you're talking about."

"Is that so? How come when I went there last night, Bingo wouldn't even let me through the door. He said I should talk to you and you could explain why."

If he'd been banned last night, I was surprised he hadn't called me on the spot. Of course, he sounded so drunk now, I was willing to bet he'd left Bingo's, started drinking, and hadn't stopped since. "Look, I'm sure it's a misunderstanding. I'll talk to Bingo and get it all straightened out." Maybe he was so drunk he wouldn't even remember this conversation.

"You better," he slurred. "Known him a long time. Don't need my nosy daughter messing in my business." He hung up before I could point out that I barely ever messed in his business, but his new girlfriend, on the other hand, was the queen of bossy.

Ten minutes later, I heard a knock on the door and opened it, expecting my Big Brother. I was surprised to see a little brother instead. My little brother.

He grabbed me up in a bear hug before I could take evasive action. He'd always been more touchy feely than me. At six feet, he was barely taller, but the skinny frame of his teen years had transformed into that of a muscular man. I might have a hard time wrestling him to the ground as I had so many times during our youth.

When he finally set me down, I backed up to get a better look. He was even more handsome than the picture on Dad's fridge. His dark brown hair was neatly trimmed—he probably paid a barber rather than using my DIY trim method. He wore tan pants and a really expensive looking sweater like it was a second skin. No one would guess that beneath the smooth good looks lurked a super nerd. I wondered if his wife-to-be dressed him.

"What are you doing here?"

"If you'd ever answer your phone, you'd know."

I shook my head and he frowned at my puzzled look. "I've been calling you for days, but you never answer."

"I have your number programmed in. Not a single call from you." My curt words were as close as I'd get to admitting I was pissed that he'd told everyone he was getting married except his only sister.

"What number do you have?"

My memory flashed back to all the blocked numbers I hadn't answered. I walked over to the kitchen counter and picked up my phone. As I scrolled through the contacts, he made himself comfortable on my couch.

"Nice place you have here."

I could hear the light vein of sarcasm running beneath his words, but I wasn't going to be nudged into a debate on better homes. "It works for me." Before he could say anything else, I strode over and shoved my phone at him. "See? There's your number."

He read the display. "Luca, I haven't had that number for months. Didn't Dad give you my new number?"

We both knew the answer. If he'd given it to Dad, chances were only fifty-fifty the information would filter through whatever alcohol haze he was in to pass it along to me. And even then, it might not be right. The harder truth was neither one of us had bothered to call each other for well on six months. And even now, the only reason he'd been calling me was to tell me about a major life event. If he wasn't getting married, who knows when I would have heard from him or him from me?

"You could've left a message. You didn't need to fly out here just to tell me you're becoming enslaved."

He laughed. "Don't flatter yourself, sis. I had to be here anyway. Wedding stuff. Don't ask me what, but it involves dinner with the in-laws. Besides, I didn't want to tell you my news in a message. I wanted to hear your voice when I told you I was getting married, and then asked you a very important question. This is even better because I can see your reaction."

Uh-oh. Visions of creepy wedding stuff invaded my brain. I prayed that six months with no contact hadn't caused my brother to forget that I hated all things sweet and frilly. Maybe he just wanted me to show his bride-to-be around. Oh no, couldn't be that. She'd grown up here. But she might not know where all the good dyke bars were. I could take her to a softball game, go out for beer after. She'd have a grand time.

Mark punched me in the arm. "Did you hear a word I said?" he asked.

Last thing I remembered was the prelude to the important question. "Guess not. What's the question?"

"I want you to be my best man, woman, whatever. I want you to stand up with me, carry the ring, make sure I don't pass out. You know, all that stuff."

He'd started out strong, but by the time he finished, he was red-faced and shy. And me? Well, I was blown away. Battling thoughts warred in my brain and I shared them. "Kind of bucking tradition, aren't you? How does your bride feel about that? She has that traditional girl kind of look about her."

He raised his eyebrows and I answered the unasked question. "Your sappy couple picture is on Dad's fridge."

"She's beautiful, isn't she?" He didn't wait for an answer. "Her family's pretty traditional, but she's awesome. You think I'd be marrying her otherwise?"

"Truth? I didn't think you'd ever get married."

"Oh. Really?"

He was genuinely surprised, which surprised me. "You know, after the great example we got from Mom and Dad? And then Mom and Larry, and Mom and Barry, and Mom and..." I was making up names, but I hadn't seen any sense in memorizing the details about our serial monogamist mother's many partners. "You know, you said you'd be an old bachelor before you ever lived with someone you'd grow to hate."

Despite my prodding, Mark's eyes still had that dreamy "other people may not be able to find true love, but I did" look. Interesting. How could we both have such distinctly different memories of our childhood, or at least distinctly different paths from it?

"I was like thirteen when I said all that."

I stubbornly refused to concede the truth of my memories. "And then you moved as far away as possible when you were old enough. You barely ever dated, even in college."

"Who had time? I was majoring in the computer equivalent of rocket science." He laughed, big and loud. "What? You thought I was going to be a lonely old man?"

"Oh." My turn to be surprised and a little embarrassed. Apparently, my memories were the ones that were skewed.

"Hell, even Dad's found a girl."

I didn't bother telling him that Maggie might deck him if he called her a "girl." Doubtless he'd find that out when he met her. Maybe I should take him over there now, have a few beers, and let him size up what his future looked like. A knock on the door rousted my memory.

"I ordered pizza," I explained as I answered the door. I shoved a twenty at the delivery guy and set the pizza on the counter. "Beer would go great with this, but my fridge is a wasteland."

He stood. "I can go get some. We have a lot to talk about."

I hadn't forgotten his "big" question, but I'd managed to duck it. Here in the apartment with just the two of us, it would be hard to avoid. I grabbed the pizza box. "Better yet, let's take the pizza to the beer. Come with me."

Maggie wouldn't be thrilled I'd brought my own food to her place, but it did mean I wouldn't have to eat a crummy turkey sandwich or run up a huge tab. Well, except for beer. I had a feeling I'd be drinking a lot of beer tonight.

Maggie rushed over the minute we walked in and sucked Mark into a huge hug. "I've heard so much about you! I would know you anywhere." She stepped back and held him at arm's length while she looked him up and down. She pulled him back into a hug and then led us to the bar.

As I'd hoped, Maggie monopolized my time with Mark. Way to avoid any personal interaction with my brother. Wasn't that I wasn't glad to see him, but I was a little leery of him. This grown-up, put together, handsome guy wasn't the nerdy little boy who hid under his bed every time our parents got into one of their screaming matches. The Mark in my mind would've shown up wearing ragged jeans, a heavy metal T-shirt, and Coke bottle glasses. He wouldn't be all gaga over a girl. He might even think they were strange and icky. We'd stayed in touch over the years, but apparently, our interactions were way more surface level than I'd realized.

"So you both like girls." Leave it to Maggie to point out our similarities. "Mark, you think Luca here is ever going to get married?"

I choked on my beer, but Mark just laughed. "I don't know, Maggie. Is she seeing anyone special?"

"Let me see, there was talk a while back about a Latin lawyer, but she turned out to be a piece of work. Maybe even a criminal." Maggie stage-whispered those last words. "And then there was this cop. Now, I don't generally like cops. They are too much in your business, but this one was real nice. Kind. And sweet."

I willed her to stop talking, but my silent pleas went unanswered. Maggie extolled Jess's virtues for a few more minutes, talking about how Jess had helped her brother, before she turned to me and asked, "You still with her? You never bring her around anymore."

I took a deep breath to force myself not to answer too quickly. "No. I mean, I was never 'with' her. She's a friend. An old friend. Just a friend."

"Right. She's not just a friend, unless she's one of those 'special friends.'" Finger quotes emphasized "special."

I was mortified. My "special" friendship with Jess was a distant memory. No matter what had happened between us last night, Jess had gone home to be with Deveaux, her new friend. Her girlfriend. It'd been hard enough hearing Jess say the word, but it felt positively nasty in my mouth. To cleanse, I spat it out. Loud. "She has a girlfriend. A doctor." I have no clue why I added the extra detail. Did it bother me that Jess found a professional more worthy of her affections than a blue-collar scuff like me?

I shook my head. No, that wasn't it. Maybe it was just that I knew the doctor wasn't all that, but Jess was blind to her faults. Of course she was. She cared about her. I didn't care about her, but even I couldn't put words to the nagging sensation that all wasn't what it seemed when it came to the doctor. And Jess deserved better than that. Way better. Yep, that's why I cared. I wanted the very best for my good friend.

I knew that wasn't all, but it was as far as I was willing to go. Right now. I needed to steer Maggie away from this line of conversation, so I blurted out, "I do have a little thing going with a federal marshal. She's smokin' hot. It's just sex, though. Nothing serious." I had their attention and I took full advantage. "Maggie, if you want lurid relationship details, you're going to have to focus on Mark. Ask him all about his future bride."

I raised my glass and toasted my own deft maneuver as Maggie began to pepper Mark with questions. I sat back and half listened to Mark tell us all about Linda, his bride-to-be, while I thought about all the loose ends in my own life. Linda was a resident at Massachusetts General in Boston, but she'd been offered a pediatric fellowship at Baylor Hospital in Dallas. Mark's geeky computer work wasn't confined by geography, which meant he could move across the country to accommodate his new wife's ambition.

My work wasn't confined by geography either. Dallas didn't have a monopoly on fugitives. I could move somewhere else, do the same thing. Wheels, guns, and a computer were all the equipment I needed. Hardin had connections everywhere, and bondsmen were loyal to a good bounty hunter. I'd never considered moving, but I wasn't sure why. Dad was here, but beyond an occasional check-in to scratch a gambling itch and to make sure he hadn't drunk himself silly, I didn't spend that much time with him. Besides, he had Maggie around now to nurse his hangovers or try to keep him from getting hung over in the first place.

My only other strong tie to Dallas was Jess. She'd been a constant in my life for so long I couldn't imagine not being able to knock on her door in the middle of the night to sate a need. But geography played a cruel joke now. She still lived only a few miles from me, but now that she was immersed in Deveaux, she may as well live across the country. Even last night, when I'd been inside her, she'd been far, far away.

Now Mark was moving back. That should be a tie for me, but he was getting married. And married people keep to themselves. They hang out with other married people and they have to confer with their spouses before they can do anything with their single friends. I'd probably talk to him about the same amount of time as I had when he lived across the country.

No ties. Nothing to hold me down. I should be basking in the simple realization of my liberty, but I felt more empty than free. I drank deeply and motioned for another the second I reached the bottom of my glass. Mark was buying, after all, and we had a lot to drink to. His impending nuptials, my solitary existence. Happy times.

Another three beers in and I began to hear voices.

"You are Luca Bennett, yes?"

The voice was quiet, but I could tell it was from behind my shoulder. Maggie and Mark were still chatting away. I don't usually hear voices after only four beers, but I had been under a lot of stress lately. I spoke into my empty glass. "Go away."

"I'm afraid I cannot. Mr. Petrov asked me to convey a message to you."

The man's voice was low, but ominous. Mark and Maggie stopped talking and stared over my shoulder. Guess the voice wasn't in my head after all. I turned around to face one of Petrov's bodyguards. Reality check. I'd been paid a king's ransom but hadn't done anything to earn it. Not that I cared. I fingered the gold coin in my pocket while I told him off.

"Look, Mr. Big Russian Guy. I work for myself." I pointed at my chest to emphasize the point. "For me. There's only me and my needs. You tell Petrov that he can use whatever powers of persuasion he thinks he has to get people to do what he wants, but I'm not on the list of those people." I could tell I wasn't really making sense, but I didn't care. I was talking to a guy whose reading list probably consisted of the label on a can of protein powder. Brawn was all he had going for him. All he needed to know was that I wasn't a lackey like him. I pulled the coin out of my pocket and dropped it on the floor between us. "Tell Petrov he can have his Imperial whatever and to leave me the hell alone."

In a surprising show of initiative, he bared his teeth and growled. "You can tell him yourself. If you're not too busy begging for mercy when you see him."

I stood up. I like to stand when I'm being challenged. Mark placed a hand on my arm, but I shook it off. I'd had lunch with an old school mobster this week. I wasn't going to be threatened by an upstart from the Baltics. I resisted the urge to poke the big guy in the chest, but I put a fierce growl behind my words. "You should leave. Now."

He hunched his shoulders once and his face smiled, but his eyes shot daggers. "I will leave, but your duty will stay. You will fulfill your duty or you will lose something valuable to you."

I opened my mouth to say that the joke was on him, that I didn't have anything of value, but the icy cold glint in his eyes took my breath away. That he wasn't looking at me, made his trance even more creepy. I followed his stare and my sight landed on Mark. And the guy standing behind Mark. Another big Russian mobster with his hand on my brother's shoulder. The tumblers clicked into place and I realized I did have something of value. Or someone of value.

I shrugged. "Him? Hell, I just met him tonight. Don't even know his name."

"And the woman you were with last night, outside Slice of Heaven?"

My gut clenched at the reference to Jess.

Mark caught my eye and then shot a glance at the hand on his shoulder. "Hey, lady, want to tell your friends to get lost?"

I offered an easy smile in response to his strained voice. "It's all good. They were just looking for directions and I told them where to go." I turned to mobster number one. "Tell Mr. Petrov I respect his confidence in my abilities, but I've got other work." I glanced down at the gold coin and said, "Make sure he gets everything that belongs to him. Or I will." I didn't care that my last words sounded like a threat.

When he didn't move, I went from bark to bite, tilting forward, in his face. "Get out. And don't come back."

They left. Without the coin. I knew they didn't leave because I told them to. They left to tell Yuri Petrov I'd been a bad girl and hadn't done what he wanted. They left to get their next orders, which wouldn't involve threats. Action would be next on their list.

I looked up to find Mark and Maggie staring at me. Worried questions in their eyes. I didn't have any answers. Hell, I didn't know what the hell was going on. Why Petrov was so bent on Bingo. Why he thought I had any influence. Why he could use his muscle to get what he wanted. I hadn't really cared before. But now that he'd threatened someone close to me, I cared. The list of people I cared about was short, which gave me even more motivation to keep everyone on it unharmed.

CHAPTER ELEVEN

I waited about thirty minutes after Petrov's goons left Maggie's before I hustled Mark out the door and drove to Dad's.

"Are you sure you're going the right way?"

"I'm taking the scenic route."

"You're scared those guys are following us, aren't you?" He shifted to look at the rear window. "I don't see anyone. Of course, I'm not sure why anyone would be out in this neighborhood."

I'd taken a winding route through South Dallas. I figured if we were going to get caught in a street fight with some Russians, chances were good the folks here would be on our side. At least we were more like the kind of white folks they were used to. Ones without an accent.

"Who were they?"

"Nobody."

"Seriously, Luca, I'm not twelve. You don't have to shield me from all the bad stuff in the world."

I looked over. He definitely wasn't twelve anymore, scared and ready to run at the first raised voice. He was a man, but he would always be my little brother. Someone I had to protect. But knowledge is power, and I could give him that much. "Bad guys. Russian mobster bad guys. They run plenty of shady businesses around town, but lately I think they're into something new or someone else's operation."

"And you're involved with them?"

"No. I mean, kind of. I'm doing a favor for a friend. It got a little complicated."

"Some friend. Is she hot?"

I slapped his thigh. "Watch it, buddy."

He laughed. "Okay, so she's super hot, but you don't want to talk about it." When his laugh faded, he scrunched up into a serious face. I recognized the expression from our youth. It was Mark's cautious, stay out of trouble face. I'd always ignored it before, leaving him behind when he wasn't up for adventure. But now instead of risking licks from Dad, the stakes were much higher. I might plunge headlong into the trouble, but I wouldn't let the people I cared about get dragged into it.

"If I could talk about it, I would, but then I'd have to—"

"Kill me? Right, I know the drill." He leaned back in his seat and I thought we were in for a quiet rest of the ride, but after a few minutes, he asked, "You think Dad can make it through a whole wedding weekend?"

I recognized the worry that had probably been stewing since his fiancée started planning this big event. Mom would be mother-in-law zilla, but zillas were to be expected at a wedding. Dad's weakness was much more subtle and likely to come out at the most embarrassing moments. Words forgotten mid-toast, stumbling into waiters passing hors d'oeuvres, arguing with the bartender about why his glass wasn't full to the top. Mark's concerns were valid. I gave the best answer I could. "He's good when he's with Maggie. She'll be there, right?"

"I assumed she'd be Dad's plus one. Guess one of your duties as best woman will be to get her there."

I knew we'd get back to that. "About that, you should probably pick someone else. I'm not big on weddings."

"You've been to so many you can't handle going to any more? Or is that you don't like cake? I find that hard to believe because everyone likes cake. Her parents are rich, so I bet it's going to be a really good cake."

"Shut up about the cake, already. You'll want me to get all dressed up. The last time I wore a dress was Easter, when I was six years old, and I'll never live down the pictures. You think I'm going to get all girly for you when you're probably paying photographers to capture every moment?"

"Fair enough. I imagine there will be a team of photographers there to capture our most wonderful day ever." I detected a slight edge to his tone. "Look," he went on, "I need someone there who's there just for me. Dad will be there for the free booze. Mom will be there for the spectacle. I've got friends who can be groomsmen, but none of them are best man or woman material. I need you to be there, by my side. For me. And I think you should wear a tux."

"A tux, huh? Mom's head will spin around."

He grinned. "Like I said, it's just for me."

"Yeah, okay, I'll do it."

I dropped Mark off at the curb. He begged me to come inside with him, but I had a long list of things I wanted to take care of, and waxing nostalgic with Dad and Mark wasn't on it. Besides, Dad was probably still pissed at me about his ban from Bingo's, and as long as I was on Petrov's shit list, it would be better if I kept my distance. I drove to the end of the street, parked in the shadows, and waited for a few minutes. When I was satisfied no one had followed me, I took off.

I considered my options. Everything—the guys Diamond wanted me to find, the Russians, Bingo—all of it, all of them, were wrapped up together somehow, but I didn't have a clue why or how. Hadn't really cared before, when finding Amato and Picone was more favor than work, but now that things were more complicated, sorting it all out seemed way more important. For a second, I considered calling Diamond and telling her to shove her favor. No amount of hot sex was worth the kind of trouble she'd stirred up.

Problem was I didn't trust her. Why had she sent me on this goose chase to begin with? Did she like watching women turn in circles for her? No, it couldn't be that simple. She was up to something, and that's exactly why I wouldn't turn to her for help now.

There was only one person I totally trusted, and I was sitting outside her house. I didn't even remember driving to Jess's place, but here I was, at the curb. And there was Deveaux's Beemer, parked in the drive, just like last time.

I weighed my options. I could drive off. And keep coming back, hoping Deveaux was gone for a while, or gone for good. Or I could suck it up and go to the door now. If Jess was going to stay hooked up with Deveaux, was I really going to stay away forever?

I took my time walking to the door. By the time I got there, I'd worked up my resolve. I was ready to face Jess and her girlfriend and act like I hadn't fucked Jess the night before.

The door swung open before I could knock.

"What are you doing here?" Her loud whisper came out like a hiss. I resisted reacting with a smart-ass remark. She was under a lot of stress, and what we'd done the night before probably hadn't helped.

"I need to talk to you. We're still friends, right?"

She sighed and motioned me in. "It's not a good time. I have a lot going on."

"I know. Maybe we can help each other out." I didn't have a clue what I could do for her, but the pained look on her face forced the promise from me. "I'll do whatever I can, but I really need to talk to you." Please don't ask me to help the doctor, please don't ask me to help the doctor.

My silent chant worked. At least for now. All she said was, "Wait for me in the kitchen. I'll be right back." She disappeared down the hall in the direction of her bedroom. I resisted the urge to follow and get a peek at the doctor who must have been waiting for her there.

Jess had one of those big, homey kitchens that people say reminds them of the family gatherings of their childhood complete with home-cooked meals and fellowship. I couldn't relate. My mother's attempts at cooking left the rest of us hungry, and we almost never invited anyone over to witness the dysfunction of a family meal.

Took her fifteen minutes to join me. Fifteen long minutes during which I considered looking for a beer in the fridge. Before last week, before I'd known about the doctor, I wouldn't have hesitated to make myself at home. Now, I felt out of place, like I didn't belong. Besides, I'd had quite a few beers at Maggie's, and Jess wouldn't approve of my drinking and driving. So instead, I amused myself by counting the tiles on her floor. At the fifteen-minute mark, I decided if she didn't come back in two minutes, I was out of there.

She showed up with thirty seconds to spare. I'd never seen her look this exhausted. She grabbed a mug from the cabinet and asked, "You want coffee?"

"Sure, if you do." Caffeine would have to be the drug of choice since I didn't have the nerve to ask for a beer. While she made a pot of coffee, I thought of about a dozen different conversation nonstarters, but silence seemed the better option. Thankfully, after a long stretch of quiet, she spoke first.

"We've been seeing each other for a while."

I nodded, not wanting to interrupt what appeared to be a full-fledged background on the doctor.

"I met her when I was at my doctor's office. It's a big office. She was there to talk to them about joining their practice. We were both waiting. We talked and, well, you know…"

I picked up the trail. "And she's smart, gorgeous. You asked her out."

"She asked me out, but whatever, it doesn't matter. We went out. We hit it off. We kept going out. We had a good time. I saw something in her, with her. I can't explain it."

She didn't have to. I'd been surrounded by enough of it lately, that I recognized the affliction—the craving for security, the need to couple, to feel complete with someone else by your side. Mark, Dad, hell, my mother was on her fourth husband trying to scratch that itch. I guess I'd always thought Jess was immune, like me. That we'd always have each other and we'd get to feel superior to the ones who wanted more. Now she was one of them and I couldn't process the change. "And now you live together."

Jess's expression turned from thoughtful to mortified. "We don't live together. She's just staying here until she finds a place."

"Sorry, I must've misunderstood something John said."

"Nobody knows my personal business but me. You want to know something, you ask me."

"Fine. Got it."

"Seriously, Bennett, it's bad enough having federal agents show up at my house. I don't need my friends going around speculating about my personal life, especially when I don't have a clue what to do about it. Besides, I thought you came over to talk about you and your problems."

I had a ton more questions about Deveaux and whatever trouble she was in, but I didn't want to be the one prying. Not tonight.

I told her essentially what I'd told John about the visit from Diamond, Yuri's gold piece, my weird lunch with Vedda's dad, and the fake prescription drug deal. I ended with the bullying I'd experienced at Maggie's bar earlier that night. "They mentioned you, Jess." I lowered my voice to a whisper. "Someone from Yuri's crew saw us last night."

Her only response was to walk over to the fridge and pull out a couple of beer bottles. She handed one to me and then twisted the top off hers and drank a long pull.

I did the same. I gave the beer some time to work its magic on her, and then said, "I'm out of ideas. I tried to give them back the coin, but they wouldn't take it. I'd drive straight to Yuri's place right now, tell him to shove it, but they mentioned you..." She looked up, but I kept talking, scared that if I stopped, we'd have one of those silly sentimental moments neither of us would be able to stand. "Mark was there. He asked a bunch of questions, but I didn't have a clue what to tell him."

"Your brother?"

"Yep. He's in town for wedding stuff. He was with me at Maggie's when Petrov's guys came calling."

"Shit, Luca. Looks like that crazy Fed got you wrapped up in a big mess."

I raised my beer bottle and toasted the air. "Women, can't live with 'em. Can't live without 'em. But beer helps."

She half-grinned and leaned forward to clink her bottle with mine. "Walk away."

"Excuse me?"

"Just walk away. Seriously, what are the chances Petrov is really going to mess with you? Because you wouldn't talk to Bingo about doing business with him? He obviously doesn't get that you're not that well connected. He'll get over it."

"Ouch. Thanks a lot."

"You know what I mean. He thought Bingo would listen to you. He misunderstood your relationship."

"What about his threats?"

"I can take care of myself. Besides, Petrov's about to have his time and attention taken up by another matter."

"Is that so? Spill."

"Not a chance."

"Not fair. Does it have anything to do with his strippers peddling fake prescription drugs? I doubt busting his clubs will keep his attention for too long. He has a ton of other enterprises."

"Stay out of it, Luca. Don't you have any real work?"

"Oh, so now bounty hunting is real work?" I took another drink of my beer. "I have had a string of good luck lately, but I've got one more case of Hardin's to do. It's a big payout, but I've been a little distracted. You may know the guy, Otis Shaw."

She nodded. "Be careful of that one. Word is he's crazy. Not legal crazy, but no telling how he'll act when you come calling. And he's huge."

"I really should go by there tonight, but I'm not in the mood to wrestle the hulk. Besides, you never know, I might still pick up Vedda's guys and that would be a decent payout. In fact, I think I might go by Bingo's place instead. See if he's ready to talk about what's bothering him."

"Don't be stupid." She glanced at her watch. "It's not even midnight. His place will be hopping. He's not going to want to mess with you when he's got a full house."

"I was thinking maybe he'd be less likely to toss me out the door if he had an audience."

Jess finished her beer and set it on the table between us. "Doesn't he shut down around three?" I nodded. "Tell you what. I'll pick you up around two thirty and we'll go over there together. He's not going to throw me out. I'll leave you two alone so you can have a heart-to-heart with him."

I tamped down my excitement at taking on this adventure with Jess by my side. Pretty strange since I'd usually balk at the prospect of a police escort. "What about…" I let my voice trail off, but I jerked my chin toward the back of the house. I hoped my reminder wouldn't make her change her mind. The idea of a late night adventure with Jess had my blood going. Even if it wasn't our usual fare. She didn't disappoint.

"You let me worry about my business. You have enough of your own shit to worry about."

Would she ever get that she was a big part of the shit I worried about?

CHAPTER TWELVE

Jess showed up at my door at two thirty on the dot. The minute I saw her, I had a hard time remembering the purpose of this late night visit. Worn jeans hugged her lean frame, a white T-shirt stretched across her chest, and her black leather jacket was a nice contrast to her slightly mussy blond hair. Either she didn't notice my appreciative look, or my lust had no affect on her. She thrust a white wax paper bag into my hand.

I shook away my lustful haze and peered inside. "Donuts, really? Isn't that kind a cliché?"

"Only if I eat them. If you eat them, it's perfectly normal."

I reached in the bag and quickly found my favorite, chocolate glazed. She did still love me after all, and the realization coursed warmly through my body. But I couldn't let the good feeling be "Your girlfriend know you're gallivanting around in the middle of the night, bringing donuts to other women?"

She grabbed the bag out of my hands and set it on the counter. "You wanna do this or not?"

This. If I knew what this was, I could answer. Was this ignoring the fact she was practically living with someone and fooling around with me? Was this actually talking about it? I wanted to know and I didn't, in equal parts. My usual MO was to ignore conflict. It would resolve eventually. Or it wouldn't, but messing around in it only got everyone dirty. But even though Jess and I had experienced conflict before, the core of our relationship had never been in jeopardy. I could count on her and she could count on me. For anything. Now that she was with Deveaux, I could feel the list of things we could count on each other for narrowing. Hated it, but would saying something make a difference? Or would I just be left lonelier still?

Not a gamble I wanted to take. I grinned to cover my aches and pulled a jacket out of the closet. Like Jess's, it was black leather. Except for my black T-shirt, we were dressed alike, and we looked like thugs looking for trouble. Not far off the mark.

I grabbed the keys to the Bronco from the hook by the door. "Let's go. And I'm driving."

Bingo's house was still lit up when we got there, but a steady stream of folks weaved down the sidewalk to their cars. A well-positioned squad car could probably initiate several DWI arrests in the next half hour, but I knew none would. Bingo's place was in the zone. Despite operating outside the law, Bingo's business was considered by many Dallas elite to be a valuable resource in the community. On any given night, you might find an NFL, NBA, or NHL player laying odds in one of his regular games. In addition to the alphabet soup of sports players, Bingo's house was a haunt for politicians, state and local. And most importantly, a few cops liked to spend their paycheck there. I wondered if any of his special guests realized he had a connection to Vedda. That was likely to be our only leverage with him and I told Jess so.

"Got it," she said. "How should we play this?"

My mouth fell open. Her badge meant she usually trumped me in situations like this, but I decided not to dwell on the balance of power. "He's pissed at me for some reason. Enough to ban me and my dad from his games. You take the lead and I'll hang back unless you signal otherwise."

"Deal."

I parked far enough away to see, but not be seen. About five minutes later, the outside lights went dark. We waited until the last car pulled away and then I drove around the corner and parked on the next street. We walked through the alley and eased up to the back door. I stood to the side while Jess knocked.

A few minutes later, Bingo's tired voice called out, "Closed."

"My partner left his wallet. He's halfway home. I live around the block and he asked me to stop by." Jess gave the name of one of the cops she recognized leaving Bingo's earlier. Worked like magic. When the door swung open, she signaled for me to join her in the doorway. Bingo's expression morphed from friendly host to annoyed resident when he saw me standing next to Jess.

"Get out."

I left the talking to Jess. She smiled at him. Probably half to disarm him and half because she'd never seen a grown man wearing a red wig and a purple satin smoking jacket at the same time. "We're here as friends. Aren't you going to invite us in?"

"I don't know you. And she…" He pointed a finger in my direction. "She's not my friend."

Ouch, that hurt. I'd been coming to his place since before I could count. I'd sat on my dad's knee while he gambled away the phone bill, the grocery money, the mortgage. I'd learned to play poker before I'd learned long division. Bingo even kept my favorite cookies on hand for years after I'd outgrown the taste. I opened my mouth to protest, but Jess intervened.

"She's your friend or she wouldn't be here, and I damn sure wouldn't be here in the middle of the night to help you out if it wasn't for her. Now, do you want to talk about Geno Vedda out here where your neighbors can hear us or do you want to invite us in?"

Pretty sure her threat about Vedda, not the assurances of my friendship, did the trick, but I didn't care. He waved us in. She hadn't flashed her badge, but she didn't need to. Just like last Saturday on the softball field, everything about her demeanor screamed cop. Didn't matter what she was wearing. When I'd been a cop, everything about me yelled dropout. Glad at least one of us had the authority to command a situation.

We followed Bingo to the kitchen. Ever the perfect host, he offered us something to drink. Jess shook her head and started to say no, but I put my hand on her thigh and squeezed. She got the message and asked for a beer for both of us. Bingo would be more likely to talk if we took advantage of his hospitality. I resisted the urge to ask if he had any cookies.

We sat around the table, nursing our drinks for several minutes before Bingo, apparently unable to withstand the silence, burst out with, "I don't work for Geno. I swear."

"We're not here to talk about Geno," I lied. We were, but I wanted him unsettled from the start. "Did you know Yuri Petrov wants a piece of your game?"

He didn't say anything, but I could tell he knew by the way he shrunk when I spoke the name. "What's up, Bingo? Why all the sudden interest in your operation?" I paused and let a thought sink in. "Or have you always had behind the scenes investors?"

He shredded a napkin into a thousand pieces before answering. "Not always."

I leaned in, like we were having this discussion one-on-one. "And lately?"

"Lately things have gotten a little out of hand."

"Whatever it is, we can help." I was only half-lying now. I'd never seen him be anything other than the friendly host, ready to take our money, but pleasant while doing it. Last week, when I'd lost money at one of his tables, I'd noticed he was a little agitated, but I'd written it off to having a full house. My mistake. "Tell us what you're in for and we'll do everything we can to help."

He pointed across the table. "How's she going to help? She's a cop."

Jess shook her head. "Not tonight. Let's just say I have a lot going on and I need an extracurricular project to take my mind off my own troubles."

"You have no idea what you're getting into."

"Try me."

He sighed and brushed aside the remnants of his napkin tearing binge. "I never run short, but last summer, when the market tanked, business started drying up. A couple of Geno's guys stop in occasionally to play cards. I cracked a joke about getting a loan."

"Let me guess, Amato and Picone?"

"You got it."

"They think your joke was funny?"

"Hilarious. They told me they knew plenty of ways I could make some extra cash, but that they didn't think I had the nerve. I told them they were right. I'm not going to turn these guys away if they want to play a game every now and then, but I know better than to get wrapped up in their kind of business. At least that's what I thought."

"Well, obviously that didn't work out so well. What happened? You got a little greedy?"

Jess shot me a shut-up look, but I didn't care. I wanted him to get to the meat of the story. Plus, I took personal offense to his remark that he wouldn't turn mobsters away, but he'd kick me to the curb after years of loyal play. I'd probably paid for a half dozen of his prized Elvis tchotchkes in the past year alone.

"If I was greedy, I wouldn't be sitting here talking to you two. I'd have never invited you in. I only want my business back. I told Amato and Picone I wasn't interested in making extra, but after my conversation with them, I started obsessing about how I was going to make ends meet. So much that when Geno himself stopped by a week later and offered to refi my place, I figured what could it hurt? Wasn't like I was going to get a loan on my own. What would I list as my job? Assets— one gambling house, a dozen decks of cards, and chips for life." He hung his head. "I should've known better, but those guys flash so much cash, I figured I could get a small piece, get back on track, and pay them back in no time. Of course, it didn't work that way. I got behind."

"Holy shit, Bingo. Geno owns your house?" He nodded, and I resisted the urge to rub it in. Everyone knows borrowing money from family is a bad idea, but borrowing from one of Dallas's first families of crime? Stellar mistake. Huge.

Jess got things back on track. "So what's the payback?"

"I operate as usual, but they have the run of the place and a guaranteed take. I will say business has picked up. Oh, and I have a place to live. Guess that's a good thing."

Business had definitely been booming tonight. And when I last played at Bingo's tables. But his clientele had definitely changed. More flash. The crowd leaving tonight looked more like a bunch of extras from Jersey Shore than the usual ball players and college students who sat at his tables.

"What about your old customers? They still come around?"

"Some, but they tend to come on different nights than this new crowd. One of them told me he didn't like the vibe anymore. But what am I supposed to do?"

"Damn shame. Your customers have always been loyal to you."

He caught the anger in my voice and rushed to respond. "You tell your dad I'm sorry. I didn't want him coming around. You know he'd feel out of place. And you, well, I couldn't let you in. You'd mess things up for me for sure."

"Well, I'm here now. And apparently, whatever Vedda thinks you're good for, Yuri Petrov thinks is worth twisting my arm and threatening people I care about. You sure this is still a gambling joint?"

"I swear, if something else is going on, I don't know anything about it." He stood up. "Wait here, I want to show you something."

I believed him, but I also believed that if something was going on, he chose not to know. Desperation made for great blinders. I turned to Jess. "What do you think?"

"I think he has no idea how much trouble he's in. He's always had an unofficial pass for whatever goes on here, but now that he's wrapped up with Geno's crew, I don't think he's safe anymore."

Bingo reappeared before I could reply. He thrust a closed fist at me. "Here, take this." I opened my hand and he dropped a heavy object in it. I didn't have to look to know what it was. Yuri must have a huge stash of these rare gold coins.

"You get this from Yuri himself?"

"No, he sent a couple of hulks to give it to me. I tried to refuse, but they forced it on me. I thought about tossing it out the door at them, but I gotta tell you, I was scared. Luca, I've never been that scared before."

I exchanged a look with Jess and she nodded for me to keep at it. "What did Yuri's guys want?"

"All they said was they wanted me to clean my house. That it was their territory now. Beyond that, I don't know. They've come back a few times on nights that Vedda's crew isn't here, but they've made it clear they want to be exclusive." He wrung his hands. "If I clear Vedda's people out, I'm in hot water with him. If I don't, then these guys come after me. What was I supposed to tell them?"

I felt his pain. I'd told them to fuck off and they'd threatened Jess. I couldn't exactly advise him to do the same. "Bingo, I need to talk to Chance alone for a minute. Do you mind?"

"Sure, yeah, I still need to clean up from the night. I'll be in the living room."

I waited for him to leave before I spoke, even though I figured he was probably listening at the door. "What do we do now?"

"You? Nothing. Time to let the folks with badges take care of this one."

"No offense, but you folks with badges wouldn't even know there was a problem if I hadn't told you."

"Don't be so sure about that."

"Give me a break." Her cagey response pissed me off. "I've been personally threatened by these guys. If you think I'm going to drop this, you don't know me as well as you think."

"Yeah, about that. What does everyone in this little bit of chaos have in common? A connection to you. Maybe if you take yourself out of the equation, we'll all be fine."

"You don't know what you're talking about." It felt like she was blaming me for everyone else's troubles. I stood up. I needed to get out of the room for a minute before I did or said something we'd both regret. "I'll be back in a minute."

I walked right past Bingo who was cleaning up the remains of a busy night. He looked up, and I pointed to the bathroom. Once inside, I shut the door, flipped on the cold water, and splashed my face. I let Jess's words roll around in my head for a few. It took a few minutes, but the cogs finally clicked into place.

Diamond. She'd asked me to look for Vedda's guys. She knew Petrov. Had even been his go-to girl for a while. She'd followed me to Bingo's on at least one occasion in the last week, and she'd been with me right before Yuri did his best Godfather impression in the parking lot of the Dusty Rose. Somehow, this mobster rivalry circled back to her. I didn't have a clue how or why, but I resolved to find out. But I had to shut Jess out of it. She and Diamond not only had the natural state versus federal animosity, Jess thought Diamond was up to no good. She didn't need any more ammunition on that front. Plus, I knew Jess would go after Diamond like a bull in a china shop. Finesse was required, which meant I probably wasn't the right one for the job either, but I had to start somewhere.

I hunted around for a towel to dry my face. Nothing on the rack, so I opened the door to the cabinet under the sink and rooted around inside. Guy was worse about doing laundry than me. In my search for a towel, I smacked my hand against the back wall. Something was off. I knelt down and looked inside, and then glanced back up at the counter. The back wall of the cabinet was about a foot less deep than the countertop. I sat on the floor and felt around until I located a spring that released a panel of what I now knew was a fake rear wall.

I didn't find any towels, but I did find row after row of burnt orange prescription bottles. I checked two and they were both full of the same pills I'd found in the bottle Laura had given me. The labels were from the same pharmacy too, which I was certain was fake. None appeared to be in Bingo's name. Looks like I had another connection back to Diamond. I shoved one of the bottles in my pocket, dried my face on my shirtsleeve, and walked back to the kitchen.

I decided to play along with Jess. Let her think she was in control. "Maybe you're right. I've got a murderer to find. I'll leave you with the non-paying gig and go collect a nice fee. Let's tell Bingo you're on it. But seriously, Jess, you better be on it. He's like family to me and he needs to come out of this okay."

"Got it."

I knew she did and I meant what I said. As dumb as Bingo was for getting involved with these guys in the first place, I felt bad for him. I wasn't all that smart myself, having gotten involved with these guys just because a sexy woman had dared me to. Time to confront Diamond and find a way out of this mess.

Jess and I didn't talk much on the way home. My sugary donut high had worn off, and all I could think about was a good night's sleep. I glanced over at Jess. She looked wide-awake. Maybe Bingo's problems would provide a nice escape to the ruckus of her home life. I'd like to think something would keep her mind off Dr. Heather Deveaux, since nothing else I did seemed to do the trick.

CHAPTER THIRTEEN

Saturday morning was super sunny, but I managed to pull a pillow over my face and sleep until noon. I considered taking the day off, but I didn't really know what that would look like. Mark was at Dad's so I couldn't steal Dad away for a trip to the casino. My television only got reception for two local channels, and there was never anything on I cared to watch. I supposed I could sleep all day, but even that gets old after a while.

Wonder what Chance and Deveaux were doing? Maybe breakfast in bed and a day of cuddling? Or would Chance keep her word and start working on getting Bingo out of his mess? Why did I care?

I thought about the prescription bottle I'd palmed from Bingo's place last night. I probably should've given it to Jess when I'd had the chance, but I hadn't. I should still call John and give it to him, but something made me feel like hanging on to it, maybe because it felt like the common thread in the fabric made up of Diamond, Bingo, the Italians, and the Russians. Maybe I was just feeling way too poetic.

I did call John. Left him a message, asking him to keep an eye on Jess, that she'd attracted some unwanted attention from some unsavory folks. A little cagey, but I didn't want to leave a lot of detail on his voicemail. I hoped after our earlier conversation, he'd get the point. I didn't mention the prescription. Not yet.

That done, my choices for the day boiled down to two options. Talk to Diamond or find Otis Shaw. I found a stray penny on my nightstand and flipped it in the air. Heads the Fed, tails the jailbird.

Tails. Today was the day Otis Shaw would go back to jail.

I considered a run, but when I stuck my head out the door to check the temperature, I nearly froze. Must've dropped twenty degrees overnight. Crazy Texas weather. After a shower, I decided to head to Maggie's for lunch out of convenience more than anything else. I'd make a burger myself if I had to.

She greeted me the moment I walked in the door and I wished I'd worn shades. Her lime green and sunny yellow ensemble burned my eyes. Her voice burned my ears. "Why aren't you with your father and your brother? They are picking out tuxedos this morning."

I could think of about a dozen reasons why I wasn't with them, especially considering what they were up to. Thank you, Mark, for saving me from this task. He had to know that getting me to agree to dress up would be enough of a chore without subjecting me to any decision-making. "They don't need me for that. What do I know about tuxes?"

She led me to the bar and pointed me into a chair. "It's not about what you know. It's your job to be there for all the little things. You know, as the best man, or whatever."

"Best woman. Or whatever. Like what little things?"

"You know, you throw him a party, you get him to the wedding, you handle the ring—"

I held up a hand to stop her. Already she'd listed way more than I was comfortable with. Show up, make sure Mark didn't throw up. That's about all I thought I was in for, and even those small tasks gave me the chills. I didn't entirely trust Maggie's version of a best whatever's duties and thought about who I could ask. Jess was the first name that sprang to mind, but I had a feeling I was just looking for a reason to call her. John was married. He would know more about the duties of a best man than any of the women in my life. Maybe I'd call him later, give him the prescription bottle in exchange for words of wisdom.

In the meantime, I needed to get Maggie off the subject and talk her into a hamburger and fries. "I'll call Mark later. I promise. But right now, I'm starving. I've been running a lot lately and I can't afford to lose weight, so I need a burger and fries, not that healthy shit you've been turning out for Dad." I whipped out a picture of Otis Shaw. "I need to nab this guy today, and turkey sandwiches on whole wheat ain't gonna cut it. Cool?"

Her expression told me I probably could have been a hellauva lot more tactful, but I'd gotten my point across. She glanced at the picture and then huffed. "It's your life. You want it to be short. Who am I to say different? Hopefully, you'll make it to the wedding. I know Mark is counting on you." She stomped off, still talking about my failing health and almost certain demise. Interesting how she'd become so in touch with what my brother wanted when she'd only just met him. Typical Maggie, meddling in everyone's business. I didn't care how much she railed as long as she brought me a plate full of fat, grease, and protein.

An hour later, I felt more like taking a nap than hunting down a felon, but I forced enthusiasm for my afternoon adventure. I filled up the Bronco and drove to Shaw's new girlfriend's place. I circled the block a few times while I considered what to do. Felt good getting back to basics. Find people, bring them in. Find more people. Easy, simple. I didn't need the complications of a cop's life. I decided to tell Diamond to screw off and give the RX bottle to John. They could each solve their own mysteries. I didn't need the trouble. A desire for simplicity was why I'd lasted less than a year on the force.

Shante's place looked empty, and this wasn't the kind of neighborhood where folks called the cops if they saw someone lurking around, but I wasn't taking any chances. I parked a street over and snuck back through the alley. Good thing I wore boots. The alley was full of empty pizza boxes and used hypodermic needles. Nice neighborhood.

The backyard was surrounded by a chain link fence I could almost step over. Not much cover. The driveway was out front, so I didn't expect to see any cars in the back, but I also didn't expect to see a swing set and a sandbox. Wouldn't surprise me if Otis was a prolific baby daddy. I'd have to be careful not to shoot up any kids in my quest for him.

After watching the back windows for about fifteen minutes, I decided no one was home. I should've walked away, gotten in the

Bronco, and set up surveillance. Thing is, I hate waiting around, especially when I know there's so much more I can be doing.

I glanced around, then vaulted over the fence. Half a dozen strides and I was at the back door. I'm not great at picking locks, but this one was simple and I was in in less than five minutes. Took less time than that to walk through the place and confirm no one was there. Satisfied I was alone, I settled in to get some intel on my jumper.

I started in the kitchen. People have a tendency to keep really important stuff in the kitchen. Like their mail, bills, and receipts, which give a history of what they like to do and where they like to do it. I found the junk drawer, crammed full of paper, and then pulled out my phone and started snapping pictures. Folks in this house weren't big on pizza, but they loved the Whataburger down the street. According to the receipts, they ate there at all times of the day, but especially late at night. I could appreciate their good taste.

I also found an account statement for a bank a couple of miles away. Based on last month, looked like someone in the family got regular government checks. I took a picture of the statement, noting the dates of the deposits. When I was done, I shoved the paper back in the drawer. I pulled up the calendar app on my phone. If the someone on the government dole was Mr. Shaw, he was due for another check in the next day or two. I walked to the front door and opened it just wide enough to stick my arm out and feel around for the mailbox. I grabbed a fistful of mail and then pulled the door shut. Mostly junk, but one envelope had that official-looking, might have a check inside look. Shaw's name beamed through the tiny window of the envelope. I'd bet the buy-in price at Bingo's it was Shaw's check. Since it was the weekend, he wouldn't be making a trip to the bank until Monday, at the earliest. I'd have to start somewhere else if I wanted to find him before then.

I put the mail back in the box and poked around the rest of the house for a few minutes before I decided Shante's house was a dead end. It wasn't even four o'clock. I wasn't likely to find Shaw and friends dining at the local Whataburger, but I drove by anyway. A quick peek in the window revealed only a few older couples. The smell of French fries was tempting, and I had to force myself not to eat a second lunch. As I considered giving in to temptation, my cell phone buzzed and Mark's new phone number blared across the screen. I jabbed the talk button. "Hey, little brother, what's up?"

"I'm at Dad's. We're about to start drinking beer and smoking cigars. Come over." He hung up before I could conjure up an excuse to miss the fun. Didn't matter, I was already turning around to head in that direction. It was the best invitation I'd had in a while.

❖

I drove by Chance's place on my way to Dad's. Didn't know what I expected to find, but the BMW was in the drive and lights were on in the living room. The happy couple was probably watching a movie. Or not. Jess hadn't seemed too happy last time I'd seen her. I wanted to give her some of her own advice and tell her to just walk away, but she needed to make that decision on her own.

I circled the block a few times and, once I was satisfied no creepy thugs were hanging out, I left. On my way out of the neighborhood, I saw a patrol car driving slowly down the street. I hoped John had gotten my message and sent someone official to watch out for Jess.

When I reached Dad's place, I fished the key from underneath the flowerpot out front and let myself in. I could smell the cigar smoke through the door. So much for Dad's good training. Couldn't really blame him, the temperature had dropped another ten degrees since I'd prowled around Shaw's place and I hadn't been looking forward to sitting around a fire in the old charcoal grill out back.

I found Mark and Dad in the kitchen and, judging by the crushed empties, they were well past caring what the place smelled like. "Hey, you two. Early bachelor party?"

Mark tipped his beer bottle in my direction and shouted, "Look, Dad, it's the best man!"

Dad wobbled out of his chair, and pulled me into a bear hug that was mostly about me holding him upright.

"Whoa there. Seems like you've been at this a while." I helped Dad back into his seat.

"You spend an entire day trying on tuxes and sampling food and you'd need to drink too."

Food? No one said anything about food. Maybe wedding planning wasn't so bad after all.

"Took me forever to get Mom to back off the morning coats and top hats."

"I don't even know what a morning coat is. But why is she even involved? Aren't your lovely bride and her mother supposed to be doing all the planning?"

"Have you met our mother?"

"Good point."

"We picked out great tuxes. We're going to look awesome."

"You're drunk."

"Maybe a little. You have something better to do?"

I considered my options. Sit outside a hamburger joint and wait for a murderer to show up. Sit outside a murderer's house and wait for him to show up. Roam the streets and hope to run into the murderer. I settled on beer and cigars. I motioned to the fancy case on the table. "Give me one of those." After I puffed the fat cigar to life, I decided to make use of the captive audience and get some answers.

I started with Mark. "Why Linda?"

"Why Linda what?"

"How do you know she's the one?" Not sure where I got the whole "one" thing. Dad may have married for life, but Mom sure hadn't. She was on her fourth number one and none of us expected it to last.

"I just knew. Know. I can't explain it."

"Try."

Dad shifted in his chair. "Hey, you two. Don't start fighting. Either of you want another beer?"

"Sure," I spoke for both of us. "And we're not fighting. I'm just curious. And Mr. Romance here can certainly come up with an answer if he tries hard enough."

Mark drank down the rest of the beer in his hand before he answered. "You'll laugh if I tell you."

I drew my hand across my heart. "I swear I won't. Now, fess up."

"We met at the hospital. In the ER. I'd sliced open my finger cooking dinner for a date, and Linda was the resident who stitched me up."

"No way. Was your date there to watch you swoon over your doctor?" He blushed his answer. "Seriously? So you ditched the date who made you cook for one who could sew. Sweet." I laughed hard until Mark punched me in the arm. "Hey, that hurt!"

"Lay off. It wasn't like that. The date was a bust anyway. On some level, cutting myself was the easiest way out of it. She even made me hail the cab for the drive to the hospital, you know, because I'm the guy. We get there and all she wants to do is bitch about how they don't have any new magazines in the waiting room. It was a Friday night. The ER was full of crazy injuries and all she cared about is the latest issue of *Cosmo*. She lasted about thirty minutes before I threw her a fifty and told her to get a cab home."

"And then you met Dr. Lovely?"

"Not hardly. Cut hand is a low priority in a busy ER. They gave me something to put on it to stop the bleeding, but I waited about four hours before being stitched up. This big Frankenstein looking guy in scrubs came over and led me to a curtain. I was so busy thinking about how clumsy he looked and how I didn't want some clumsy guy stitching me up, that I didn't notice Linda in the room. She had her back to me, but then the guy left me there, and she turned around, and bam. That was it."

"No way. 'That was it'? What does that mean? Hot doctor turns around with a needle in her hand, ready to stitch you up after you've spent hours waiting, after what was probably significant blood loss, and what? You instantly fall in love?"

Mark leaned forward, all intense. "No, see, that's it. I know I didn't fall in love right there, but everything else in the world fell away. For about ten seconds, it was me and her and nothing else. No whiny date, no crazy ER. We both just stared at each other. Like we'd met before. An instant connection. It sizzled."

"You sure that wasn't flesh burning in another part of the hospital?"

"Fine, you can laugh all you want. Point is, I had a feeling and I went with it. I waited a week, then I sent flowers and asked her out."

"And now you're getting married."

"Yep. Can you believe it?"

I didn't, but the main reason was sitting across the table from both of us. I shot a pointed look at Dad and then stared Mark down. "Maybe I didn't think it was in our genes to find true love."

Dad perked up enough to offer his opinion, complete with slurs. "Whadda mean? True love is grand. Trick is to never let it go once you find it." He wobbled to his feet. "I gotta pee. Be right back."

Mark and I watched him pinball down the hallway. Once he was out of sight, I grilled Mark. "How well do you know this woman? You're really going to move back just because she got a job here? What about your life, your friends back east?"

"Uh, I haven't run any background checks on her, but I'm pretty sure they wouldn't let her be a doctor if she was a crook. Yes, we're moving back here. In case you forgot, I have ties to Dallas too. Duh. And there's a big airport here with lots of flights. My friends can visit me and I can visit them, but Linda's my first priority. That's what being a grown-up is all about."

I did my best to ignore the dig, but I couldn't deny that my questions for him were a lot like questions I had about my own life but didn't want to face. Questions I wanted to ask Jess but wouldn't dare. How well did she know Heather Deveaux? She let her move into her house and ignored her friends for the sake of a woman. And how about those background checks? A quick check might have turned up reasons not to date the hot doctor. Why hadn't Jess told me about her budding relationship? Why did I care so much? Why was I having such a hard time stopping?

"What's the matter? Don't you think you'll get married someday?"

I was saved from answering, when Dad chimed in, "Yeah, Luca, what about that nice cop that hung out at the hospital when you were all shot up?"

Okay, so I was only delayed from answering. Thanks, Dad. "That nice cop isn't as nice as she seems. And she's just a friend."

A friend I used to get naked with on a regular basis. Now we just do middle of the night missions together and I go home alone while she curls up with her lawbreaker lover.

Mark wasn't going to let me off the hook so easily. "I have no idea who you're talking about, but if not the nice cop, then maybe someone else? Seriously, Luca, you've never even considered settling down?"

I hadn't, not in the way he meant. I owned a car outright, I worked for myself, I'd lived in the same apartment for years. To me, that was settling down. Mark and Dad believed you weren't truly settled down until you were coupled up—a notion I wasn't buying. Besides, what woman was going to change to fit my lifestyle? And I for sure wasn't changing for anyone. My fling with Ronnie Moreno this past summer had been a study in how certain lives don't mix. Fancy house, fancy car, big aspirations. I'd known from the start it wouldn't work out, yet I'd let myself get a little too close. No good came of it, and I wasn't going back there. A fling maybe, but settling down? No way I'd ever even consider it. Not unless I could find someone like me.

Jess flashed in my mind. Now she was dating the woman with the fancy car, fancy clothes. Just like Ronnie, turned out her lover wasn't all she appeared to be. Jess and I were more alike than anyone realized, even us. I had a sudden craving for the easy relationship we had before Heather Deveaux entered the picture, and I realized that being with Jess was the only time I ever felt fully settled. But that wasn't the same thing as being settled down. Was it?

CHAPTER FOURTEEN

I woke up in my childhood bedroom, half in and half out of the twin bed with the flowered comforter my mother had insisted on and we'd been too broke to replace after she walked out on us for a better life. I'd been too drunk last night to either drive or care about the flowers.

My mouth was coated with cigar smoke and a layer of beer. Ugh. I rolled out of the bed and wandered into the guest bathroom. Toothpaste and a toothbrush of unknown age and origin were in the medicine cabinet. I brushed holes in my teeth trying to get rid of the rank taste of the night before.

Back in the bedroom, I checked my phone. It was seven a.m. and the house was dead quiet. Perfect time to make my getaway. I'd slept in my clothes, so I was ready to get out. I grabbed my boots and carried them to the front door. I had my hand on the doorknob when my plan was thwarted.

"Leaving without saying good-bye?"

Mark was dressed for a jog. Not the way I dressed for my morning run. He wore matching sweats and running shoes that probably cost more than my monthly rent. I lifted my boots. "I'd go running with you, but I didn't dress for it."

He strode over to the door. "I'll walk you to your car." He didn't say a word as we walked to the Bronco, but his expression told me he had something super serious on his mind. He climbed into the passenger side and I braced myself for a heart-to-heart.

"Spill it."

"Breathe, Luca. I just wanted to talk to you without the rest of the crazy family around."

"So talk."

"You really okay? I mean you live alone. Your work's kind of dangerous. That guy at the bar the other night seemed pretty intense."

I stared at my little brother and tamped down my first response which was something along the lines of where do you get off trying to act all protective, Mr. Computer Nerd? But it wasn't like him to meddle in my business, so I tempered my reaction. "Dad put you up to this?"

"No, hell, no. I mean, he and I did talk about you a little before you got here last night, but I'm genuinely concerned. You are my best man after all. You need to stay in one piece at least until the wedding." His smile was cautious, tentative.

"I've managed to stay in one piece this long. I think I can manage."

"How many times have you been shot now?"

"Not as many as I could've been."

"That's comforting."

"Why the sudden interest in my health?" It wasn't a toss-off question. I really wanted to know why he suddenly cared so much about the sister he only talked to a couple of times a year.

He shifted in his seat. "I guess I just miss my family. Linda's got a huge family. They'll all be at the wedding, and I suppose I'd like the few relatives I have to stay intact long enough to be present for the big day."

"And after, I can go out and get myself shot up again?" I smiled so he would realize I was teasing and we both laughed.

"Yeah, that's about right. But you'll have to wait until you turn the tux in. I'm not buying a tux with bullet holes in it just because you couldn't go for a day without getting into trouble."

I punched him on the arm. "Go for your run and don't worry about me. I'll show up for your big day and I may even leave my gun in the car."

"Don't you mean guns?"

"Whatever."

He opened the door, but leaned over and gave me an awkward hug before exiting. "I'm leaving this afternoon, but I'll call you with details about the wedding."

"Do I need to throw you a silly bachelor party?"

"No worries, I can take care of my own party. You just show up. That's all."

He wanted more than that. I could tell by the look in his eyes, but it wasn't a party he was after. He wanted his big sister. To stand by his side, to be proud of him. I would and I was. I'd tell him later when he wasn't being such a sap about it. For now, I only said, "No worries. I'll be there."

I drove by Jess's house again after I left Dad's. I planned to do a quick drive by, then head home to get some real sleep in a real bed. I circled through the neighborhood and didn't see a patrol car. Didn't surprise me since I doubted they'd put round-the-clock surveillance on her place based on my word alone. And there was the fact she was a cop and they probably expected she could take care of herself. Despite my drive-bys, I thought the same thing. Until I pulled up in front of her house and saw the front door standing open without a soul in sight.

I slammed the Bronco into park, jumped out, and ran to the door. Jess would never leave her door wide open. When I reached the entry, I pulled out my Colt and slowed down. Wouldn't do to go charging into who knows what. I eased into the foyer and glanced around. Nothing seemed out of place on the inside, but my heart was beating so loud I was sure you could hear it down the street. Something was wrong. Really wrong.

Maybe Jess wasn't here and Deveaux left the door open. Maybe the Russians took them both. Wait a minute. I backtracked and peered out the front door. The driveway was empty. No Beemer in sight. I walked toward the garage and looked through the glass. Jess's Mustang was inside. So either they both left in Deveaux's car or Deveaux left on her own. Or…

A million thoughts ran through my head, but they all came back to the front door and the fact it was open. Before I could process what was going on, a loud voice took over.

"Put the gun down. Slowly. Then turn around with your hands over your head."

I recognized the voice, but I couldn't place it. She spoke cop, but it wasn't Jess. Only one way to find out and live to tell about it. I set the Colt on the ground and turned around with my hands laced behind my head.

"Nice. Now, on your knees."

Damn. It was Officer Hotstuff, make that Pryor, the one that tried to arrest me while I was stalking Henry Marcher. What was she doing here if she was assigned to patrol South Dallas? I asked and surprisingly, she answered.

"Special duty. Funny you should ask, since you seem to get around a lot. Don't tell me you're looking for a jumper here."

"You're the funny one. This house belongs to a cop. A cop who appears to be missing. Any chance you could work on that case and stop pestering me?" I knew I should employ some diplomacy, but I didn't have it in me. Not for her. Not until I knew where Jess was and that she was safe. Next thing I knew, the rookie had me cuffed. Damn.

"Get up. I have work to do and you're going to sit in the back of my car until I get it done."

I stood and silently wished I'd taken a shower before I'd left Dad's. I could feel alcohol oozing from my pores and I knew I smelled. Book-in at the county jail on a Sunday morning wasn't going to be much fun, and this chick was going to enjoy every minute of it. I strongly considered making a break for it, but she looked like she was anxious to fire her gun and I wasn't a small target. I settled on diplomacy. "Look, if you'll just call John Ames, tell him who I am, he can explain why I'm here. Detective Chance is a friend."

"Sure. You go sneaking around all your friends' houses with guns drawn."

"Fine, don't call him. He's the one who ordered surveillance in the first place." I prayed I was right. "You can explain to him why you let something happen to his partner while you messed around with me."

The look of uncertainty on her face told me she wasn't sure whether to believe me, but she didn't completely think I was lying. I kept talking. "Think about it. She's gone and her front door's open. No sign of forced entry, so you know I didn't break in. But you also know she's in danger or you wouldn't have been assigned to watch her place. So, apparently, something happened to her on your watch and now that you know that, you're standing here with me while the bad guys get away."

She lowered her gun and I knew I had her. She walked over and picked up the Colt. "Come here."

I followed her to her squad car and watched her remove the bullets and then place my gun in her trunk. She undid the cuffs, and then motioned for me to sit in the car. "Stay put. I'm going to check things out."

She walked to the front of the house and mimicked my earlier stealth entry. I stayed put until she was out of sight. Then I pulled the Sig she would've found if she'd patted me down and stepped out of the car. I was pissed the department had sent a bumbling rookie to take care of Jess, and I'll be damned if I was going to sit around and wait for her to assess the situation. I made it two steps when I heard another voice behind me. "Luca, what the hell are you doing?" I recognized this one too.

I took a second to holster the Sig before I turned around. I didn't think Jess would shoot me, but we definitely weren't connecting lately, and I didn't want to take any chances. When I was finally facing her, I was both relieved and sad to see she looked as worn out as I did. My relief faded quickly into anger. "Where have you been? There's a cop inside your house looking for your dead body. Your front door's wide open and you were nowhere in sight."

"I went for a run. Heather must've left the door open." She looked at the ground. "The lock's tricky." She started to the door. "Who's inside?"

"Officer Pryor. You know, the one who thinks I'm a common criminal. She took my gun. You're going to have to get it back. And you need to get a different girlfriend if she can't learn to shut the door."

"She going to shoot me if I sneak up on her?"

"Who? Your girlfriend?"

"No, jerk, Pryor."

"Probably."

"Fine. I'll wait out here." She pushed off the car and paced. Something was wrong. Wasn't like her not to just charge in and take care of the situation. And the way she'd glossed over my mention of Deveaux. Not like her not to bite back. On her next pass, I grabbed her arm.

"What's up with you?"

She shook out of my grasp. "What's up with *you*?"

"Nothing, but I'm not the one acting weird. Where is your girlfriend, anyway? It's pretty early to be out and about on a Sunday morning."

"Right back at you."

"Seriously, Jess. What's going on?"

"She's not my girlfriend."

"Oh, we're back to that, are we?"

"She left."

"I get that. Where did she go?"

"I told her she couldn't stay here until she cleared things up with the Feds. She checked into the Ritz until she figures out if she's even staying in Dallas. I don't know what she's going to do." She sagged and I reached over to pull her toward me, but she jerked to attention and I heard footsteps behind us. I turned around to see Officer Busybody approach.

"Detective Chance? Are you okay? Is she bothering you?"

Before I could muster up a smart-ass remark, Jess pulled her aside and they held a whispered conference. When they broke apart, Pryor opened the trunk and pulled out my Colt. She handed it to me with a huge frown, then got in her car and drove off.

"What now?" I asked Jess.

"You go home. I go in my house." She stalked off toward the house and I followed. She hadn't even asked me why I'd come by and apparently didn't care, but I had a lot of questions, and I wasn't leaving until she answered some of them.

When she reached the door, she shook her head, but left it open and I followed her inside. I was prepared to have to wrestle information out of her, but I wasn't ready for what happened next. As soon as I stepped over the threshold, she reached back and slammed the door shut behind me and pressed me against it. Her lips were on mine before I could register what was going on, and my reflexes gave in before I could process. I didn't need to—this was natural. While we exchanged hungry kisses, I reached my hands under her shirt and slid them up to her breasts, pinching, rubbing, pulling her closer. She pushed off me for a second and ripped her shirt over her head, then fell back against me like she'd been sucked by a vacuum.

My head swam and I had one of those out of body moments, where I was watching the action. And the action was good. Jess was all over me, one hand on my crotch, one hand up my shirt, her lips switching between my lips and my neck, powerful, insatiable. I wanted this, her wanting me like this, but it felt too much like the hasty fuck outside of the strip club. Quick, unfulfilling, regrettable.

I wanted more. As she started to slide her hand into my jeans, and I pulled out of her kiss long enough to gasp, "I'm filthy. Let's shower. Then let's do it in the shower. Then in bed. Let's do it all day."

I may as well have thrown a bucket of cold water at her. Pow. Spell broken. The glaze in her eyes fell away and she stepped back. "Sorry, I don't know what got into me."

I stayed in place, but reached out. "Don't be sorry. This is good, but it can be better. Don't you think?"

Her face was a mask. I couldn't tell what she thought, but I could tell the moment was gone. We weren't having sex, casual or otherwise. Not today.

"Look, I'm tired. Maybe you should go."

I stared at her, trying to figure out what had changed. Despite her attempt at defiance, I saw hurt in her eyes. I hadn't put it there, but I wanted to erase it. She'd been fine with the idea of a hasty lay, but the moment I'd suggested something more, the stakes were too high. A good friend would've given her what she needed, but I feared a quick fuck would leave us both empty, and the realization was my very own bucket of cold water.

I'd never questioned what we had. Whether it was enough, whether it had any meaning beyond friends fulfilling a mutual need.

Until now. In this moment, I recognized Jess wanted to fuck away her hurt. I'd always known that on some level, but for the first time, I realized I wanted to be more than a placeholder for something or someone better. For a lover.

I wasn't mad, I didn't feel used, but I did feel done. It was time to go. Jess would have to mourn Deveaux some other way, and I would find a different way to give her what she needed. I closed the distance between us and did my best to ignore her slight flinch as I leaned in. "I'll leave now, but I'm not gone." I kissed her on the cheek and left her standing in the doorway.

❖

As I pulled away from Chance's place, I left an urgent message with dispatch for John. I may not be able to give her what she needed, but I could make sure she was safe.

My apartment was exactly the same as I left it. Lonely. A definitive bachelor pad with heaps of dirty laundry and empty to-go containers. I would not be getting any awards for housekeeper of the year, and I had no desire to do anything about that today. As I walked to the bedroom, I started pulling off clothes. I tossed them into one of the several piles on the floor and then climbed into the shower. Not gonna lie, I was still aroused after my close encounter with Jess, and I considered taking care of myself under the hot stream of water, but the idea of utilitarian sex didn't have the same appeal it used to. What the hell was wrong with me?

I ran out all the hot water before I stepped out and toweled off. A loud knock on the door caught me before I could find something clean to wear. Not entirely sure I even had any clean clothes, I wrapped the towel around my waist and went to the door. I barked, "Who is it?"

"It's Collier. We need to talk."

"Go away. I'll call you later."

"What's the matter, Bennett? You have an early morning date? Or did she just not leave from last night?"

That did it. I was pissed now. How dare she show up whenever the hell she wanted and turn my life upside down? I swung the door wide and watched while she sucked in her breath. "What's the matter, *Marshal* Collier? Never seen a half-naked woman before? Oh, wait, you used to make a living out of being half-naked, and this"—I pointed at my chest—"well, you've seen this several times now. Still not used to it?"

She stepped in and shut the door behind her. "Someone has a chip on her naked shoulder. Want me to kiss it and make you feel better?"

She said it like a dare and I took her up on it. I dropped the towel and pulled her toward me, taking the kiss she'd offered before she could react. She resisted for a second and then melted into me. I drew power from her submission and I pressed harder with my body, my hands, my lips. As if I could force fuck the rest of my day into oblivion.

When I finally came up for a breath, she spoke one word. "Bed?"

One word shouldn't have been enough to shake me out of my trance, but it did. Hard. I stepped back and then, suddenly embarrassed, I reached over and picked up the towel. She placed a hand on my arm before I could wrap it around myself.

"Something I said?"

I shrugged her off and hid in the towel. Not entirely sure what was wrong with me today. Two hot women wanted to fuck me, and here I was, holding out for more. Silly, really, considering I'd never cared about more before. Never even believed in it. Not sure I believed in it now. All I had to do was drop the towel and I could spend the next few hours engaged in my favorite means of forgetting. After the morning I'd had, I deserved it.

I stared into Diamond's eyes and realized that even if I wanted what she had to offer, she wasn't the one I wanted it from. "Nope, nothing you said. I just changed my mind. Got a lot to do today."

Her piercing look told me she didn't buy my rambling lie, but I didn't care. I wanted her to leave and then I'd figure out why I'd suddenly lost my way, turning down sure sex while I examined my feelings. Who was I?

I was the person who was escorting Diamond Collier to the door. The person determined to keep our relationship all business. I held the towel with one hand and turned the doorknob with the other. "I'll call you when I find Amato and Picone."

She paused as she crossed the threshold. "Oh, about that. That was the reason I came over. That matter's been taken care of. Thanks for your help, but we've got it under control." She blew me a kiss and disappeared down the walk.

Chapter Fifteen

I should've gone back to bed. Chance didn't want my help. Diamond no longer needed my help—a fact that festered although I couldn't quite put my finger on why. I'd wanted her to leave, but I hadn't realized when I turned down her advances that that was the last time she'd be offering. Diamond had found her guys. She didn't need me anymore. Well, I didn't need her either, but I liked the idea of having a fallback, especially now that Jess was no longer interested in playing that role.

That wasn't right either. Jess seemed perfectly content to keep our fuck-buddy status, but something had changed. Her need had an edge to it. Different from the raw cravings we'd always shared. Maybe her relationship with Deveaux ramped up the dangerous, forbidden factor of sex with me. If her relationship was really over, if Deveaux had really left, would things change between us? Did I want them to?

I didn't know and didn't want to think about it. I did know that the last thing I felt like doing was driving around Otis Shaw's baby mama's neighborhood, hoping to catch him out and about. Besides, after spending the night on an ancient twin mattress, I didn't think my hungover self could handle a takedown.

Instead, I spent the day doing things I don't normally do. I made my bed, did laundry, then took another shower to try to get the smell of alcohol out of my system. I ended my housckeeping in the kitchen where I tossed the remains of some unidentifiable meal from the inside of the fridge and actually wiped a couple of surfaces down.

When I finally shut the refrigerator door on my half-ass cleaning job, I realized I couldn't clean away whatever was eating at me. The schedule on the refrigerator door told me where I needed to be.

I traded my boots for my running shoes, grabbed my guns, and headed out the door. For once, I would be early. Cold day for a softball game, but it was the second to last game of the season and, knowing Texas weather, the last game would be played under a hot sun. I would have much rather been running, but I wasn't here to play. Not softball, anyway.

As I pulled into the parking lot, I scanned the cars, but Jess's old Mustang was nowhere in sight. I forced myself to look for silver BMWs and sighed with relief when I didn't see a one. Maybe Jess was late. She'd had a lot going on today. I decided to wait in the car, with the heater on. I'd sit here until I saw her, made sure she was okay, and then naptime for me. I parked the Bronco in the center of the lot and started surveillance.

About five minutes later, the lot started to fill up, and uniformed dykes of all shapes and sizes started filing onto the fields. I glanced at the clock. Game time was only a few minutes away. I must have missed her. No way coach would show up this late to her favorite sport. I cut the engine and crawled out. Freaking cold, especially after snuggling in the warm cocoon of the car. I glanced around, but still no sign of Jess's car or Jess. I could trudge over to the field and see if she'd managed to get by me, or I could drive away and let her take care of herself.

I got back in the car and leaned toward the latter. Didn't look like any crazy Russians mobsters were lurking. Besides, my being here was probably more about me than concern over Jess's safety. This morning, I'd gotten all worked up and she was just out for a run. She didn't need me lurking around, trying to save her. She'd be just fine without me. I looked at my cell and made a vow. Once John called me back, I'd fill him in on the new developments about Deveaux and make sure he had a decent watch on Jess, and then I'd back off. Leave Jess to manage her own fallout.

A sharp knock on my window caused me to toss the phone to the floor. I grabbed the Colt out of her holster and turned to the glass, barrel first.

Nancy held up both hands and assumed a mock "please don't shoot me face." I holstered my gun and lowered the window. "You scared the shit out of me."

"Sorry, pal. Thank goodness you're here. We're down one player and we'll have to forfeit if you don't get your ass on the field like five minutes ago."

"Hold on. I'm not playing."

"Then what are you doing here?" She reached for the door handle and yanked it open.

"Who's not here?" I had a sudden sick feeling in my gut.

"Chance. Didn't show. Didn't even call."

"Not like her not to get a sub."

"What are you talking about? You're the sub."

"I'm—" I started to say more, but shut up. It was totally out of character for Jess not to show up or at least find a replacement. Either she was love-struck or something had happened to her. She'd been out of sorts this morning. The logical conclusion was she was mourning on her own, but I didn't feel like being logical. But I also didn't feel like raising the alarm without something to back it up. I'd go by her house, check on her, or I'd call John one more time and nag him into doing it. "Nance, I'm sorry, but I can't stay. I gotta take care of something really important."

"Luca, we'll have to forfeit. Chance will have your hide."

My cell phone, still on the floor, rang loud. I offered a grimace to Nancy. "Sorry, I have to take this." She gave me the evil eye and stalked off. I scooped the phone off the floorboard, and started to hit ignore. I wanted to drive away, not talk on the phone, but I checked the caller ID in the unlikely event it was Jess.

It wasn't.

"Hey, John, I've been waiting for your call. Sorry to bug you on a Sunday, but I went by Jess's place earlier and the cop the department assigned to watch her is a piece of work. Maybe you could swing by later and check on her. Her lady friend moved out and she's not herself right now."

"Where are you?"

The question had me shaking my head. What did it matter where I was? "At the softball field, but she's not here. That's my point." I was rambling and I knew it, but I couldn't seem to stop talking. John finally cut me off with a question designed to get my attention.

"Your friend, Bingo? He's in trouble. You might want to get over here."

And click, the line was dead. I roared the Bronco to life and spun out of the lot. I didn't have a clue what I'd find when I got to Bingo's place, but John's calm tone didn't fool me. I braced for big trouble.

❖

The place was crawling with cops. I circled the block a couple of times before I even found a place to park, and then I went in search of John on foot. Yellow tape and a burly guy in uniform tried to keep me from my mission.

"Step back. This is a crime scene."

I resisted shooting a look at the boldly marked, brightly colored tape and asking him if I looked like I couldn't read. Instead, I said, "I'm looking for Detective Ames."

"He's busy."

Master of the obvious. "I'm sure he is, but he asked me to come by. Said he had some questions for me about B—" I stopped myself and searched my memory for Bingo's given name. "Uh, Mr. Hubbard. I'm sure he'll appreciate it if you tell him I'm here." There, I'd managed to wedge one true statement in my little spiel. He had called me and suggested I come over. Wish he'd been a little longer on detail. Might've helped me bluff better.

Apparently, whatever I'd said was enough to send Officer Gatekeeper in search of John. I paced outside the tape for what seemed like forever. When he finally showed up, he looked haggard, stressed.

"John, what the hell's going on?"

He motioned for me to follow him, and we walked a healthy distance away from the swarm of cops. Despite the fact we were out of range of listening ears, he whispered. "I shouldn't even be talking to you about this."

I matched his whisper by keeping my own voice low. "I wish I knew what 'this' was."

"When's the last time you were here?"

As much as I trusted him, I spent a minute assessing his reason for wanting to know before I answered. Did whatever was going on have to do with Bingo's gaming? Or the prescription bottles I'd found tucked away in his guest bath? A quick look around told me whatever "this" was, it was way more serious than gambling and drugs. The crime scene techs were out in full force, and the medical examiner doesn't make an appearance unless there's a body to haul off. I made a snap judgment to tell John whatever he wanted to know.

"Friday night. Actually, more like Saturday morning." I didn't add "with Jess," but I suddenly realized if John was here, she should be too. Maybe that's why she wasn't at the softball game. "Is Jess inside?"

His face scrunched like I'd asked him something hard to cipher. I pushed harder. "She's not at her regular softball game. Have you called her?"

"Yeah, but I had to leave a message."

"Not like her not to answer her phone. And that doesn't bother you?"

He pointed at Bingo's house. "Only thing bothering me right now is what's inside there." He took a deep breath. "You still have a picture of those two guys you were looking for?"

Amato and Picone. I pulled out my wallet and thumbed through the contents for the photos. I moved slowly, trying to process why I was standing outside Bingo's house with a fleet of cops and crime scene techs, why John was asking about these guys, the ones Diamond said had been taken care of. When I found the photos, I handed them in John's direction, face down, but kept a tight hold on a corner. When he realized I wasn't letting go, he sighed. "Trust me, Luca. Just let me see them."

He was tired, worried, and harmless. I had to trust him if I wanted any more information. I flipped the photos over and released them into his grasp. He studied them for a minute and then handed them back to me.

"That's it?"

"You can stop looking for them."

That wasn't news, but his expression was different from what Diamond's had been. Hers conveyed her job was over, but John looked like he had even more work ahead. There was something he was leaving out. I felt dense, like everyone around me got the punch line to a joke, while I was left sorting out the lines. "You told me to trust you. Spill."

He pointed at the photos I held in my hand. "Those guys are lying on Bingo's living room floor. Dead."

I didn't give a shit about the guys, but my thoughts raced ahead. "Where's Bingo?"

"Being questioned."

"Why aren't you the one questioning him? Isn't this your case?"

"I wasn't the first on the scene. I'm just an assist."

Maybe his secondary role explained why he wasn't as concerned that Jess hadn't responded to his call, but a whole lot of other questions were still unanswered. Why had he called me here? He could have ID'd Amato and Picone without me. "What can you tell me?"

"Not much. Bingo called this in. Said he came home, found these guys, already dead."

"Dead how?"

"Shot in the back of the head. Execution style."

"And you don't believe him because?"

"For starters, they're in his house. Follow that up with they've been messing with his business." Jess must've told him about that. Before I could ask, he counted off on his fingers. "Opportunity, motive."

Means. "You found the gun?"

"Not yet."

I didn't even try to stop the rising tide of anger and my voice showed it. "Let me get this straight. You think Bingo's smart enough to hide the weapon, but dumb enough to leave the dead guys in his own damn living room?"

"Lower your voice." John glanced around. "I don't know what the hell to think. I'm just telling you the facts. Bingo says he's been out running errands all morning. He's got receipts, and a neighbor can vouch for the fact he got back to the house just minutes before he called 911. ME's going to give us an approximate time of death, but until then we can't really pin down Bingo's alibi. For all we know, those bodies could've been there since last night."

My mind started spinning. Toupee wearing, Elvis loving Bingo would go to great lengths to protect his business, but shooting two guys in cold blood? I'd never believe it. Besides, how would he have even managed the feat? Two Italian hoods, enforcers, come to his house and he somehow disarms them, gets them to lie on the floor, and then shoots them both dead? Unbelievable. I couldn't wrap my mind around it, but as I tried, another answer, much more plausible, popped into my head.

"Petrov."

"What?" John looked at me like I had Tourette's.

I didn't disappoint as I spewed a string of words that made perfect sense to me, but made me sound like a crazy person. "Petrov. The Imperial. Threats. Fake meds."

He shook me like he could make all the words fall into intelligible sentences. It worked. I took a deep breath and then let loose with complete thoughts. "What if Petrov arranged this kill? Makes perfect sense. He's been trying to get into Bingo's business. Even gave him one of those fancy gold coins like he gave me. I think all this has something to do with the fake prescription meds the Feds are interested in. There are tons of them in there."

"Slow down. What are you talking about?"

"Chance and I were here the other night. Bingo told us that Yuri's guys had been to visit. Told him to clear the Italians out and let them have the run of the place. Yuri even gave him one of those coins, like he gave me. I'm sure Bingo can show it to you."

"Yeah, okay, I can ask him about that, but all that could mean is that he was highly motivated to get rid of the Italians."

"Give me a break. Have you met Bingo? No way he overpowered and shot those guys."

"Maybe not. And what did you say about prescription drugs? When I talked to Jess she didn't mention anything about it."

Uh oh. Time to confess I hadn't told her. I hadn't told anyone. The bottle was still in the glove compartment of the Bronco. "Hang on." I retrieved the bottle and handed it to him. He rolled it in his palm, reading the label.

"Looks a lot like the one you gave us before."

"Sure does. Did you get any leads from Candy the other night?" So much for my resolution to stay uninvolved, leave the ruckus about prescription fraud to the Feds and the cops. But now Bingo was swept up in it, and I cared what happened to him. It would be too easy for the cops to decide he was responsible for the dead guys in his living room, close the case with an easy arrest.

"She wasn't exactly cooperative. Told us she didn't know what we were talking about. To talk to her lawyer, who just happens to be some chump on Petrov's payroll."

"Of course. But what about all the bottles in Bingo's place? Vedda was probably dealing here and Petrov wanted a piece of it. Bingo's place is perfect. Think about all the rich college kids who are in and out. He already has a ready and willing client base."

"Except there's one problem with your little theory."

"What's that?"

"Crime scene's been all over the place. Only one prescription bottle in the place and it's from a legit pharmacy. Viagra, in Morris Hubbard's name."

I pointed at the bottle in his hand. "I'm telling you, his guest bathroom cabinet was full of bottles, just like that one."

"And Chance saw them too?"

Shit. "She was a little preoccupied."

"I'll take that as a no."

"Since when is my word not good enough?"

"Settle down. I'm just being devil's advocate here. You've known Bingo most of your life, right?"

I got it. A prosecutor would tear my testimony apart. But this was more about getting the cops to follow up on a lead. We were a long way from a trial, and if we could sort this out, we'd never get there. My dormant private investigator juices were flowing. "Look, just promise me you'll ask Bingo about it. He hasn't lawyered up yet, right?" John shook his head. "Don't you guys usually take that as a sign he's got nothing to hide?" I didn't wait for the answer. "Ask him about the pills. And ask him about the gold coin. And promise me you'll let me know if you decide to arrest him." I barked out the instructions as I ran back to the Bronco.

"Yeah, I'll let you know. Where are you going?"

"I have an idea. I'll be in touch. Tell Bingo, I'll put him in touch with a lawyer."

I started the car with one hand, while I dialed a number on my cell phone with the other. I listened to the rings as I sped away from the crime scene, planning what I'd say when she picked up the line. Five, six, seven. Finally, the line connected and I started talking over the voice on the other end. "We need to meet, right now." I paused for a response, but all I got was the repeat of the automated message: "The number you've reached has been disconnected."

In a fit of anger, I tossed the phone to the floorboard. Damn you, Diamond Collier.

CHAPTER SIXTEEN

Diamond's last words to me echoed loud. "That matter's been taken care of. We have it under control."
I'm not a conspiracy theorist. I'm one of those people who think the simplest explanation is the most likely way things went down. But I couldn't ignore the coincidence. Amato and Picone show up dead in Bingo's house hours after I'm told "that matter's been taken care of."

If some crazy government plot was at work, I wasn't sure what I could do about it. I could show up at the marshal's office and demand answers, but that was likely to get me thrown out or even arrested. I didn't have a way to get in touch with Diamond other than the useless phone number she'd given me. Any other law enforcement agency was likely to think I was a kook for thinking the government might have been involved in a murder.

And maybe I was. Maybe what I told John about the Russians had been spot on. Petrov wanted to take over Bingo's gaming house. The fact he had one of his girls selling the same fake prescriptions out of his club that I'd seen stocked at Bingo's place convinced me that was part of the reason why. But leaving dead bodies in someone's living room seemed kind of extreme, even for these guys. Bingo didn't need that strong of a threat. Anyone who knew him, would know he would've caved easier than that. And now that he was a suspect in the murder, there wouldn't be any gaming at his place for the foreseeable future. If Petrov's guys had done this, they'd shot themselves in the foot.

Still, I couldn't shake Diamond's words. "That matter's been taken care of." Maybe it was something simple. Like maybe the Feds had started the turf war between Vedda and Petrov to draw them out and it got out of hand. Diamond had been at my place around eleven this morning. Suddenly, knowing what time these guys had been offed seemed very important to me. I'd pumped John for all the information I could right now. Besides, he probably didn't know the answer yet. But when the reports started coming in, I wanted to make sure I had access. This was personal, not just because Bingo was involved, but because I didn't want to think I may have been fucking a cold-blooded killer.

I swung by Jess's house. I rang the bell and snooped around, but no one answered, and her car wasn't in the garage. Would've been too easy. The one other place I could imagine she'd be was at work, but if she had been, she would've been with John at the crime scene.

Maybe she'd shown up at the softball game after all. I scrolled through the numbers in my phone until I found Nancy McGowan's. She put the number in herself one day when she was flirting. She picked up on the fifth ring, right when I was about to hang up. I charged through the usual hey how're you doing stuff and got right to the point.

"Did Chance show up at the game?"

"Hey, Luca, nice of you to check in."

"Nance, I'm in a hurry here. I need to talk to Chance."

"Of course you do." She dripped a lot of innuendo into the four words. Enough to get me to rise to the bait.

"What's that supposed to mean?"

"Nothing."

"Right." I couldn't explain why her sass pissed me off, especially since I usually shrugged it off, but today it bothered me. A lot. "You got something to say, just say it."

"She has a girlfriend, you know."

I heard the slur in her voice. She was probably enjoying a few beers after the game. If they'd won, a few shots as well. Nancy was a gossip, but for some reason, I'd never thought she'd gossiped about me. Or Jess. We'd been careful to keep our relationship under wraps, although lately there hadn't been much to hide. Guess we hadn't done as good a job as we'd thought. Or at least I hadn't.

I fought a strong desire to deny Nancy's unspoken accusation, defend my own honor, but what was the point? Besides, her implication was pretty damn close to the truth. Maybe it was Jess's honor I wanted to defend.

"I know she has a girlfriend. I know all about her. I need to talk to her about work. It's important. Do you know where she is?"

"No, Luca, I don't. But I'm at Sue Ellen's if you want to come by." She paused and I heard the distinct sound of a drink being gulped down. "And I don't have a girlfriend."

Have another shot, Nance. "Thanks, but I'm working." I hung up before she could say more she would regret later or more I didn't want to hear.

I drove in aimless loops around the city. Everything Jess had said to me that morning tumbled around in my mind. She'd been upset, even if she hadn't wanted to show it. She'd given Deveaux an ultimatum. While she was in limbo, she tried to fuck away the uncertainty with me. When I turned her down, would she have gone in search of someone else to help her forget?

No, Jess wasn't a quitter. She didn't walk away. She'd stood by me when I'd left the police force all those years ago, but she'd never understood my decision to bail when things got tough. She would never have done the same thing. Wasn't in her DNA to give up. She wouldn't write off Deveaux until she knew for sure the doctor wasn't going to get her shit straightened out.

I drove with purpose now. The Ritz Carlton was downtown. I sure wasn't dressed to wander around in a fancy hotel, but then again, I never was. If Jess wasn't there, maybe I could get the doctor to give me a clue about where she might be. I hated the fact that she might know more about Jess than I did, but I swallowed my feelings. Had to if I wanted to see this through.

Deveaux answered the door in a hotel robe, her hair still wet from the shower. This wasn't going to be pretty. I took a deep breath and pushed my way in the room. Figured she had her chance to keep me out when she looked through the peephole. Once she opened the door, all bets were off.

"Is she here?" I didn't even pretend to have a different reason for being here.

Deveaux heaved a dramatic sigh and sat on the bed. "Not right now, but she will be back."

"Don't worry. I'm not here to interrupt your lovefest. I have a work-related reason I need to talk to her."

"You have no idea what's going on here, do you?"

"I know enough."

"I'm leaving town."

"You really can't go fast enough."

"Is there a particular reason you don't like me? Or is it all jealousy?"

If I ignored her, would she go away? I tried for almost a whole minute, but she showed no signs of disappearing. "I've known Jess a long time. I have no need to be jealous."

"I'm sure you tell yourself that. And it probably works for you. Most of the time."

I shot a look at the door. When she'd said Jess was coming back, was she talking today? Because no way was I having this conversation with this woman. The robe didn't help. If Jess walked in right now, no telling what she'd think. "Do you want me to wait outside while you get dressed?"

"I'm not getting dressed."

Fine. She wanted to play poker? She had no idea who she was messing with. "Tell me why the Feds are so interested in you. You run away from Chicago to avoid a trip to the pokey?"

The only hint she was the slightest bit unsettled was in her eyes. I thought I detected a trace of fear, but she covered it quickly. "Is that really any of your business?"

I didn't hesitate. "Yes. Like I said, I've known Jess a long time. She's an honorable person, and she deserves someone who isn't going to smear her good name. Besides, it's not like I can't find out on my own. Wouldn't you rather tell me your version?"

"You should be a federal agent. You sound just like them."

"But I bet your lawyer told you not to fall for their tricks."

She nodded. "Actually, he told me not to talk to anyone. Including Jessica."

Ugh. I was willing to bet no one other than Jess's parents and elementary school teachers had ever called Chance Jessica. Did she like being called that? How could I not know the answer?

"Fine. You don't have to tell me anything. I'm sure I can figure it out on my own. You're fairly young, for a doctor. You like fast cars, fancy clothes." I waved my arm to indicate the room we were in. "Swank hotels. Probably a lot harder to manage all that when you've got mountains of med school bills hanging over your head. You decide to take some shortcuts. Do some procedures that aren't exactly necessary to collect from Medicare. It's pretty easy, not much oversight. You decide to do it some more. How am I doing so far?"

"If you think I'm going to confess my sins to you, you are sorely mistaken."

"'Confess your sins'? Isn't that a bit dramatic?"

"Maybe. But maybe everything isn't black and white. Is everything so cut-and-dry in your world, Luca Bennett?"

"I didn't come here to talk about me."

"I'm sure you didn't. At least not to me. You came here for Jessica. Isn't that right?"

"It's not like that."

"If you really believe that, then you don't deserve her."

She was like a dog with a bone, but I wasn't biting. "You said she'd be back?"

"Any minute. She had to make a couple of calls. Private."

Doubtless she'd had messages from John and who knows who else about the murder at Bingo's place. She might have even headed straight over there. There was no reason for me to stay here. I could catch up with her later. Curiosity about Deveaux wasn't worth the third degree. I walked to the door. "Tell her I'll call her later."

"Oh, I'll tell her, but don't be surprised if she doesn't call you back right away. She and I have a lot to discuss."

I hated her. Everything about her. She made me feel dirty and I wanted to put distance between us. I wanted to put distance between her and Jess, but Jess saw something in her. Maybe it was caring. Deveaux cared about Jess. The lady may have shady ethics, but she gave Jess something she wanted. Couldn't fault her for that, but I didn't have to stick around to see it play out. I left.

At the elevator, I did that thing people hate and punched the button repeatedly as if it would make the car come faster. Didn't work, but when the doors finally slid open, I came face-to-face with Jess. Guess my button pushing had done something.

She stepped out of the car, but I didn't get in. She frowned and shook her head. "What are you doing here?"

"What are you doing here?" I'm excellent at playing a five-year-old.

She glanced down the hall toward Deveaux's room. "Something tells me you already know."

"I know you're here with her. I know you're not working. I know you didn't keep your promise."

"What the hell are you talking about? What promise?"

"Don't tell me your phone hasn't been ringing off the hook. Two of Vedda's guys executed in Bingo's living room and you don't know a thing about it?"

She nodded. "Yeah, John just called. I'm going to meet him at the station."

"Little like shutting the barn door after the horse has been stolen."

"If you have something to say, say it. Quit with the innuendo."

"You said you would watch out for him. You promised him. You promised me. Then bang, less than forty-eight hours later, two mobsters wind up dead in his living room and he's on the hook for their murders."

"And you think he didn't do it?"

"And you think he did?"

"I don't know what to think, but I promise I'll keep an open mind. Just so you know, we're not lead on this case, so we won't be making the calls."

"John already told me. Bingo needs a lawyer."

"You're right about that."

"Speaking of lawyers, what's your doctor friend doing on that front?"

"Did you talk to her?"

"Not much. She's not big on sharing. Jess, what's going on with you two? She's trouble. You should keep your distance."

"I've never run from trouble."

She hadn't, thank God. If she had, we wouldn't have stayed friends after I left the force and we never would have made it all these years later. Trouble was I couldn't define what we were and suddenly I wanted to. The woman behind the door was Jess's girlfriend. Was I a friend or just a fuck buddy? Did it matter?

Only if I wanted something more. No reason to name what we were except to measure it against what we weren't. I'd let Deveaux get inside my head. What I had with Chance was good. No reason to fuck it up by thinking about what it could be, wouldn't be. Her quiet voice interrupted my thoughts.

"I should go. Luca, trust me. I got this."

I glanced at Deveaux's door to signal I knew where she was headed. Jess might be in love, or something she'd mistaken for it, but she wasn't going to jeopardize her career over a woman. Not a woman like Deveaux, anyway. I needed to let her handle the situation her own way. Trust she'd do the right thing. I nodded. "Okay. But promise me you'll keep me updated on what's going on at Bingo's?"

"I will." She walked a step away from me, then turned back and fixed me with a stare. Her gaze burned my defenses.

"What?"

"Nothing, it's just…" She looked at the floor and apparently found the design in the carpet to be captivating. Now she was scaring me. What could be so hard to say?

"Spit it out."

She looked up and stared again. I couldn't get a read on her sudden loss of speech, but I prodded her by raising my eyebrows.

"Just promise me you won't do anything crazy."

Her voice was soft, her request almost a caress. Sometimes I hated how well she knew me. When I wasn't liking it.

"Crazy? Sure, I promise—nothing crazy."

I could think of a bunch of other ways to define all the things I was about to do. I didn't need to add crazy to the list.

I tried to call Diamond twice more on the walk to where I'd parked the Bronco. Same message, disconnected. I even went as far as looking up the number for the U.S. Marshal's Service. I knew their offices were in the federal building just a few blocks away, but it would be locked up tight on a Sunday. The guy that answered the phone said he didn't have a Diamond Collier on his list, which could mean a host of things. Diamond Collier wasn't her real name. She worked for an office in a different district. Or she wasn't really a U.S. Marshal.

I knew she was a federal agent of some kind, so I wasn't going to jump to any big conclusions, like she'd gone rogue. Besides, what private interest could she serve by starting a turf war? More likely the reason she wasn't on the list was the name thing or she was working out of a different office. Still, I couldn't put off a lingering suspicion. Why was she suddenly unavailable, her phone disconnected? Wasn't like she was working undercover and had to burn her identity. But her comment about how the matter had been taken care of festered like a splinter working its way to the surface.

This whole deal got under my skin. Even if Bingo hadn't been involved, I'd want to solve the puzzle. Jess's warning had been warranted. My MO was to charge in, shake things up, and see what I could make of the mess, but whoever had set up Bingo was a pro, and my usual methods were likely to get someone killed. Probably me.

It had been a long day. Charging in could wait.

When I got to my apartment, I shucked off my boots and jeans and set up shop on the couch with a beer and my laptop. The signal from my neighbor's Wi-Fi was weak, but not weak enough for me to want to pay for my own service. I held the computer at the best angle for reception and began my research.

A Google search for fake prescription meds yielded dozens of results. According to Dan Rather, counterfeit prescription drugs were a huge problem, flooding the market with dangerous substitutes for the real thing and allowing addicts to dope up under the guise of medicine. Dan the man relayed a big story about a Chinese national caught selling all kinds of fake meds to a bunch of Feds in ICE and Homeland Security.

Chinese, Italians, and Russians. Great. Bingo had stumbled into the United Nations of crime.

I spent the next hour reading articles and watching video about the scourge of counterfeit meds, until I ran out of beer and the signal started to wane. It wasn't late, but I lacked energy to do anything that required putting my pants back on. Sitting around in my underwear made me think of Jess. Bet she was still working, or maybe she was on her way back to the Ritz where she'd put on one of those fancy robes and join Dr. Deveaux for a drink on the balcony. My hand strayed to my crotch, but I wasn't in the mood for me.

I wondered if Mark had left town yet. I dialed Dad's house and he picked up on the first ring and let me know Mark had flown out a couple of hours earlier.

"He said to tell you he'd be in touch about the wedding. He left one of the fancy invites for you over here."

"When's he moving out here for good?"

"A couple of weeks before the big day." He paused and I heard a gulp followed by the unmistakable sound of a can being crushed. Maggie must be working late at the bar and Dad was enjoying a night alone. "You get things straightened out with Bingo? Maybe we can catch a game."

I took a deep breath and braced for his reaction. "Dad, Bingo's place is closed for a while."

"What did you do to piss him off now?"

If only it were that simple. "Nothing. He's gotten himself in some trouble. Until it gets sorted out, I don't think he's going to be back open for business."

"Those shady guys that've been coming around. I bet they're to blame."

I had a feeling the shady guys he was referring to were dead now. Maybe at the hand of a new set of shady guys. "What do you know about them?"

"Not much. A new crowd's been hanging around his place lately. Lots of flash and show. Not Bingo's usual customers. Seemed like they had the run of the place. Wondered when Bingo was going to get around to throwing them out, but I guess they got him in trouble before he had a chance."

"Looks like." I didn't see any need to tell him the worst of it. "I've had a long day, so I'm going to turn in. I'll come by next week and we can find some trouble to get into."

I hung up, shut down the laptop, and crawled into bed. Tomorrow, I'd make a few calls, see that Bingo was hooked up with a good lawyer, and then I'd find Otis Shaw, collect a big payout, and take the next week off. Jess could investigate crime, explore whatever she had going on with Dr. Deveaux. Me? I'd sleep, drink, and gamble. Life had gotten too complicated. It was time to simplify.

CHAPTER SEVENTEEN

I crawled out of bed Monday morning after a fitful night of sleep. I'd had some version of the wedding dream, but this time Bingo was there, on stage with the band, crooning Italian ballads like a sorry Frank Sinatra cover. He looked old, tired, and his toupee was barely hanging on for the show. At the break, he passed a hat, asking for help with his legal fees.

I resolved to get the attorney issue out of the way as soon as possible. I'm not fond of criminal defense lawyers. I know they serve their purpose, but in my opinion, they are not much better than the folks they represent. Ronnie Moreno had proved my theory. I called Hardin and got a couple of names.

After a run and a shower, I felt and looked slightly human. I made a withdrawal from my coffee can so I could gas up the Bronco and I hit the streets.

This morning, the crime scene tape was confined to Bingo's door instead of a three house radius. I knocked without a lot of confidence. John had promised to let me know if they arrested Bingo, but even if they hadn't, I seriously doubted he would spend the night here. I pulled my notebook and a pen from my back pocket and started to write a note. Wasn't sure how much I wanted to say on something that would be sticking out his door. Luckily, I was saved from thinking too hard by the guy I was trying to rescue.

"Luca, what are you doing here?"

He looked like hell, worse than he had in my dream, mostly because he'd completely abandoned the toupee and his head was a misshapen gourd. I considered whether I had a baseball cap in the car I could loan him and how I could offer it without hurting his feelings.

"I stopped by to check on you." I thrust my note at him. "Hardin suggested these attorneys. Call one. Don't try to handle this by yourself."

"You think they're going to arrest me?"

"I don't have a clue, but it makes sense they'd settle on the easiest explanation."

"I didn't kill those guys."

"I know." And I did. No way this beaten down guy could have committed cold-blooded murder. He didn't have it in him, either physically or mentally. "I think you were set up."

"Why would someone do that?"

Good question. I hadn't given it any more thought since my thoughts dead-ended the day before. "I don't know, but I'm sure if you tell your attorney everything you told Detective Chance and me, they'll develop some leads. Did you give the gold coin to the cops?"

He sighed. "I don't have it anymore. I hocked it."

"Damn. Did you at least tell them about the prescription drugs Amato and Picone were selling from your place?" I laughed at his look of surprise. "Seriously, the drugs were right there in your guest bathroom. Not exactly a secret operation."

He at least had the decency to look embarrassed. "Vedda's guys cleared those out the day after you were here with your friend. Said they needed them at another location. I'm sorry I didn't tell you about the drugs. I was scared. And now, why bother telling the cops a bunch of stuff I can't prove? Does it even matter?"

Maybe not. I still had my gold coin. I could give it to John and hope it helped back up Bingo's story, but I doubted anyone would care. Without anything definitive to tie Petrov to the action at Bingo's place, no one was going to go poking in that hornet's nest. Maybe the ME's report would clear Bingo. If those guys had been killed during the time he could prove he wasn't home, it would go a long way to showing he wasn't involved. I tamped down the running string of questions in my head and said, "I'm sure it'll all get sorted out." I pointed at the paper in his hand. "Call one of those attorneys. Tell them everything and watch your back. If someone would go this far to set you up, they won't mind going a step further."

He nodded gravely, signaling my blunt assessment had hit home. "I'm just here to meet the clean-up crew. I'm staying with my sister for a few days until this is all straightened out."

I'd never pictured Bingo with a family of his own. After all this, I wasn't sure I'd ever look at him the same way again. His house had been a safe place, my haven for exercising my second favorite vice. Would he ever reopen, or did the legacy end here? I didn't want to think about it. We exchanged cell phone numbers and I drove off.

Otis Shaw's favorite check cashing store was five minutes away from opening when I pulled up. I parked a few doors down and set up watch.

I didn't have to wait long. At eight thirty sharp, a huge guy, who made Henry Marcher, my jumper from earlier in the week, seem like a midget, crawled out of a Cadillac Seville, circa 1980, and walked in the store. I wrote down the plate number and considered my options. I'd definitely need to show firepower to take this guy in. He was way over my weight class. I wondered if he was armed. I already knew he wasn't shy about firing a gun. Last thing we needed was a shoot-out in front of a store full of cash. No doubt the employees had guns under the counters and they'd probably join in the fight. Someone, probably me, would wind up full of holes.

I decided to wait in the car and follow him to his next stop. Guy with a pocket full of cash wouldn't wait long to spend it. He confirmed my hunch when he pulled up in front of the nearest Whataburger. If I played this right, Otis Shaw would be buying me breakfast.

I resisted the urge to follow him inside. Instead, I grabbed the Colt from my holster, draped a jacket over my arm, and waited by his ride. When he finally burst through the doors with three sacks of steaming takeout, I realized why it had taken him so long.

"Git off my ride." His words were muffled, probably because of the wad of food lodged in one side of his jaw. Guess he couldn't wait until he got home or at least into the car.

I adjusted my jacket just enough so he could see the gun, not enough to start a panic among the exiting customers. "Mr. Shaw, Hardin Jones needs to see you. Come with me and we'll get things straightened—"

I barely got the last word out before I was clobbered by a cloud of orange and white striped bags. Didn't hurt, but the fist that followed them packed a mighty punch. I doubled over and Shaw swiped me away from his car door like I was made of paper. I resisted the urge to shoot. Too many bystanders. He started the Cadillac and I jumped up, hauling one of the bags with me and ran to the Bronco.

I did my best, but he had too much of a head start. I lost him at the next intersection when I got blocked by a huge-ass truck and he made a left turn against the red light. If I hadn't just caused a scene at the Whataburger, I would've risked it and run the light too, but I didn't need to chance getting pulled over and questioned about what I was doing pulling guns on people outside a fast-food joint. Well, at least now I knew Shaw wasn't going to behave in public. I'd have to wait and catch him without an audience.

When I got home, I rummaged through the bag I'd managed to save. Two biscuits with bacon and egg. Hash browns. Gravy. The morning hadn't been a bust after all.

After breakfast, I contemplated my next move. It'd been a pretty full day already. I was wavering between a short nap and a long nap when John called. I picked up on the first ring.

"I have good news and bad news."

"Let's hear it." I didn't bother specifying the order.

"Based on the ME's time of death, Amato and Picone could have been killed during the time Bingo was out running errands."

"I'm guessing that's the good news. And the bad?"

"They weren't killed at Bingo's place."

Too much breakfast, too little sleep made my mind sluggish. "What does that mean?"

"Jensen," he referred to the lead detective on the case, "thinks it means he killed them somewhere else and brought them back to the house."

"You realize how stupid that sounds, right? And Bingo is supposed to have done this by himself? You've met him, right?" I raised my voice just in case he wasn't getting how worked up I was.

"Settle down. I'm with you. Something fishy about all this, which is why we haven't made an arrest. We planned to talk to Bingo again, but he's lawyered up."

"Pretty smart if you ask me."

"Pretty sure it was your idea."

"Sue me." I started to tell him to call me back when he had something of substance to report, but then I remembered the stupid gold coin. "Where are you now? I want to give you that Imperial. Bingo said he got one just like it from Petrov. I'm telling you it's his 'you're in my debt now' calling card."

"You mean the one he conveniently hocked and lost the pawn ticket? His lawyer told us. You should keep yours. You can help him pay for his lawyer out of it. Looks like Bingo was strapped for cash, which Jensen figures is a motive for getting rid of the Italians."

"Did this guy just make detective? Bingo's business is done. This little incident has shut him down. Do you think Bingo executed two guys with a gun you can't find, loaded them into his car, hauled them home, and dumped them into his living room?"

"Yeah, I told him your theory about Petrov and he thinks that's Bingo's ace in the hole. Show of loyalty to Petrov by taking out the Italians." He kept talking over my grunted protest. "Don't shoot the messenger. Between you and me, I think Jensen wants a stat more than he wants to dig. I'll do as much as I can, but like I told you before, I'm not the lead on this one."

I caught a lot of "I"s in what he said and asked, "What does Chance think?"

"You haven't talked to her?"

Way to change the subject. "Not since she first found out about all this. And she was a little preoccupied at the time. Don't tell me you haven't seen her."

"I've seen her, but we haven't talked much. She's out canvassing the neighborhood with a couple of uniforms while I'm here dealing with the ME and the lab." He waited a beat, then added, "She feels real bad about what happened."

About ditching me for the doctor? About being with the doctor in the first place? About leaving Bingo hanging out to dry? I did and I didn't want to know the answer. "Yeah."

"What about that U.S. Marshal you were so hot on? Wasn't she the one had you looking for Amato and Picone in the first place? Why don't you hit that and see what you can find out?"

"'Hit that'? Really, John? Don't try to talk like a hipster. Not you. Not you at all. Besides, like every other woman in my life, she's disappeared."

"Rough."

He had no idea.

Nap didn't take. Didn't get anywhere close to sleep. I needed to be doing something, but I didn't have a clue what. Someone ordered a hit on Vedda's guys. Most likely, it was Petrov, but why? If he wanted Bingo's place for business, it was stupid to make it a crime scene. Petrov's success was due to his brains. Leaving Vedda's guys dead at Bingo's wasn't a smart move for anyone who wanted a piece of Bingo's business.

So who had an interest in closing his doors for good?

The Feds. If Bingo's house had become a hotspot for organized crime, they'd want to shut it down. They must have known something was up there, otherwise, why would Diamond have been looking for Amato and Picone in the first place?

I shook my head. I may be a renegade, but the idea that government agents had killed a couple of suspects and left them where an innocent man would be blamed was too much for me to take in. The whole thing stunk, and I had a strong desire to clear the smell.

Clock read two p.m. The biscuits and gravy were a distant memory. I had a trace of a plan, but I'd definitely need a good meal before I took it on. I dressed and armed up, pulled the Imperial coin from my coffee can, and walked over to Maggie's. Middle of the day, the only customers were a few regular drunks, hunched over the bar. Place was so quiet, my entrance made a big bang, and Maggie flew out of the kitchen to welcome me with a flurry of observations.

"You! Where have you been? Your brother left town. Your dad isn't eating right and he's drinking too much. I think he's sad. You should go see him."

I didn't have the heart to tell her his mourning had more to do with his favorite gambling place being shut down than any kind of empty nest syndrome. "I'll go see him soon. He said Mark left my wedding invite at the house."

She presented a creamy colored envelope with a wax seal. "He gave it to me. Said I'd probably see you before him."

I took it and hefted the weighty envelope in my hand. "Fancy." I slid a finger under the flap and broke the seal to find another envelope inside. *Luca Bennett and Guest.*

"You gonna bring someone?"

And guest. What the hell? Like I was the host of this shindig. I was a guest myself. And I'd be busy doing best man things, whatever those are. My thoughts rambled on and Maggie poked me in the side.

"Are you?"

"Am I what?"

"Are you going to bring someone to your brother's wedding?"

She said the words real slow, but it didn't help. I blurted out, "I don't have anyone to bring."

Maggie grunted and folded her arms. "And that's your problem."

"Maybe it's not a problem. I'm happy being on my own." The slight tinge of dishonesty stung and I rushed to cover. "I mean, I'll have things to do. You know, for Mark. Wedding things. Right?"

"Sure, if you're set on going alone. Besides, you'll be all looking good in your tux. Wedding will be full of single women, all sentimental about romance. You'll have your pick of the lot."

The image of scads of well-dressed women, teary-eyed and romantic, caused me to feel suddenly claustrophobic. Not my usual reaction, but nothing had felt usual lately, and I didn't want to talk about it. "You have any decent food?"

"And by decent, you mean fat and grease?"

"How well you know me."

"Maybe it's better you stay single since you're going to die young."

She was all talk. I knew that once she got over trying to change my dad—who was never going to change—she'd be back to serving up food that tasted good instead of food that was good for us. After staring me down, she stalked off to the kitchen mumbling about calories and cholesterol.

An hour later, fueled by a cheeseburger with extra bacon and a big basket of fries, I'd finally figured out my next step. Hell, if I was going to die young, I may as well go out blazing.

CHAPTER EIGHTEEN

Judging by the cars, Slice of Heaven was busy for a Monday night. Good. Better chance Candy would be working. John and Chance may not have been able to get her to talk, but they were constrained by pesky rules, like the Constitution. Me? Not so much. I'd let my Colt do the convincing.

I'd considered driving straight up to Petrov's house. I'd been there before, last year when I'd hunted Diamond down, but the reception had been icy at best. His goons had frisked me and taken my guns. Besides, the place was a fortress. Better to stir things up and get him to come to me.

I ordered a draft beer and pretended to drink it while I scoped out the place. No sign of any of Petrov's regular security detail. Good, because I was prepared to shoot up the place to get some info. After a few minutes, I slipped the cocktail waitress a twenty and told her I was hungry for some Candy. She motioned for me to follow her to one of the rooms in the back. The room was utilitarian. A couch, a small table, and a dimmer switch on the overhead light. The light was low and I didn't change it, hoping the couch didn't have too many remnants from prior customers.

I didn't have to wait long. A few minutes later, a perky brunette in a thong walked in, shut the door behind her, and joined me on the couch.

"I heard you were in the mood for something sweet."

"Do they teach you to talk like that at stripper school?"

The perkiness faded fast. "You have cash or not?"

I reached into my pocket and pulled out the Imperial. "Will this do?"

I barely caught her flinch before she morphed back into vivacious mode. "If that's real, we can work something out."

I set the Imperial on the table and leaned back into the couch. "Tell me everything you know about Yuri Petrov's prescription drug business."

Candy was fast, but the sight of the Colt stopped her before she got to the door. I pointed to the place on the couch she'd just abandoned. "Hey, now, we were just getting started."

"If I scream, two very big guys will be in here in seconds."

"I'm sure they will enjoy cleaning up the blood. Have a seat."

She sat as far away from me as she could get. "What do you want?"

"I told you. You know the cops are already interested. Why don't you fill me in about Yuri's new business and I can get them out of your hair?"

"I don't know anything."

"Not what I heard." I cocked my gun, but didn't point it at her.

Perky, vivacious—all gone. The girl next to me on the couch was a puddle of nerves. She'd talk. I just had to wait her out.

"Look, I'm in college. This is how I pay my way, but the club hasn't been as busy as it used to be. Economy and all." I nodded to keep her talking. "Yuri's guys offered a few of us extra work, peddling prescription drugs. I needed the extra cash, so I said hell yeah. They wanted me to sell on campus, but I know better than to risk getting thrown out of school, so I just sell to some of the girls at the other clubs. I figured that was low risk."

She had a brilliant business mind. "You know where Yuri gets the stuff?"

"Not a clue."

She was telling the truth. "You have some on you now?" I was regretting giving John the only proof I had. Wouldn't hurt to have more on hand.

She shot a look at the Colt and her face fell. "No. I don't suppose you'd believe me if I said I could get some and be right back."

"I believe you'd bring something besides fake meds back. Just a few more questions and I'm out of your hair." I holstered the Colt as a sign of goodwill. "Ever been to Bingo's place?"

"Bingo? What's that?"

"What college you go to?"

"UTA."

Not in Dallas. Okay, I could buy she'd never heard of Bingo. I pulled out the ratty photos of Amato and Picone. "How about these guys?"

She reached for the photos and I watched while she stared too long for someone who'd never seen them before. Finally, she handed them back. "Maybe. They look kind of familiar. Maybe they're customers."

"Well, they're for sure not college students."

She giggled, a bit of the bouncy co-ed showing through. I decided to get out while she was feeling all happy-go-lucky.

"I'm taking off." I stood and picked up the Imperial from the table. "You give me a five minute head start and I promise I'll never bother you again. Just do me one favor."

She nodded and I handed her the coin. "Don't tell a soul you answered my questions, but make sure Yuri's guys know I asked." I pointed at the coin. "Show them the special tip I gave you." I strode out of the room before she had time to respond. Needed to make some tracks. Once Yuri found out I'd been in his club, pumping his girls for information, he'd be on my tail and fast.

Outside the club, I paused briefly to flick a glance at the wall where Jess had fucked me for the last time. I rolled the thought around in my head. After seeing her playing white knight for Heather Deveaux, I realized it probably had been the last time, and I cared more than I wanted to.

Shake it off. I'd been feeling weird ever since I'd left Maggie's. Damn wedding invite. As if it's not bad enough I'm going to a wedding, I got a plus one invite. Like showing up stag was a big fail. Whatever.

My silly attempt at introspection almost made me miss seeing him. Otis Shaw in his ancient Cadillac Seville, pulling out of the lot at Black Lace. I cut off two cars to try to slip in behind him, but he made the turn before I could catch up.

It was late. A man leaving a strip club would likely be heading home this hour. Question was, which home? His baby mamma's house or his girlfriend's? Odds were on the girlfriend's place. I made the drive out to Cedar Hill in record time. The lights were still on which was a good sign. Shaw's car wasn't out front. I took a pass through the alley. No Caddy. Either I was wrong or he hadn't made it here yet. I couldn't imagine he'd want to get it on in a house with a screaming baby. I decided to hide out and wait.

An hour later, the house lights went out and I decided he wasn't coming. On my way home, I drove back by Dalia's place, just in case watching strippers had made him reminisce about the mother of his child. Not a sign of him there either. Maybe he'd found a third option. How could a hood like Otis Shaw have so many choices and I couldn't even come up with a plus one to take to my brother's wedding?

I rolled out of bed Tuesday morning, restless and edgy. Waiting wasn't my favorite thing to do, but surely Petrov wouldn't take long to react to my questions from the night before.

I threw on sweats and a jacket to cover the two guns I wore. Until he showed his hand, I wasn't taking any chances on getting caught without a decent amount of firepower. Probably should've skipped the run, but I needed to pound out the nervous energy ramping up in my brain.

A mile in, I was exhaling big frozen puffs of air, but the rote activity felt good. With each footfall, I stomped out all the useless wanderings in my head. Today, I would catch Shaw. I'd turn him in and see if Hardin had new work. If I went on about my regular routine, all the other pieces would fall into place. Petrov would show up and I'd get answers about Bingo. Deveaux would go back to Chicago and my relationship with Jess would return to normal.

Normal. Was it normal to screw your best friend? Was your best friend really your best friend if a woman could come between you? Had anything really changed, or was it all in my head? Maybe this is how all friends are—coasting along nicely until we meet "the one," and then everything had to shift, to compress, to make space for what was most important. And normal got redefined.

Fucking brain. Couldn't turn it off. I had to actually do something if I was going to have a shot at putting Jess out of my head. I ticked off a mental list: find Shaw, get an update on the investigation from John, check in with Bingo. It was a good list, a busy list, a list that didn't include anything having to do with Jessica Chance.

❖

Shaw wasn't at Dalia's or Shante's. Unless he'd dumped the Cadillac, which I highly doubted. I decided to run by Black Lace later and show his mug shot around. Maybe he'd found a new lady friend to shack up with. Amazed me how many women were quick to overlook the fact the guy was a felon.

Next item on my list was a call to John. I'd already checked the morning paper. No word on Bingo being arrested which meant the cops were still investigating, whatever that meant. I tried the station first and waited through the rings, deciding whether I'd tell him about my visit to Petrov's club. I'd resolved to keep it to myself when the line finally connected.

"Chance here."

I considered hanging up.

"Is anyone there? I can hear you breathing."

I took a deep breath. "It's me."

"Oh." Even tone, a hint of surprise, but not disappointment. Shame on me for reading so much into a two-letter word.

"I was calling John."

"He's in a witness interview."

I perked up. "Witness? On Bingo's case?"

Her voice got whisper low. "No. We're not on that case anymore."

"Well, John said you were only backup. Any reason you can't still give me a hint about what's going on?"

"Guess I should've been more clear. We, as in the entire department, are not on that case anymore. Feds grabbed it."

"You sound relieved."

"Yeah, well, normally I'd be pissed, but this case was a mess. It's your fault, anyway."

"Excuse me?"

"Something about that pill bottle you gave John got the DEA all over us. They took Bingo's case and every fake prescription case vice had working. You cut our work load substantially. I should thank you."

Diamond. She'd been working the prescription drug angle. Not a job for a U.S. Marshal. Was she really DEA? It would explain why she'd been looking for Amato and Picone who'd apparently gotten into the fake meds biz. But why lie to me and say she was working for the Marshal Service?

I needed to sort this out, but first I needed to end this awkward conversation with Jess. She wasn't herself. When she told me about the Feds taking over their case, I would've expected her to sound pissed, but she only sounded tired. "You okay?"

"Sure, what else would I be?"

I didn't have an answer for her non answer, so I let it ride and attempted casual conversation. "Mark left town."

"I thought he was moving here."

"He is. He just had to go wrap things up back east. He'll be here a couple of weeks before the wedding."

"Is he excited?"

"I guess. Kind of overwhelmed I think. His bride-to-be seems pretty fancy. Got the invitation, and I swear it's like something the royal family would send out, wax seal and all."

"I don't know, maybe that's normal."

Normal. I was starting to hate that word. "Is it normal to bring a guest?"

"What?"

"My invite said 'Luca Bennett and Guest.' Am I supposed to bring someone or will they care if I show up alone?"

"Pretty sure that's your choice. You want to take someone?"

Normal. If things were normal we wouldn't even be having this conversation. I didn't know jack about weddings, but I did know that if things were normal, Jess would go with me to the damn thing. She'd help me navigate my way through all the customs I was completely unaccustomed to. She'd make sure I wouldn't make a fool of myself in front of all my brother's fancy new relatives. She'd tie my tie and make sure I didn't drip anything on my shirt, at least not before the ceremony. Because that's what friends do. When things are normal.

But nothing was normal between us anymore. "Hey, I've got another call coming in," I lied, "I'll talk to you later."

"Sure. And, Luca?"

"Yeah?"

"You should definitely take someone."

Nope, nothing was normal.

CHAPTER NINETEEN

The U.S. Marshal's Service office was in the Earle Cabell building in downtown Dallas. Downtown wasn't my favorite place. Parking was expensive and I hate driving around on streets that pedestrians think they own. I decided against taking out a woman eating a sandwich and talking on her cell phone who stepped right out in front of me, but only because I didn't want the delay of having to deal with the accident report.

On my fourth circle around the block, I finally scored a metered spot. I stowed my guns in the hidden compartment of the Bronco's floorboard. Lots of layers of security in this building and, in jeans, boots, and a black leather jacket, I already looked a little out of place. No need to add an arsenal to the mix.

The Marshal Service was divided into two groups. Young, fit, law enforcement types, ready to take on the adventure of chasing down bad guys on the lam, and old, not so fit, Walmart greeter looking folks who were content to act as courtroom bailiffs, telling people when to stand and sit, and getting coffee for jurors. Took me a few minutes, but I finally located the office for the young and fit types and, after a trip through another metal detector, stated my business.

"I have an appointment with Marshal Diamond Collier." Best to lie with confidence and make the other side think they were the ones who'd messed up the calendar.

The receptionist scrunched her brow, and I was waiting for her to tell me that no such person worked there, but instead she took my name and asked me to have a seat. Maybe they were trained to call for backup when nefarious types showed up. She scurried away and I pretended to read a three-year-old Time magazine. Good to know my tax dollars weren't being spent on updated subscriptions.

About twenty minutes later, I heard a click and the door next to the receptionist desk opened. I didn't expect Diamond to show up, but if I was looking for hot women, this one would do. Maybe the Marshal Service had placed an ad for new recruits, highlighting that only good-looking blondes need apply.

"Ms. Bennett?"

I stood up to compensate for not being armed, but since she matched my height and build, it didn't have any impact. "That's me."

"You have an appointment with Diamond Collier?"

The lack of a title in front of Diamond's name didn't get past me, but so far this was surreal. She was acting like I really had an appointment and I played along. "I do."

"Then I'll need you to come with me."

Weird, but it wasn't like I was going to tell her no. I stayed a step behind, enjoying the view, as she walked us to the bank of elevators. She punched the button for the sixth floor lobby. Maybe this was her orderly way of showing me out of the building.

"Mind if I ask where we're going?"

She cut a quick smile. "I don't mind."

Pure cop. I decided against giving her the satisfaction of ignoring further questions and let my mind wander. Didn't have to wander long. In a few minutes, the car stopped and she led me down a hall that led to a cafeteria. Maybe she was going to buy me an early dinner.

No such luck. Food service had closed for the day, but the seating area was open. She motioned for me to stop just outside the door. "Wait here." She stuck her head in the entrance and glanced around. "Okay, go on in."

"Are you this clandestine about all your meals?"

She ignored my question and pointed to a table in the corner of the room with one occupant. I knew before she turned around it was her. Blondie waited by the door and I joined Diamond at the table.

"Do you actually work in this building or is this another of your many and varied covers?"

"Sit down."

I flicked a glance at Blondie who was standing sentry at the door. "She's staying?"

"I trust her. Anything you want to tell me, you can say in front of her."

"Well, that's the thing. I don't know that there's anything I want to tell you. I came to get answers, not give them."

"I can't promise you I can tell you everything."

"At this point, anything would help. How did you know Amato and Picone were dead before their bodies were found?"

"I didn't. Not for sure."

"Then why did you tell me to stand down? What was it you said? 'That matter has been taken care of.' What the hell did you mean by that?"

She ducked the question. "I got called to a different aspect of the investigation. More pressing matter. You know how it is."

No, I didn't. My most pressing matters involved putting gas in my car and paying my rent, not choosing which crime family to investigate or which undercover identity I was going to assume. "Not what I heard. I heard you guys snatched the case from the local P.D. Seems like if it was that important, you wouldn't have been reassigned so quickly."

"Gee, wonder where you heard that. Detective Chance pissed that she lost the case?"

"Actually, I don't think she gives a shit." I immediately regretted opening up a discussion that included Chance, and I quickly changed the subject. "Why did you tell me you worked for the Marshal Service?"

"Seemed easier."

"Lying usually is."

"I'm with DEA. We've spent a lot of time building a case around these fake prescriptions. I told you what I could."

"You can tell me more now. Like why you called me off Amato and Picone, conveniently right before they turned up dead?"

A minute passed. Then another. "We've been working on this case for a while." A beat passed. "We heard chatter."

Chatter. They must have a wiretap on Petrov's operation. Probably how they found out Amato and Picone were trying to cut in on his business and certainly how they'd figured out Petrov had taken care of the problem.

She must've sensed my question because she held up a hand before I could get the words out. "You know I can't tell you more."

She didn't need to add how sensitive this information was. I got it. "You still have a tap on Petrov?" I prayed she didn't ask why I wanted to know. I'd been considering a visit to his house if he didn't show up to find me first. Might be handy to know if the place was bugged.

She didn't ask, but the look on her face was odd. Surprise, maybe? "Petrov? Uh, no. We're focusing our efforts on a different angle."

"And you don't really care about what happened at Bingo's? Let me guess, you all only took over the investigation to keep it under wraps so you could play some other game. Am I right?"

"The murder's not our focus."

"Even if Petrov ordered the hit?"

"We have bigger fish to fry."

I took a stab. "Like the supplier?"

"It's a big operation. You should let us handle it."

"Doesn't sound like you are handling it. What about Bingo?"

"I don't think they have enough evidence to prosecute him. If he's innocent, he'll be fine."

"Spoken like a true purveyor of justice."

She looked at the door and I followed her glance. Blondie was like a castle guard. All stoic and acting like we weren't having a heated conversation yards away. I looked back when I felt Diamond's hand on my arm. "Look, I'm just doing my job."

"Your job sucks."

"I can't get involved in every little detail or I lose sight of the big picture."

"Which am I?" I already knew the answer, but I wanted to hear her say it.

"What?"

"A little detail or the big picture?" I shook my head. "Never mind, don't answer that."

Her hand trailed down my arm and she stroked my fingers. "Don't be like that."

I didn't want to be. Like that. I wanted to be like this. Sitting alone—or semi alone, anyway—with a beautiful woman who wanted me like I wanted her. Did I want Diamond? I'd wanted her for sex, no doubt, but I'd gotten that and I wasn't satisfied.

"Maybe we should see each other outside of work. You know, like a date?"

"You're kidding, right?" I shot a look at Blondie, as if to ask her to join in my disbelief, but she stood ramrod straight, staring into the hallway.

"What, you never eat dinner before you fuck? It would kill you to have a conversation first?"

Did I? Would it? Before I had a chance to consider the questions, she threw a couple more out.

"Or is it that your heart belongs to someone else? Maybe a certain cop we know?"

There was a layer of real curiosity beneath the teasing tone, but I chose to write it off to the fact that she or one of her pals may have seen Jess and I going at it outside Slice of Heaven. Hope whoever it was had enjoyed the show because I wasn't giving up any details about my relationship with Jess. Truth was, I didn't know what I would say even if I wanted to share.

"Are you asking me out?" I started to warm up to the idea. Not the date part, but the get my mind off whatever was going on between Chance and Deveaux part.

"Maybe. What would you say if I said yes?"

"I don't dress up, I don't eat fancy food, and I don't like being without my own ride."

She laughed. "Assuming I could meet all your requirements, what would you say?"

"I'd say you were fucking with me."

"Assume I'm not."

"You like weddings?" I wanted to reel the question back in the minute it left my lips.

"What?"

"Never mind." I stood up. "Look, I gotta go. You may be off the case, but Bingo's my friend and I'm not letting him twist in the wind while you guys figure out who's in charge."

Her hand was back on my arm. "Don't do anything stupid."

Another woman warning me away from my own tendencies. Get in line. I shook her hand off. This one didn't have the power to tell me what to do. "No worries. I have a plan. Maybe I'll pay Geno Vedda a visit. You may not care about the truth, but I bet he will."

I strode past Blondie and willed a plan to form. Nothing about weddings and dates, only business. I'd been kidding about Vedda, but maybe it wasn't a joke. After all, who would have the biggest stake in finding the real killer? Geno Vedda, of course.

Was he even missing? Funny how Diamond didn't seem as hot on finding him as she had when she'd shown up on my doorstep over a week ago. I may not know where to find Geno, but I knew where I could find his dad. Lunchtime tomorrow, I'd be pitching my theory about Petrov to the head of the Vedda family, hopefully over a big platter of Mangia crab claws.

After I left the federal building, I did what was becoming my usual loop around Dallas looking for signs of Shaw, including a trip to Black Lace. The girls there recognized him, but they didn't have a clue about how to get in touch. Maybe his night away from Shante and Dalia had been a one-night stand. Hope he'd worn a condom or there'd be one more baby mamma waiting on him to get out of the pen.

Tired and hungry, I picked up a pizza and a six-pack and headed home. I changed into sweats to watch TV on one of the two channels that came in on my ancient TV. I was the best date I would ever have.

❖

When I woke up close to lunchtime the next morning surrounded by empty beer cans and dried up pizza crusts, the thought of crab claws made my stomach turn. Maybe I wasn't my own best date after all. The pain in my head at the sound of my ringing phone confirmed it.

"Yeah?"

"Luca, it's Bingo."

I sat up, surprised. I didn't think he'd ever called me on the phone before. Then I remembered that I'd left my number on the note with the names of the lawyers Hardin had provided. "Whatcha need?"

"I talked to a couple of those lawyers. They want big bucks to take a murder case. I'm thinking I should just go downtown by myself, talk to the cops, and see what we can work out. Can you talk to your friend? The one who came with you the other night?"

That was a loaded question. "Probably not a good idea. She's not on the case anymore. The Feds have taken over and you definitely don't want to go marching into their offices. Best advice. Sit tight and don't talk to anyone." Too bad Ronnie Moreno wasn't still in town. I'd make her take Bingo's case pro bono after all the trouble she'd been. But she was in D.C., so I'd have to solve this one on my own. Guess I'd have to try to stomach the crab claws. "I have an idea. I'll call you when I have some news."

Mangia wasn't too terribly busy yet, but again I told the hostess I'd order from the bar instead of taking a table. The same blond bartender was pouring drinks, and she still reminded me of Jess. I ordered a beer, mostly so I could take my time scoping out the place, but I enjoyed the fact she was easy on the eyes. I was surrounded by folks that looked hungry, not vigilant. Not a one of them looked like guards for a mobster. Maybe Anthony Vedda was having lunch somewhere else today. A half a beer later, I left my barstool to find out.

The unmarked room was where I remembered it, but this time it was guarded by a tall, bald guy with big bulges under his suit coat. I had bulges of my own, but the kitchen of a popular restaurant is no place for a shootout. I decided to start with words and resort to guns only if necessary. "I'm Luca Bennett. I'd like to talk to Mr. Vedda."

He stared at me, through me really, but didn't move a muscle. Acted like he hadn't even heard me. I stared back, feeling a little foolish for engaging in this childish game. Just when I was about to break—damn, this guy was good—the door opened. I recognized the guy who came out. He was one of the ones around Vedda's table when I'd been here the last time. He glanced between me and Staring Man, apparently undecided about the situation.

I stuck a hand out at him and he took it on impulse. "Luca Bennett. I'm here to see Mr. Vedda."

He nodded and ducked back in the room, shutting the door behind him. I wasn't sure whether to wait or give up, but he was back before I could give it a lot of thought. He told Staring Man to frisk me, and a minute later, he'd taken all my guns. All the ones he found anyway. I had a tiny .22 and a switchblade in my boots. No one ever seemed to check there.

I was ushered into the room, but I could tell right off the bat, hospitality was not the word of the day. Cruel and unusual punishment. The table was full of wonderful food, but I wasn't offered a seat. Anthony Vedda slowly chewed his food and carefully wiped his lips with a linen napkin before deigning to address me.

"Ms. Bennett, your former calling card is no good to you now."

Bingo. "I think that's a mistake."

"Oh, you do? Are you saying that I make mistakes?"

"Everyone makes mistakes. Especially if they don't have all the available information."

"Indeed. What a wise observation." He was mocking me. He waved a hand to the other men sitting around the table. "Why don't you enlighten us? Tell us all the information, so that we may refrain from making mistakes in the future."

"Bingo didn't kill Geno's—" I searched for a word that sounded more acceptable than hoods. "Employees."

"And I suppose you know who did?"

"I have a good idea. Based on my observations." I couldn't help myself. "I think Yuri Petrov had Amato and Picone killed. Dumped them at Bingo's place to shut him down. Petrov was trying to take over the house for his own purposes, and Bingo resisted." Okay, that was a slight exaggeration since Bingo wasn't a resisting kind of guy.

"Amato and Picone were in the way. He had them killed and left them at Bingo's place to teach him a lesson."

"Interesting story. You have proof of this?"

"Bingo is not a killer."

He waved a hand, dismissing me. "You have no proof."

"I have no proof." Pretty sure that even if I'd held on to the gold coin, it wouldn't have made an impression. "Only my word that Petrov personally told me about his interest in Bingo's business, and we both know Petrov can be very persistent about his business. He wanted sole control."

"Yet, you thought it was a good idea to come here today?"

I almost cracked that I'd hoped I could wrangle a good meal out of it, but the sense of humor in the room was lower than low. I took my best shot. "I guess you don't care if Petrov takes over your business."

"I am no longer a businessman. I am retired. I do not have interests outside of good food"—he picked up a glass—"good wine, and spending time with good friends. Perhaps you should develop similar interests instead of pursuing matters that do not concern you."

What had started as a friendly sounding spiel ended with a harsh tone, and I could tell I was being dismissed. No crab claws for me. But I didn't want to leave empty-handed. "Okay, I get it, but what about Geno? Don't you think he'd be interested in hearing what I have to say?"

"My son is not your concern." He paused to take a sip of wine. "And if you choose to make him your concern, you will become mine." He offered a fierce stare that turned into an engaging smile so quickly I had to question whether it had happened in the first place. "I trust you will find other pursuits. More profitable ones, less dangerous." He raised his glass in a mock toast. "To life!"

I got it. Both the overt and covert threats. And the dismissal. Keep asking questions, keep looking for Geno, and they would take me out. The Vedda family had something to hide, and I'll be damned if I was going to let it stay hidden.

CHAPTER TWENTY

Thursday morning, after my run, two giant cups of black coffee, and a donut the size of my head, I took to the Internet to find out whatever I could about Geno Vedda. Nothing pisses me off more than being told not to do something. I got why Anthony Vedda might not believe my theory, but I'd be damned if he thought he could wave me off the case. I was damn frustrated at the lack of response from anyone. Vedda had pretty much ignored my theory, Diamond had moved on to other matters, Jess and John were off the case, and so far Petrov hadn't taken the bait I'd left for him.

My searches didn't turn up anything I didn't already know. Geno's front was the restaurant industry, but everyone assumed he ran a ton of underground enterprises that made him the big bucks he was known for. He probably had at least a dozen setups like the one at Bingo's. I'd need to be a lot better connected if I wanted to find Geno, let alone talk to him. Guess I'd hoped that I'd get his father all riled and then he'd call his son and unleash him on Petrov. They'd duke it out and Bingo would be vindicated.

Not a very well thought out plan. Even if Vedda took on Petrov, whoever emerged victorious wouldn't give a rat's ass about Bingo. Did I really think one of them would march up to the Feds and say, "Hey, it was so and so, not Bingo. Make sure you clear his good name, okay?"

Not gonna happen. But if one of them admitted it to me, I could be a witness. Maybe someone would believe me.

In an effort to keep from getting riled, I told myself I'd worry about it when the time came. Right now I needed to focus on finding Shaw. I inspected my coffee can and pulled out some cash. The bank was getting low. I'd need to find Shaw if I was going to keep eating, and I'd need to eat if I was going to have the energy to take him down. Chicken, egg. Looked like a trip to Maggie's was first thing on my list.

After a stare down, she compromised by bringing me a cheeseburger and a salad. No fries. On the house. Since I wasn't paying, I didn't gripe, but the salad went untouched. I'm always hearing news stories about salmonella from lettuce, but I'd never heard of an outbreak of food poisoning after French fries. Give me a good batch of grease any day of the week.

Maggie sat across the table and stared while I worked my way through the non healthy portions of my meal. She had a goofy grin on her face, so between bites I asked, "What's up?"

"I'm excited about the wedding. Aren't you?"

Uh no, I wasn't. Nervous maybe, but excited? Not really. I knew that wasn't the appropriate answer. "It'll be nice. I guess."

"It'll be more than nice. Fancy flowers, fancy church. Mark's bride is beautiful. It will be a splendid day."

I almost threw up a little in my mouth. Who knew Maggie was a sentimental freak? Did I dare tell her I was kind of dreading the big event? I was supposed to wear a tux, give a toast, and who knows what else, but everything on the list was completely foreign to me. I risked a tiny overture. "I've never been to a wedding before, let alone had to do anything at one of them. Any pointers?"

Should've kept my mouth shut. Or brought along a notebook and pen to write down the long litany of tasks and pointers Maggie reeled off. When she finally stopped talking, all I could remember was I was supposed to hold on to the ring until Mark needed it, make sure he didn't chicken out, and say something nice to the happy couple in front of loads of people during the reception. Tall list. No wonder I was anxious. Friend in trouble, big role at wedding, Jess in the clutches of a viper. I had a lot going on.

As if on cue, more trouble walked in the door. Petrov had sent the same two guys. Probably their punishment for not getting me to comply the first time. I pushed my now empty plate away and stood. Maggie followed my gaze and said, "Uh oh."

I pointed a finger at the booth. "You stay here. I mean it." I didn't trust her not to fly at them like a bat out of hell. I'd started this rumble. If anything happened to her because of it, I'd never forgive myself.

I met them halfway from the door. "Gentlemen, let's take this outside."

Thug Number One nodded and waved a hand to usher me out. Petrov's Bentley was waiting. Thug One patted me down, took the Colt and a look down my shirt, probably making sure I wasn't wearing a wire, and then motioned for me to climb in. He crawled in after me, and I found myself in the middle of a thug sandwich, facing Petrov and his fancy dog.

Petrov spoke first. "You know where I live, yes? You cannot just come to see me instead of causing trouble at my club?"

"I have a phobia about big houses. Besides, your house isn't a good place to speak freely." He raised his eyebrows. "The Feds are listening in."

"And you know this because?"

I wanted to establish credibility, but I didn't want to go so far as to throw Diamond under the bus. Petrov had a lot of reasons to want her completely out of the picture. I pulled a lie out of my ass. "Bingo is my friend and his lawyer has connections. Not everyone is so good at keeping secrets. You arranged the hit on Vedda's guys and set Bingo up to take the fall. I get that it's all just business to you, but like I said, Bingo is my friend."

A slow smile crept across Petrov's face and I wanted to punch it off. The thugs seated next to me must have sensed my agitation because they leaned forward, like they were ready to body block me from the big guy.

"You have a lot of nerve, accusing me of murder." He flicked a glance at his bodyguards.

"It's not like it's a secret. Since your house is bugged, the Feds already know. Just a matter of time until they arrest you."

"Yet, they haven't." He leaned forward. "My house is clean. I spend good money to make sure it is a safe place. Daily. And I didn't set up your friend. He was my friend as well, and working with him was profitable. I do not cut off my nose to spite my face. But there is nothing I can do for him now. His situation has attracted too much attention, and he is no help to me anymore. If you want someone to blame, you should look elsewhere." He waved a hand at his burly friends and the one closest to him opened the door while Petrov dismissed me. "Now, I suggest you go find something else to do. My business is no longer your concern."

I stood in the parking lot, slowly digesting what he'd had to say. He had to be bluffing. Of course, I was probably crazy to think he'd cop to murder. I guess I just thought he might do a little bragging. Guys like him think they are untouchable. But something he said lingered: "working with him was profitable." He hadn't worked with Bingo. Vedda was working with Bingo. Petrov wanted in, had even come to me to get Bingo to work with him, had shown up at Bingo's with his you-owe-me gold coin, but Bingo was too scared of Vedda to get in the middle. The only way Petrov could've been making a profit at Bingo's was if he were in business with Vedda and that was unlikely. Guys like Vedda and Petrov don't share.

Vedda. Maybe his guys were working against him and he offed them himself. Maybe Vedda thought Bingo was helping Amato and Picone betray him. The more I maybed the situation, the more I liked the idea. Neat and tidy. Now, someone just needed to prove it and Bingo would be in the clear.

Wait a minute, if the Feds knew Amato and Picone were dead based on chatter and they weren't listening to Petrov, then they must have been listening to Vedda. Which meant Diamond and her seeking justice pals already knew Vedda had taken out his own guys. She had the means to clear Bingo right now, but instead she'd ripped the case from local law enforcement and was holding on until she could get something bigger out of it. She wasn't worried about Bingo getting charged because she knew he wouldn't be, but she didn't care if she left him twisting in the wind.

If this was all true, then I should be relieved that Bingo would come out okay. Problem was I didn't trust Diamond. Not enough to leave Bingo's fate in her hands. I could think of only one person I trusted completely, and I dialed her number before Petrov even made it out of the parking lot.

❖

Jess showed up only twenty minutes after I called. Considering she lived thirty minutes away, I guess I'd exaggerated the urgency of the situation.

I'd thought about asking her to meet me at my place, but my place was for fucking, and since we didn't do that anymore, I settled on Maggie's. Only risk here was Maggie asking nosy questions about why I didn't ask the nice, pretty cop on a date. After Jess had helped her brother out, Maggie thought she was golden. She didn't understand why I didn't put a ring on her finger and march down the aisle.

Whatever.

Maggie practically skipped on the way to seat us in the best booth in the place, and then hurried off to get our beers. Likely she'd show up with her own and try to dominate the conversation so I launched right in.

"Petrov just came to see me. He didn't have anything to do with Bingo's situation. At least not the dead guys in the living room part of it. You need to talk to whoever you can and yank this thing back from the Feds."

Jess held up a hand. "Slow down. You're talking crazy. What? Petrov paid you a visit and charmed you into thinking he's a great guy?"

"It's not like that."

I managed to get the story of my visit to Diamond and Petrov's visit to me out before Maggie reappeared. In addition to three beers, she served up a big plate of fried onion rings because she knew they were Jess's favorite. Sucking up to potential girlfriends for me meant healthy eating went out the window. I was cool with that. Maggie settled into the booth next to me and motioned for us to continue our conversation. "Eat, talk. Don't mind me. I'll just keep you company."

She stayed put through my annoyed stare, so I kept talking. "It makes perfect sense. Diamond said they'd heard chatter about Amato and Picone—the guys found dead at Bingo's place," I added for Maggie's benefit. "I assumed they'd had Petrov's place wired, but they're listening in on Vedda."

"I thought you said Geno Vedda was missing."

"I think she lied to me about that. Maybe she was just trying to get me interested, like if I thought by looking for his guys, I might also find Geno, then I'd be more likely to take on the case."

"But if they were working for Vedda and she had him wired, wouldn't she know exactly where they were?"

"Okay, okay, obviously I haven't figured it all out, but I'm telling you, when they died, those guys worked for Petrov and I think Vedda took them out when he found out they turned."

"So, what are you going to do about it?"

"That's the thing. I already talked to Diamond. She says she's off the case, bigger fish and all that. I think she knows exactly what happened and doesn't plan to do anything about it."

"That sucks, but now that the Feds have taken over, if they're not going to pursue Bingo, he'll eventually be cleared."

"Cops. You think everything is black and white. Bingo will never be cleared. The Feds will just close their investigation without making an arrest. Bingo will be out of business. Permanently."

"Let me see if I get this straight. You want me to interfere with a federal investigation so I can clear your friend and allow him to reopen his gambling house so you can blow all your money close to home?" She shot a look at Maggie who nodded that she agreed it was one of my more stupid ideas.

"I want you to do what's right. Or I will."

I didn't try to hide how pissed off I was. Did no one else give a shit about leaving Bingo twisting in the wind? I started to get up, but Jess grabbed my arm.

"Calm down. Let's talk."

She was right. She was usually right. I didn't have to like it, but I should at least listen to what she had to say. I slid back into the booth. "Okay. What ideas do you have?"

She released her grip on my arm, but she didn't move her hand. "Give me twenty-four hours. I'll make some calls, see what I can find out. If I don't make any progress, we can talk again and make another plan. But seriously, Luca, if you go charging around, you're likely to get Bingo killed. Let's try it my way first. I promise you, I will do everything I can."

I couldn't ask for more. Well, I could, but there was nothing more I wanted from her. As far as Bingo was concerned, anyway. I plunged into another subject. "Diamond asked me out on a date."

Jess slowly pulled her hand back across the table. "That's nice."

"I may have asked her to Mark's wedding."

"I'm sure you'll have fun." Jess's frown told me she hoped I'd have anything but.

"I'm not sure I really asked her. I may have just mentioned it." My rambling trailed off. I didn't have a clue where I was going with this. The words were just stumbling out of my mouth.

Maggie tried to save me by chiming in. "She's nervous about the wedding, being the best man and all." Only Maggie would try to rescue me by sticking it to me in my most vulnerable spot. And she kept right on going. "Detective Chance, I hear you have a girlfriend. A doctor, no less."

"Actually, no, I don't. No girlfriend, doctor or otherwise."

Maggie flashed me a harsh look, and I knew she thought I'd made her a liar. I started to protest, but Jess beat me to the punch. "She left town. Turns out she was more trouble than I was interested in taking on."

A wave of relief washed over me, and I had to resist the urge to smile. What kind of reaction was I supposed to have? Jess didn't look happy, but she didn't look sad either. After what Jess had said the night we met at Slice of Heaven, about how her "friends" knew about Deveaux, I decided she was throwing me a bone. But I guess I was still pissed off at the slight. "Do all your *friends* already know?"

Ouch. I could see by the pain in Jess's eyes, I'd hit a nerve. "No," she said. "No one else knows. She left this morning."

My anger deflated, but I had another question. "Is she coming back?"

"Wouldn't matter if she did." Her response was exactly what I wanted to hear.

Maggie reached over and gave Jess's arm a tight squeeze. "Can't believe she took advantage of a nice girl like you."

Maggie didn't even know Deveaux, but she acted like she and Jess were the best of friends, commiserating about being jilted lovers, apparently assuming "more trouble than she was worth" was a euphemism. I cleared my throat to remind them I was still here, and Maggie seized on the reminder, looking pointedly back and forth between the two of us. "Well, that makes things different now, doesn't it?"

I knew what she was implying, and I prayed she didn't say more. But since nothing, including prayers, usually dissuades Maggie, I pointed at the bar. "Maggie, looks like that guy over there needs something."

She twisted in her chair. "I don't see anyone."

"He's there, behind that woman." I pointed at a big group. "He was waving over here at you."

She stood and looked around, finally walking over to the bar. I could tell she didn't believe me, but what was she going to do? When she was finally out of earshot, I said, "Sorry, didn't know she was going to glom on to us."

Jess crossed her arms. "She's trying to set us up, you know that, right?"

I knew she was right, but I was too busy trying to figure out Jess's reaction to respond. Her tone was easy, light. She wasn't annoyed, maybe a little amused. "How about we get out of here while she's distracted?"

"Deal."

I left Jess's side and walked over to Maggie as we were leaving. "We gotta go. Put dinner on my tab?"

"On the house." She looked over to the door where Jess was waiting for me. "You should ask her to the wedding."

"Not gonna happen."

"Scared she'll say no?"

I didn't like being called scared, even when it might be right on. "Leave it alone, Maggie."

"Fine, I'll leave it alone, but alone is what you're going to be. For the rest of your life, until you learn to grab the opportunities that are right in front of you. What's the worst thing that can happen?"

A bunch of responses came to mind, but one kept repeating. She could say no. I'd always taken Jess for granted, solidly confident she would always be there for me. Lately, my confidence had been battered and I wasn't in the mood to take risks. Not as far as she was concerned.

I joined Jess at the door, and we walked into the parking lot. Two blocks and we'd be at my place. We wouldn't have to talk there. Instead, we could rip off each other's clothes and settle into the only feelings I'd ever been comfortable with—the rush of arousal, the explosion of an orgasm.

But we were past that. Problem was, I didn't know where that left us. "Do you want—"

Jess stopped me from saying more. "I'm sorry about what I said."

"Huh?" I honestly didn't know what she was talking about.

"The friend thing. At the club. I didn't mean it. We are friends. Good friends. I should've told you about Deveaux. Don't know why I didn't."

She was lying about that last. She knew it and I knew it. She didn't tell me because she didn't know how I'd react. And since I hadn't reacted well, I guess she'd been right to keep it to herself.

"I was a jerk. I'm sorry."

"I think we might be even."

"I want you to be happy. It's just…" I let the words trail off not because I didn't know what to say, but because I figured she already knew the rest and saying it out loud would just make us both uncomfortable.

She saved me the trouble. "Are you really nervous about the wedding?"

"Maybe a little."

"You'll be fine. He's your brother. Just focus on him and don't worry about the rest. It'll take care of itself."

I doubted that was true, but I nodded anyway. And then I jumped off a cliff. "You could come you know."

"What? And hang out with you and your date?"

I flashed back to my dream, make that nightmare, with Diamond and Jess, both at the wedding. "She's not my date. I didn't really ask her."

"'Didn't really ask her?' Seems like you might want to figure that out before you go asking anyone else."

"I didn't ask her. For real. And I'm not asking you like a date." The lie was easier than I thought it would be. "We'd go, like friends. You could make sure I don't do anything stupid. You're good at social stuff and I could really use your help."

"You're a real charmer."

"You'll go?"

"I'll think about it."

"Yeah, okay. That's good."

We both stood in the parking lot, out of things to say. This awkwardness wasn't us. All I wanted in that moment was to get back to where we'd been, before Deveaux, when our roles were defined and we both knew what would happen at the end of a night, but I knew it wasn't going to happen. In the meantime, one of us needed to make a move, and I decided to step up. "Guess I'll head home. Got an early morning planned. You'll call me if you find out anything?"

"Absolutely."

She walked to her car and I resisted the urge to call her back since I didn't know what I'd do if she turned around.

CHAPTER TWENTY-ONE

I got out of bed the next morning ready to make some cash. Now that I'd placed Bingo's fate in Jess's capable hands, I could concentrate on finding Shaw. By the end of the day, I'd be standing in Hardin's office collecting my fee.

Outside it was pitch-black. I couldn't wait for daylight savings time to end. I didn't mind the dark at night, but in the morning, it sure was hard for me to get going. First stop, the dumpy convenience store around the corner for coffee. I knew I'd regret it if I wound up having to stake out Shaw's place, but I'd probably fall back asleep on the drive over without it.

After careful consideration, followed by a coin toss, I decided to start at Shante's place. Since Shaw had gone to the trouble of having his government check mailed there, he obviously thought of it as his permanent, at least for now, residence. I pulled onto Interstate 30 and merged into traffic. A lot of it. Who were all these people who not only rose before the crack of dawn, but had to actually be somewhere before the sun came up?

Early morning work is an anomaly for me, but I hadn't slept well the night before, and I'd finally decided to get up and scratch the last thing off my to-do list. Fairly certain my lack of sleep had something to do with my evening with Jess the night before.

I tallied the events of the night. Deveaux was gone. Jess apologized, kind of, for being a bitch. She said we were friends and she meant it. I'd been worried about our friendship, so I should be relieved, right?

I wasn't. Something big had changed between us. Our normal deal would have been to end up in bed, but we'd walked away from each other. Friends without benefits. Like normal people. Maybe that was the problem. Jess and I, what we had, had never been normal. I wasn't sure I liked normal. Well, shit, I knew I didn't like normal, but I was willing to give it a try if it meant I got to keep my best friend.

I focused on the road. Once I made it through the Mixmaster, traffic going my direction tapered off as most of the folks out and about this early were headed toward Dallas instead of away from it. I took my exit and noticed a big Chrysler sedan change lanes and exit right behind me. Gave me a little pause, but I shook it off. Petrov wouldn't let any of his guys drive an American made car. Plus, I didn't think he considered me a threat, even though I'd accused him of murder the day before. I was a nuisance that he only noticed when he needed my special brand of pestering.

Shante's neighborhood was quiet. Either these people didn't work days or they'd already left for work. It was seven fifteen and the sun was just beginning to edge into view. I turned onto her street and noticed the Chrysler keep on going.

From down the street I could see Shaw's car parked in Shante's front driveway. I needed to park close enough to Shante's house that it wouldn't be too hard to get Shaw in the car, but far enough away to keep him from recognizing my ride. I drove around the block and settled on a space on the cross street, three houses down from Shante's. Before I climbed out of the Bronco, I loaded up. Two pairs of handcuffs, the Colt, the Sig, my favorite knife, and a twenty-two in each boot. I pulled my hair up and tugged on a Rangers ball cap. The team was in the pennant race for only the second time in over fifty years, and everyone in the city was a Ranger fan right now. I figured the cap might buy me some goodwill with nosy neighbors, and, combined with a pair of dark sunglasses, it might keep Shaw from recognizing me right away. My final accessory was a clipboard I pulled from the backseat.

I was on my way to the house, working on a plan to get Shaw to the door, when front doors started flying open and the street filled with kids. Okay, so maybe it was only a few doors and about half a dozen kids. Of course, it was a school day, one of those facts of life I don't relate to because I don't have kids of my own and no one in my circle of acquaintances does either.

I ducked back to the Bronco to wait them out. The kids dawdled, but I couldn't really blame them. I skipped a ton of classes when I was in school. Boring, useless shit, like algebra and poetry. Besides, it was too early for anyone's brain to take in information. If classes had started after noon when I was in school, I would have been valedictorian.

When the kids finally scattered off to school, I started back toward Shante's with a plan. I was giving away free Ranger playoff tickets for folks who would invite me in and answer a few survey questions. No one in this city would turn down an opportunity to win seats to one of the rare postseason games. By the time Shaw figured out I was bluffing, I'd have him in cuffs.

I'd reached the sidewalk in front of Shaw's house when my phone rang. I glanced at the screen. Jess. Maybe she'd gotten hold of Diamond first thing and was calling to report in. I started to answer, but I saw someone peeking out of the curtains of Shaw's house and decided I better make my move before whoever was inside decided I was up to no good.

The woman who answered the door must have been Shante. She looked like a slightly younger version of Shaw's baby mamma, Dalia. He'd probably keep repeating the pattern—get one woman pregnant, find another, younger model, get her pregnant—for the rest of his life. I gave Shante a year at best.

I mustered my most engaging smile and plunged into my made-up spiel. "Hi, I'm with the Dallasites Who Care Foundation. We're conducting a door-to-door survey and, if you'd be so kind as to answer just a few questions, you could win tickets to see the Rangers in the playoffs."

"I don't want to buy nothin'."

She was brilliant. I tried again. "That's the beauty. You don't have to. We're a nonprofit. We don't sell anything. But the Rangers gave us tickets to help with our efforts to gather information for the survey. All you have to do is answer some questions. It'll take ten minutes, tops."

I was doing my best to imitate survey takers everywhere, but I knew I sounded inane. I was about ready just to pull the Colt and muscle my way inside, when she nodded and swung the door open wide.

"Yeah, okay. I can do that."

As I followed her into the house, I said, "Is your husband home? It really helps to get the couple's perspective on these questions. And that way I can justify giving you some extra tickets."

She pointed at a rickety metal table in the kitchen. "Wait here. I'll get him."

While she was gone, my phone rang again. Jess. Five minutes and I could call her back, but trying to talk on the phone now would totally wreck my plan, to the extent I had one. I shut off the ringer and started to put it back in my pocket when I felt the buzz that told me I'd received a text. I studied Jess's message, but it didn't make sense.

Vedda's there. Get out.

Vedda's where? Here in Shaw's place? Not likely. And how did Jess know where I was? I took a second to type, *I'm good. Will call u in a few*, and then found a place to hide while I waited for Shaw to appear.

A few seconds later, I heard voices. Hers pleading and his grumbling. I bet she'd had to wake him up for this golden opportunity. He'd never forgive her when he figured out his trip downtown did not include a championship baseball game.

When they emerged from the hallway, I was ready. I pushed Shante out of the way and snapped a cuff on Shaw's wrist before he knew what hit him. I pointed the Colt in his back and said, "Mr. Shaw, let's try this again. You missed your last court date, and I'm here to take you in."

I should've brought a bazooka. Shaw roared and body slammed me back into the wall with superhuman power. The force of the jolt knocked the Colt from my hand, and while I tried to catch my breath, I watched it skitter across the floor.

Shaw, on the other hand, was headed to the back of the house. I retrieved the Colt and took off after him. For a big guy, he sure had speed. He was out the door and in the alley before I made it over the chain link fence. Guess I was going to get my morning run after all.

We tore down the alley, huffing and puffing. At least we were running in the direction of the Bronco. If I couldn't catch him on foot, I'd jump in the car and run him down. As long as he was mostly alive, I could still collect my fee. We were only a few yards away when the game changed.

The Chrysler I'd seen earlier spun around in the street and stopped square in front of my car. Before I had time to process what was going on, I heard another set of tires squealing and saw another car pull in behind mine.

Jess's text. Vedda. He must have followed me this morning, and now he had me surrounded. Car doors started to open. I glanced at Shaw. The big guy was frozen in place, likely confused. I barked at him. "These are cops. Here to take you in. They're pretty pissed at you. Get in the Bronco, and I'll make sure you stay safe."

Only took him a minute to figure out he had better odds against me than he did against two cars full of folks with guns. He opened the passenger door of the Bronco and started to climb in. I hunched behind him, but Vedda and his sidekick were too fast.

"Luca Bennett. I hear you've been looking for me."

Geno Vedda motioned for his lackey to stay put, and he walked toward me. The H & K submachine gun in his hand was the only thing that kept me in place. We both looked back at the other car, but if anyone was inside, they were hugging the floorboards. Geno jerked his chin at the Colt in my hand and I set it on the ground.

"I'm not looking for you, Geno." I pointed at Shaw, who was completely confused about what had just happened. "I'm in the middle of a job. If you'd like to talk, maybe we could do it when I'm done." I'd learned to bluff from my dad. He'd be so proud of me right now.

"That's not what I heard. I'll take care of your little job right after I take care of you." He raised the gun.

I was all out of bluff. I was going to get blown to bits, in the street, two steps away from having a jumper in custody. I'd spent my whole life living by the seat of my pants, never thinking about the future, never caring about the end. But I cared now. Big-time. What had I texted to Jess? *I'm good.* Well, I was anything but, and I'd never have the chance to change that.

"Police! Drop it, Geno."

Jess? I glanced to my right and there she was. She'd never looked so good, and it wasn't just the fact she was holding a big ass gun of her own. As glad as I was to see her, I didn't want her to be in the middle of this. Her Glock was no match for the submachine gun in Vedda's hand.

"Go away, Chance. I got this." Once again with the bluffing, but she wasn't buying it.

"Doesn't look like it, Bennett. Get down."

Vedda looked between us and laughed. "Don't worry, ladies. I have enough bullets for you both."

Ladies. Like I wasn't pissed off enough before. I spent the next second trying to figure out how to get my Sig out of my holster before Vedda could get off a shot, but another voice, from my left this time, distracted me.

"Come on, Geno, put it down."

John stood at the front bumper of the Bronco with a big ass gun of his own. Geno's guy started to edge away while his boss tried to figure out where to focus his firepower. He settled on Jess, shouting over his shoulder to John. "Drop your gun, or I'll shoot your partner."

"I don't know, she's a pretty good shot," John yelled back at him.

"We'll see."

I saw his finger squeeze the trigger and I lunged. As Vedda and I both fell to the ground, I heard gunfire, lots of it and the sickening sound of bullets making their mark followed by a cry in a voice I knew all too well.

I hate hospitals. I'd counted the ceiling tiles about a hundred times. Read the instructions for the adjustable bed and resisted the urge to turn on the TV because I didn't want to wake the sleeping patient. The minute Jess's eyes fluttered open, I pounced. "You realize the only reason they kept you overnight is because you're a cop, right?"

"Pay's for shit, I may as well get some benefits." She was unflappable, even after being shot.

"You're surprisingly chipper for someone who just woke up."

Jess looked up at the clock over the hospital room door. "You're one to talk. How often do you get up this early?" She stared into my eyes. "You look like shit. Let me guess, you didn't sleep at all. Have you been here all night?"

I shuffled under her gaze. "No. I took a break to get something to eat downstairs. I expect to be admitted for botulism any moment."

She used her good hand to point at her left arm. "So what's the verdict?"

"You'll be fine, but you're going to have a scar. Bullet grazed your arm. They gave you antibiotics and doped you up on killer pain meds." I pointed at the door. "John's outside. He was here last night, but you were kind of out of it. I think they gave you the really good stuff."

"See what you could've gotten if you'd stayed on the force?"

Totally like her to make light. I wasn't quite there. "That bullet was meant for me. If you hadn't showed up, no telling what might have happened."

"Aw, shut up. Besides, if you hadn't knocked Vedda down, his aim would've been a hell of a lot better. You don't need another scar to add to your fancy collection. This is my first. I hear the chicks dig them."

I leaned over and kissed her forehead. "You're right about that. How did you know Vedda was tracking me?"

"I tracked Collier down Wednesday night and talked to her about your theory. Cop to cop, she confirmed it, but told me to butt out. Yesterday morning, she calls me first thing to tell me they picked up talk on the wire at Vedda's place about taking you out. Vedda was on the move and he'd called some of his guys to say he'd found you and where. He must have followed you from your house. Officially, Collier wasn't authorized to do anything about it since they had bigger plans for Vedda, but unofficially, she wanted me to know. She basically admitted the only reason she'd asked you to look for Amato and Picone in the first place was to stir things up. They had a warrant to listen in on Vedda, but they hadn't been able to connect Petrov to his operation. You were the catalyst to draw out the players.

"John and I were at the office when she called. We busted ass getting to you."

"I'd be dead if you hadn't."

"Thank John. He drives like a demon."

I let her bout of humility go. She didn't want me to fuss, and I got that, but I'd have to find another way to make up for the fact she'd saved my life. I'd knocked Vedda off balance, but it was her bullet that took him down.

"Yeah, I definitely owe John one. He took Vedda's bodyguard down. You want me to send him in? If I don't soon, he's going to bust down the door."

"Sure, in just a sec." She pointed to the space on the bed beside her. "You get Shaw?"

"He was so freaked out, he probably would've turned himself in. He may be a thug, but he's small-time compared to Vedda and his gang. I don't think he'd ever seen a submachine gun up close. I cuffed him to Vedda's car and let the cops take him in." I'd traded cashing in on Shaw for a ride in the ambulance with Jess.

"I'll make sure you get credit."

I shook my head. "I don't care."

"You will when you're hungry and you can't afford to eat."

"I'm good."

"Are you?"

"I am. You?"

"Golden."

I was certain we both knew we were talking about more than our health. The air between us was suddenly thick with stuff we needed to say, but neither one of us seemed ready to. I stood up. "I should bring the gang in. If you're ready for a crowd."

"Who else is out there?"

"Besides John? Your entire softball team and a few other cops."

I started to the door, but she called me back.

"Luca?"

"Yes?"

"I think I may take you up on that invite, if it's still open."

Took me a minute to realize what she was talking about. "Mark's wedding? What changed your mind?"

"Aw, you know, you'd just get into trouble if I'm not there."

"Maybe I like trouble."

"Fine. Go by yourself. I was only trying to be nice."

"I'm kidding. Go with me. I'll stay out of trouble."

"Maybe we can get into trouble together."

I liked the sound of that.

CHAPTER TWENTY-TWO

Three weeks later...

I stared at the bag hanging on my closet door. I'd picked up the tux yesterday. Tried to pay attention to how the guy had dressed me, but I was fairly certain I didn't remember all the snaps and buttons, let alone how to tie the tie. I took a deep breath and unzipped the bag. The fancy black suit mocked me, but with only an hour until I had to be at the church, it was time to tackle the beast.

My phone rang and I glanced at the number. I'd expected it to be Jess, but it was a number I only recognized because I'd gotten two other calls just like it when I'd been at the tux place. Wasn't a local number. I let it go to voicemail, again. I had enough going on today. Didn't need to deal with phone calls from strangers when I couldn't even figure out how to get dressed.

Fifteen minutes later, I'd managed to put on pants and a shirt. Considering how many tiny buttons I'd had to fasten, I was pretty darn proud of myself. I was staring at the dreaded tie and the silver and onyx cufflinks—a present from Mark—when a knock on the door signaled relief was at hand. I opened the door and gaped.

"Wow." Someone hadn't had trouble getting dressed. Jess walked in the room, shaking her head.

"You're not dressed yet?" she asked.

"You look fantastic." She did. Her little black dress hugged her hips and hit at the exact right spot on her thighs. Tall black heels.

Well-toned calves. Breathtakingly beautiful. I'd never seen her like this, and as much as I wanted to savor the sight, all I could think about was unzipping her dress and ripping off all the little buttons I'd worked so hard to fasten.

She must've read the look in my eye because she shook a finger in my face. "You need to get dressed."

I ignored her warning, instead touching her half-bare shoulder. "No scar?"

"Oh, it's there." She grinned. "It's the only reason I didn't go strapless."

"Good thing since I wouldn't be able to concentrate if you did. I think I'm supposed to be in charge of a ring, give a toast, shit like that. If you were wearing any less, I'd say let's skip the whole thing."

She placed a hand on my chest and pulled me close. Her breath was warm in my ear. "Later, okay?" I answered with a kiss. Slow, deep, the kind of kiss that ends with two people naked, rolling around in bed. Or on the floor. Or wherever. Through the haze of hormones, I felt her push me away. She led me to the bedroom, but she made it clear we had a singular purpose, and it didn't involve sex.

"Where's your tie?"

I pointed to the dresser. "Over there with the damn cufflinks."

"Thwarted by your wardrobe?"

"I'm thwarted by a lot of things today."

She kissed me on the cheek and then started on the cufflinks. She fastened them so deftly, I felt like a complete klutz for all my earlier efforts. When she placed her hands around my neck and started messing with the tie, I felt something completely different. She focused on the errant ends of the tie, but I focused on her. The funny way she held her tongue while she concentrated on the task. The slope of her neck—smooth, kissable, gorgeous. She'd dressed for me, I was certain. She knew how important this day was. How nervous I was at the big role I had to play, at the fact I'd be seeing my nothing's-ever-good-enough mother for the first time in ages.

Why should I be surprised? Hell, she'd taken a bullet for me. She'd always been there, no matter what else was going on in her life, no matter how much of a shit I'd been. She was the one who'd sat by my hospital bed, who always answered my late night calls, who knew me like no one else. And still, she stuck around.

But she wouldn't always. Deveaux had been a close call. Jess had started to fall and, if Deveaux hadn't turned into a felon, she might be wearing that slinky black dress for a night out with the doctor. At some point, true love trumped friendship. Even I got that. Would I lose Jess? Was it only a matter of time? Could I, would I do anything to stop it?

She leaned back to inspect her work, and then she looked into my eyes and said, "You look like you want to say something."

I swear she could read my mind. "Do you miss Deveaux?"

"No," she answered quickly. "I miss the thought of it. Love, romance, all that. You know what I mean?"

I did. Probably for the first time ever. Could I have that? Could I have that with her? "Jess, I don't really know how to say this, but I—"

A sharp knock on the door interrupted me. I ignored it at first, but whoever it was persisted. I leaned in and kissed Jess on the lips. Light, but with a promise of more. "Don't move. I'll be right back." I hurried from the bedroom to the door, anxious to get rid of whoever had interrupted what I'd had to say. Maybe the few seconds' delay would give me the time I needed. I knew what I wanted to say, but I wasn't sure how to say it without sending Jess running.

I threw the door open and sucked in a breath. Ronnie Moreno stood with her hand raised to knock again.

"I need your help," she blurted. "I've been calling, but you didn't answer, so I took a chance you'd be at home."

I stared into Ronnie's deep brown eyes and suddenly I had no words. Not a one.

THE END

About the Author

Carsen Taite's goal as an author is to spin tales with plot lines as interesting as the cases she encounters in her career as a criminal defense lawyer. She is the author of seven previously released novels, *truelesbianlove.com*, *It Should be a Crime* (a Lambda Literary Award finalist), *Do Not Disturb*, *Nothing but the Truth*, *The Best Defense*, *Slingshot*, and *Beyond Innocence*. She is currently working on her ninth novel, *Rush*, a romantic intrigue. Learn more at www.carsentaite.com.

Books Available from Bold Strokes Books

Battle Axe by Carsen Taite. How close is too close? Bounty hunter Luca Bennett will soon find out. (978-1-60282-871-1)

Improvisation by Karis Walsh. High school geometry teacher Jan Carroll thinks she's figured out the shape of her life and her future, until graphic artist and fiddle player Tina Nelson comes along and teaches her to improvise. (978-1-60282-872-8)

For Want of a Fiend by Barbara Ann Wright. Without her Fiendish power, can Princess Katya and her consort Starbride stop a magic-wielding madman from sparking an uprising in the kingdom of Farraday? (978-1-60282-873-5)

Broken in Soft Places by Fiona Zedde. The instant Sara Chambers meets the seductive and sinful Merille Thompson, she falls hard, but knowing the difference between love and a dangerous, all-consuming desire is just one of the lessons Sara must learn before it's too late. (978-1-60282-876-6)

Healing Hearts by Donna K. Ford. Running from tragedy, the women of Willow Springs find that with friendship, there is hope, and with love, there is everything. (978-1-60282-877-3)

Desolation Point by Cari Hunter. When a storm strands Sarah Kent in the North Cascades, Alex Pascal is determined to find her. Neither imagines the dangers they will face when a ruthless criminal begins to hunt them down. (978-1-60282-865-0)

I Remember by Julie Cannon. What happens when you can never forget the first kiss, the first touch, the first taste of lips on skin? What happens when you know you will remember every single detail of a mysterious woman? (978-1-60282-866-7)

The Gemini Deception by Kim Baldwin and Xenia Alexiou. The truth, the whole truth, and nothing but lies. Book six in the Elite Operatives series. (978-1-60282-867-4)

Scarlet Revenge by Sheri Lewis Wohl. When faith alone isn't enough, will the love of one woman be strong enough to save a vampire from damnation? (978-1-60282-868-1)

Ghost Trio by Lillian Q. Irwin. When Lee Howe hears the voice of her dead lover singing to her, is it a hallucination, a ghost, or something more sinister? (978-1-60282-869-8)

The Princess Affair by Nell Stark. Rhodes Scholar Kerry Donovan arrives at Oxford ready to focus on her studies, but her life and her priorities are thrown into chaos when she catches the eye of Her Royal Highness Princess Sasha. (978-1-60282-858-2)

The Chase by Jesse J. Thoma. When Isabelle Rochat's life is threatened, she receives the unwelcome protection and attention of bounty hunter Holt Lasher who vows to keep Isabelle safe at all costs. (978-1-60282-859-9)

The Lone Hunt by L.L. Raand. In a world where humans and praeterns conspire for the ultimate power, violence is a way of life… and death. A Midnight Hunters novel. (978-1-60282-860-5)

The Supernatural Detective by Crin Claxton. Tony Carson sees dead people. With a drag queen for a spirit guide and a devastatingly attractive herbalist for a client, she's about to discover the spirit world can be a very dangerous world indeed. (978-1-60282-861-2)

Beloved Gomorrah by Justine Saracen. Undersea artists creating their own City on the Plain uncover the truth about Sodom and Gomorrah, whose "one righteous man" is a murderer, rapist, and conspirator in genocide. (978-1-60282-862-9)

Cut to the Chase by Lisa Girolami. Careful and methodical author Paige Cornish falls for brash and wild Hollywood actress Avalon Randolph, but can these opposites find a happy middle ground in a town that never lives in the middle? (978-1-60282-783-7)

More Than Friends by Erin Dutton. Evelyn Fisher thinks she has the perfect role model for a long-term relationship, until her best friends, Kendall and Melanie, split up and all three women must reevaluate their lives and their relationships. (978-1-60282-784-4)

Every Second Counts by D. Jackson Leigh. Every second counts in Bridgette LeRoy's desperate mission to protect her heart and stop Marc Ryder's suicidal return to riding rodeo bulls. (978-1-60282-785-1)

Dirty Money by Ashley Bartlett. Vivian Cooper and Reese DiGiovanni just found out that falling in love is hard. It's even harder when you're running for your life. (978-1-60282-786-8)

Sea Glass Inn by Karis Walsh. When Melinda Andrews commissions a series of mosaics by Pamela Whitford for her new inn, she doesn't expect to be more captivated by the artist than by the paintings. (978-1-60282-771-4)

The Awakening: A Sisters of Spirits novel by Yvonne Heidt. Sunny Skye has interacted with spirits her entire life, but when she runs into Officer Jordan Lawson during a ghost investigation, she discovers more than just facts in a missing girl's cold case file. (978-1-60282-772-1)

Murphy's Law by Yolanda Wallace. No matter how high you climb, you can't escape your past. (978-1-60282-773-8)

Blacker Than Blue by Rebekah Weatherspoon. Threatened with losing her first love to a powerful demon, vampire Cleo Jones is willing to break the ultimate law of the undead to rebuild the family she has lost. (978-1-60282-774-5)

Silver Collar by Gill McKnight. Werewolf Luc Garoul is outlawed and out of control, but can her family track her down before a sinister predator gets there first? Fourth in the Garoul series. (978-1-60282-764-6)

The Dragon Tree Legacy by Ali Vali. For Aubrey Tarver time hasn't dulled the pain of losing her first love Wiley Gremillion, but she has to set that aside when her choices put her life and her family's lives in real danger. (978-1-60282-765-3)

The Midnight Room by Ronica Black. After a chance encounter with the mysterious and brooding Lillian Gray in the "midnight room" of The Griffin, a local lesbian bar, confident and gorgeous Audrey McCarthy learns that her bad-girl behavior isn't bulletproof. (978-1-60282-766-0)

Dirty Sex by Ashley Bartlett. Vivian Cooper and twins Reese and Ryan DiGiovanni stole a lot of money and the guy they took it from wants it back. Like now. (978-1-60282-767-7)

The Storm by Shelley Thrasher. Rural East Texas. 1918. War-weary Jaq Bergeron and marriage-scarred musician Molly Russell try to salvage love from the devastation of the war abroad and natural disasters at home. (978-1-60282-780-6)

Crossroads by Radclyffe. Dr. Hollis Monroe specializes in short-term relationships but when she meets pregnant mother-to-be Annie Colfax, fate brings them together at a crossroads that will change their lives forever. (978-1-60282-756-1)

Beyond Innocence by Carsen Taite. When a life is on the line, love has to wait. Doesn't it? (978-1-60282-757-8)

Heart Block by Melissa Brayden. Socialite Emory Owen and struggling single mom Sarah Matamoros are perfectly suited for each other but face a difficult time when trying to merge their contrasting worlds and the people in them. If love truly exists, can it find a way? (978-1-60282-758-5)

Pride and Joy by M.L. Rice. Perfect Bryce Montgomery is her parents' pride and joy, but when they discover that their daughter is a lesbian, her world changes forever. (978-1-60282-759-2)

Ladyfish by Andrea Bramhall. Finn's escape to the Florida Keys leads her straight into the arms of scuba diving instructor Oz as she fights for her freedom, their blossoming love…and her life! (978-1-60282-747-9)

Spanish Heart by Rachel Spangler. While on a mission to find herself in Spain, Ren Molson runs the risk of losing her heart to her tour guide, Lina Montero. (978-1-60282-748-6)